TEMPT ME

Steamy Secrets, Book One

DIANE DEMETRE

LUMINOSITY PUBLISHING LLP

TEMPT ME
Steamy Secrets, Book One
Copyright © October 2019 Diane Demetre

Paperback ISBN: 978-1-9993066-4-9

Cover Art by Poppy Designs

DEDICATION

I am forever grateful for the still, small voice within that guides me and illuminates every step I take.

I must also thank the big, loud voices of love and encouragement from my family and friends, who stood by me as I embarked on yet another chapter of my life.

Big thanks to my husband who believed in my dream to become an author and sincere thanks to the lovely Kate Miles and Elizabeth Tasker from Luminosity Publishing, who made my publishing journey so delightful.

And to my readers, for without you, being published means nothing. Thank you for spending your valuable time with me. Steamy secrets are always best shared.

QUOTE

Dance is the movement of the universe concentrated in an individual. You were once wild here. Don't let them tame you.

— Isadora Duncan

SPRING 1999

CHAPTER ONE

FRIDAY

M**ICHELE'S HIGH HEELS CLATTERED** a staccato rhythm as she dashed into Divinities. "Sorry, I'm late. I couldn't find a park anywhere. I ended way up the street. Don't these footpaths piss you off? Obviously designed by a man."

With her pale blue dress fluttering at her tanned thighs, she swirled into the café out of breath and cranky. "Bloody pavers catch my heels every time." She tossed her tote bag on the floor and dropped into the spare chair, giving her heels a cursory inspection. She clucked irritably at today's damage. Another pair ruined. Flicking her hair behind her shoulders, she wriggled upright and blew air kisses to her three girlfriends already seated.

"I know. I'm forever buying new shoes." Dressed in a designer white linen pantsuit, Julie lifted her long leg in the air for all to admire her latest addition. A gold three-inch pump dazzled in the sunlight, a perfect match for her new gold handbag, perched on a chair beside her.

"God, Julie. You mightn't have been a professional dancer, but with those legs, I swear you've got an alter ego performing as a Radio City Rockette," Michele said.

"I've got you to thank for that. All those private dance classes for the past twenty years have certainly paid off." Julie waved her foot aloft for added effect.

"Mmm, sweetie. I love them." Cindy grabbed Julie's foot to check the brand stamped under the sole.

"For goodness sake, Cinderella, put your leg down before we're all blinded by the glare of your priceless shoe," SallyAnn said with a droll smile. "Some of us can't afford such luxuries, you know." She glanced down at her beige ensemble. "Unlike you high-powered businesswomen who can support your champagne tastes, my beer budget mostly goes to the kids."

Julie's leg recoiled back under the table in double time. "Sorry, SallyAnn. You still look lovely, though. I can buy you a pair if you like?"

"Don't be silly. I was only joking." SallyAnn crinkled her nose and squeezed Julie's arm. "Richie buys me the niceties of life whenever I need them. I just don't need them as much as I used to. It's more about the house and the kids nowadays."

Continuing with her own train of thought, Michele swivelled from Cindy to SallyAnn. "Remember when we were dancing? Here on the coast back in the eighties?"

"I do," SallyAnn said. "I miss those days." She gazed out into the distance at the waves crashing on the beach and raked her elegant fingers through her short platinum hair.

"Me too," Cindy agreed.

"But at least you're still in showbiz, producing shows for clubs and corporates. You still get some of the buzz," SallyAnn reminded Cindy.

"And, Michele, you've still got the event business," Julie said.

"I'm home playing chauffeur, nurse, mother, wife and happy homemaker. Not that I mind. I love Richie and the kids, but I do miss the dancing," SallyAnn said with a familiar longing in her voice.

"I know what you mean. Nothing beats that feeling of when you're waiting in the wings, ready to go onstage. Then the light hits your face and bam! You come alive and all you want to do is dance. Nothing compares to that. Right, girls?" Michele stared hard at SallyAnn and Cindy, whose own recollections transformed their faces, making them look years younger. Silence, wistful smiles and vigorous head nodding were agreement enough.

"And the after-show parties you had were even better," Julie said, joining them in a trip back to their halcyon days.

"You mean the men you had at the parties were even better." Cindy smiled and cocked a brow at her.

"Mmm, them too." Julie smirked.

Michele waved her balletic hands in the air. "The ubiquitous chorus line, that's what we are. Though not quite with the precision of the four swans from *Swan Lake*, we've each given our best performance, to star and shine in our own lives."

"Goodness, 'Chele, that's an awfully grand statement," SallyAnn said, "but you're right. We had a great time, and I wouldn't change it for anything."

"Me either. It was the best." Cindy pushed her unruly blonde curls from her face.

"I love you, girls." Michele reached out for a group hug.

After a few more minutes of happy memories and mutual adoration, Michele clapped her hands, calling them to order. She paused for dramatic effect then tapped out a triumphant tempo on the table with her long nails. "Ladies, I've made a decision. Tonight, I'm going to go out and get laid."

Michele's three friends glanced at each other but made no reply.

"I've been in monogamous relationships all my life since I was fourteen. I've never had any sort of casual sex, ever! I'm through being such a 'good girl.' If I don't do it now, I never will."

"Good for you. It's about time. In all the years we've been friends, I still can't believe you've never had a one-night stand. Seriously, sweetie, you're forty-two!" Cindy said as if for the hundredth time.

"Just because you were a late bloomer and had lots of partners to make up for lost time, doesn't make you the expert, you know," Michele said.

Julie nodded. "I agree with Cindy. Look at you. You're a gorgeous, sexy woman and you still look fabulous. I can't understand why you spent the last sixteen years with little to no sex in your life, playing babysitter to that sexually confused husband of yours. Up until now, I've not said anything but since you're finally divorced, I will. Sixteen years is more than what you get for murder. Time you got out and got some." She slapped the table like a judge with a gavel. Decision made.

"Look, it wasn't that bad. Adam and I had a good creative working relationship with the event business, so the sex wasn't that important." Even as she listened to her explanation, Michele winced at how lame it sounded.

Julie screwed up her nose in disgust. "Everyone needs sex. You've been missing out. Go out and get as much as you can while you look as good as you do. You owe it to yourself."

All eyes turned to Michele in silent affirmation. Get as much as possible before gravity takes hold and the hormones wither and die.

A young waiter, sporting a blinding smile and a taut body to which his thin polyester shirt and tight jeans clung for fear of rejection, happened into their view with perfect timing. Discounting the thought of desiccating hormones, the women shifted their gaze to the Adonis, taking the grand tour up and down his torso.

"Are you ready to order, ladies?" Pad at the ready, pen poised, he was doing his utmost to ignore the visual excursion his customers were taking over his body.

"Of course we are, gorgeous, but are you on the menu?" With her usual candour, Julie posed the question lurking unspoken in everyone's mind.

"Sorry, no. But if you come back tonight, I think my name's on the dessert menu."

More clapping and laughter erupted as Cindy praised his quick response, "Touché, sweetie. Well served."

"Mmm, I do hope so." Julie shot the final remark at the waiter, staring him down as she flashed a challenging smile. Amid titters and flirtatious chitchat, orders of coffee and tea were taken by the blushing subject of the women's attention.

After he made a hasty retreat, the focus turned to SallyAnn who, having been married for the past fifteen years remained the poster girl for all the fairy tales professing the dream of meeting Prince Charming with the 'happy-ever-after' ending.

"Well, 'Chele, you do what you have to but just keep yourself nice." SallyAnn's advice elicited the usual eye-rolling and lampooning. "It's a very different world out there than in our day," she added, fiddling with the sleeves of her cardigan.

"For God's sake, SallyAnn, how old are we? We're not dinosaurs yet you know," Michele said.

"I don't mean it that way. It's just different. The tone of dating has changed, the men aren't as gracious. It's a whole new world."

"I know that. But I think you're missing the point. I don't want to date anyone. I just want to get laid." Michele beseeched the heavens for help like a good Shakespearean actor.

Other lunchtime diners looked over at the four well-dressed women and smiled at Michele's strangled cry for satisfaction. The giggling and nodding of heads from some of the other women in the café proved Michele was not alone in her plea, while a couple of the men debated whether to make an approach in answer to her prayer.

"I'm forty-two, newly divorced and now it's my time. I'm going to have some fun and enjoy my brand, new single life."

"Sweetie, we're so happy for you but to be honest, we all thought your marriage would've ended sooner. You certainly put up with a lot for a long time," Cindy said.

"I guess so. But you know me. I grew up on an emotional diet of the *Wonderful World of Disney*. I blame Walt for my slightly skewed relationship expectations," Michele said with a flicker of amusement. "All that 'clap your hands' stuff and dream of Prince Charming. Tinker Bell has a lot to answer for."

"Well, you gave it your best shot," SallyAnn said. "You played the roles of wife, business partner, dance teacher and life coach for Adam. You were the best thing that ever happened to him."

"That's for sure. And I must say I'm proud you didn't play victim any longer," Julie added.

"I know," Michele said. "I mean, it didn't come as a big surprise really. Adam was bisexual when we got married and his occasional dalliances with men didn't bother me too much. But when he started doing the beats and then not telling me, that was the last straw. I just couldn't stand the deception any longer."

"I would've cut his balls off," Julie hissed, scissoring her fingers for effect.

"I must say, 'Chele, you handled it well, though," SallyAnn said. "Not sure if I could've been so understanding and forgiving."

"I guess, but Adam and I spent lots of good years together. I figured what's the point in throwing out the baby with the bathwater. I'd always thought he was more gay than straight anyway. So, as I say, not really such a big surprise in the end," she said with a shrug.

"You're amazing." Cindy leaned over and stroked Michele's shoulder.

"Well, it's all in the past now," SallyAnn added.

"Yes. I've played to the final curtain." Michele's arms flew outward and she took a seated bow. "You know, girls, I can't remember the last time I had sex, and I certainly can't remember the last time I had great sex. So, I've decided it's time I got some."

"You go, girl," Julie said. "There're lots of men to choose from out there. Remember with one of those" — she pointed to Michele's crotch as she cocked her sculptured eyebrow — "you can have as many of them as you want." She flourished her hand toward the two men sitting at a table just out of earshot, who acknowledged her gesture with expectant boyish grins.

Spurning their eagerness with a giggle, Cindy agreed. "Julie's right, sweetie. You can have any man or men you want. So be choosy."

"I intend to be. It's a strange feeling, though. It's like I've got this wicked voice inside me, screaming out for some erotic fun and serious satisfaction."

"You sure it's just not Tinker Bell all grown up still clapping her hands?" Julie asked, and they all laughed.

Michele pulled a face. "Very funny."

Right on cue, the waiter returned with their orders, dispensing them amidst more flirtatious banter. On his exit, all eyes turned to Michele.

"Then it's settled. Tonight's the night." Julie raised her coffee cup to the centre of the group.

"Absolutely." Michele lifted her cup to toast.

"Time to go out and get some sex," Cindy said holding her peppermint tea aloft.

"Just make sure he's not a serial murderer," SallyAnn quipped and joined in the salute to Michele's forthcoming adventure.

~ ♥ ~

MICHELE PUT HER MAKEUP purse in her handbag and glanced at her watch. In the entertainment business, it was known as 'beginner's call,' the last five minutes before the curtain goes up and the time to take one last look in the mirror. Following dancers' tradition, she gave a slow twirl, casting a tentative eye at what she'd chosen. This evening called for the drama of black; an off-the-shoulder tight black top cinched into even tighter black jeans tucked into black knee-high suede boots. A little hesitant whether her selection erred on the trampy side of style, she reassured herself that since she hadn't been able to get into these jeans for a couple of years, damn it, she'd wear them. From the song list stored in her memory, the old Hollies hit, "Long Cool Woman in a Black Dress," provided the silent soundtrack to which she completed her makeup and hair. As a dancer, she'd become adept at these essential pre-show preparations. Her tousled tresses and flawless skin tones with fashionista smoky eyes demonstrated she knew her craft well.

By the time she strode out her front door, her body tingled with the familiar sensation of opening-night jitters. Her heart rate quickened, her shoulders were pulled back, her tummy was sucked in and the dancing queen was emerging. Tonight was another opening night, and the audience, whoever he was, was going to get a performance of a lifetime.

~ ♥ ~

STEPPING OUT OF THE taxi into her new life, she was an unrestricted free agent under a kaleidoscope of neon billboards and flashing lights. Like most Saturday nights, bachelor herds of young men prowled the arcades and avenues, indecisive as to which club or into which stripper's G-string they'd throw their week's wages, while flirty young girls flounced along the glitter strip in their tight dresses secretly looking for Mr Right.

Seems blind faith in Walt's fairy-tale endings is still alive and well in tinsel town, she thought as she put a little extra chutzpah in her step.

Everywhere the smell of salty air and sex twitched at her nostrils. This was her city, an ever-changing, improvised scene of characters performing under the bright lights, looking for the cues, delivering their best lines. "Okay, girl. Eyes, tits and teeth," she reminded herself as the first flutter of nervous excitement threatened to overwhelm her. This old theatre trick to overcome the nerves an entertainer feels just before curtain-up had been taught to her many years before. Put a sparkle in your eyes, stick your chest out and smile big enough to crease the corners of your eyes, and you're on your way. It's showtime.

She strutted down the street to the city's beat, sensing men stop and turn, as if aware of her sexual quest.

"Going my way, sweetheart?" came the first inquiry from a rangy looking specimen.

"I don't think so," she said with a polite smile.

"What about you and me, doing the horizontal mambo?" The second inquiry growled from a leather-clad, tattooed man who looked like he'd just cocked his leg from his Harley.

"Maybe another time." A bigger smile creased her face, but she didn't break stride.

Listening for her cue, she chose the club for her mission based on the bass beat of its music and the quality of its departing clientele. Speakeasy was a vibrant, well-known bar tucked away from the boisterous crowds. Scrutinizing her with a smile, the brick wall doubling as a bouncer stepped aside, his eyes appreciating both her genes and those she wore as she sashayed past. On entering the venue, she was swallowed up in a sea of churning people ensconced in the mating game. Up close and personal was the *modus operandi.*

"This is the place. Let's go." Her inner sex goddess's approval propelled Michele further into the throng.

FOR THE PAST DECADE, Michele's curiosity in spirituality had led her to explore a variety of self-discovery practices including past life regression, rebirthing, yoga, and meditation. After years of going within with Shirley MacLaine, the pivotal moment had occurred during a three-day kundalini meditation retreat when she heard her guidance.

Michele referred to her invisible intuitive self as the Goddess and this relationship proved to be peaceful, insightful and oftentimes irreverent. Never more so than when the Goddess displayed her unfettered divine sexuality as Michele's inner sex goddess, who had recently manifested herself with a wicked *joie de vivre.* With the Goddess's calm counsel, Michele came to realize her marriage and recent divorce were not mistakes at all, but inevitable crossroads in life's dance. And so tonight, at yet another juncture, she followed her inner guidance.

SQUEEZING HER WAY THROUGH the nightclub crowd, Michele made for the bar where she stepped nimbly into a space just vacated by a large Negro man.

"I must try one of those as well," she mused to herself, watching his tight buttocks retreat.

"All in good time," came consent from within.

Leaning across the bar to be heard, Michele ordered her poison. The service was fast, the vodka and tonic cold and the music hot. With all the accoutrements to suit the scene, she settled in to scope the room, enjoying the buzz of sexual energy.

It took only thirty minutes before an extra drink arrived in front of her. The bartender pointed to the big guy at the other end of the bar who tipped his glass and smiled. She accepted his offering with a reciprocal gesture. Her drink patron stood nearly a full head height above everyone else and was built like an Arnie Schwarzenegger double with a twist of Crocodile Dundee about him. Accentuated by his casual clothes, his face and manner had Aussie written all over them. After an initial assessment, Michele gave him only fleeting attention as she'd already chosen her mark for the night; the young bartender with the trim body, aquiline face, and gelled hair.

The night progressed, and another couple of drinks arrived compliments of the titan, who remained fixed as if supporting the other end of the bar. She acknowledged each drink with a gracious smile, which he returned with the unwavering stare of a wildcat, mouth curled waiting for its prey to make a move.

While the bartender showed initial interest in her flirtations, he disappeared at the end of his shift leaving her advances unrequited.

Nothing new there, she thought, *God, what's wrong with me?* Feeling the familiar sense of rejection left over from years living with her husband, she sculled her drink and turned to leave.

But there he stood, her drinks benefactor, wearing an inscrutable expression as he blocked her exit. From a distance he'd looked a solid guy, however up close he must've been virtually a hundred kilos of pure muscle.

With a smile twitching his lips, he initiated the conversation. "You're the horniest thing I've seen in years. Why are you chasing pencil dicks?"

His brash opening remarks pinned her to the spot and, as a half-smile flitted across her face, she took a closer look at this man with the roguish sense of humour. He wouldn't be classed as typically handsome, but his sheer presence and blunt approach caused her skin to tingle. Impeding any escape, he flashed a wide, white smile, and waited for a response. His eyes, a vivid marine blue, twinkled with life experience and his collar-length soft brown hair framed his sun-tanned face. He encroached into her personal space, towering over her with the promise of a real man, and he smelt good. The scent of masculine musk mingled with the bittersweet overtones of a world-class aftershave triggered a positive response in her brain.

"Thanks for the drinks. That was very generous of you. And your name is . . .?"

"You can call me Mark. And you are?" His voice was like the breath of a friendly dragon, warm and playful.

"Michele." Her initial obligation to be polite since he'd spent money buying her drinks had softened to casual interest. "Tell me a little about yourself, Mark."

"Not much to tell really. I'd rather talk about you."

"Either you're very chivalrous or very secretive. I suspect it might be the latter. You don't give too much away, do you?"

"Not only good looking but clever as well. What is it I can do to make you choose me instead of that gay bartender?"

Shit, she thought. After all she'd been through, she'd chosen a carbon copy of her ex-husband. Why hadn't she'd seen it? But it wasn't too late to save the night. "Well, I guess you can buy me another drink, Mark."

When he leaned across to order another round of drinks, the muscles in his neck and arms flexed as they took his weight, stretching his shirt across what appeared to be an extraordinarily muscular back. Conducting a quick appraisal, she noted his faded blue jeans belted at the waist accentuated his solid thighs and taut buttocks. Her lips curled in approval when she spotted his neat, clean boat shoes. Her mother had always said you can tell a lot about a man by his shoes.

"Forget about the shoes! This is it. I'm telling you. Don't miss out on this one." Her sex goddess had made her decision for the night. However, Michele wasn't yet convinced.

"That's an interesting ring you're wearing," she said, spying an emblazoned gold ring on his right forefinger. "What is it?"

"Oh, this is just a dress ring."

"It looks terribly official." Clasping his hand in hers, she turned his fingers to the light. It'd been so long since she'd held another man's hand that the weight, structure, and size triggered a slight stirring below her waist.

Their drinks arrived and Mark toasted. "Cheers, baby."

He stepped into her space and exhaled. When his breath skimmed over her hair, she closed her eyes to savour the moment, losing herself in his presence. She'd not experienced this primal attraction before. It was raw and untamed. She could all but hear his heart beating a mantra in his chest. *Tempt me, tempt me.* Though she'd never thought of herself as a temptress, it was a role she'd like to explore. She opened her eyes and met unwavering gaze.

He leaned closer. "How're you doing?"

"I'm fine thanks." Though the heat in her groin indicated otherwise. "In fact, I'm very fine."

"Really? Do you know what fine means?"

"I think so. What do you think it means?"

"Frustrated, insecure, neurotic and emotional." Using the increasing crowd as an unspoken excuse, he pressed in further toward her.

She tingled all over. "Well, I may be frustrated but I don't think the last three describe me in the least." She averted her eyes, thinking that small act would break the mounting tension between them. It didn't. He continued smiling down at her, cocked his head and tugged his right hand. Much to her surprise, she'd taken hold of it again, turning the ring on his finger around and around.

She dropped his hand as if on fire. "Oh, sorry."

"No, don't do that. I was enjoying it." He lifted her hand and held it in his.

"Forget Walt Disney and Prince Charming. Let's get this party started. She who dares wins."

Michele ignored her inner advice. "Is this the game, is it? Will you pretend to be my Prince Charming?"

"If that's what you want, that's what I'll be. However, I've got more to offer than Prince Charming. We can do things together you've only dreamed of, and I imagine you mightn't have done. But with that body, you were made to do."

When he took a long, deep inhale he seemed to extract her essence, devouring every inch of her, physically, mentally and emotionally. His crotch pushed harder against her, scorching like a hot iron, branding her as his. Though her head spun, and her body shrieked, she met his force. The time had come. It was now or never. With a slow, deliberate gesture, she placed her empty glass on the bar, matched his blistering gaze and took the leap.

"Okay. You. Me. Now."

Without a word, he smiled as if it'd been a forgone conclusion. He wrapped his arm around her waist and ushered her outside into the chill of the night. But it had little effect on the sexual heat rising in her body. She wanted to be on their way. To get this party started. She'd never felt this eager before and it excited yet frightened her a little. Within minutes, she sat pressed beside him in the back seat, virtual strangers in an unexpected time and place.

During the drive, Michele managed a few furtive glances at this man who'd charmed her so simply. With powerful thighs wrangled into his jeans, biceps bulging at the short sleeves of his loose-fitting cotton shirt and a torso resembling the bulk and promise of a treasure chest, he was all man. Like an innocent Aladdin, she imagined the delightful treasures that might lie within, never considering she may be about to open Pandora's box. Although he was relaxed and confident in his own skin, his rugged face bore signs of a tough life. He didn't speak or touch her. Yet an animal magnetism seeped from his body, prowling across the seat to settle in her lap, making her quiver with anticipation. While she fidgeted in a futile effort to relieve the mounting tension, he turned with a half-smile, like a doting parent reassuring a child. Then he resumed his invisible sexual assault on her body once more.

During this electrified silence came SallyAnn's warning. "Off to who-knows-where with a stranger. No one knows where you are. You don't know where you're going. Have you lost your senses?" The thought and image of SallyAnn's concerned face rattled around in Michele's mind, but there was no turning back now. As the cliché warned, the die had been cast.

EVENTUALLY, THE CAB CAME to a stop. When she stepped out into the cool air, Michele was at an exclusive marina which unfolded before her like a lavish sound stage. Superyachts and spectacular cruisers were secured along multiple mooring arms, listing in a gentle rhythm. With a new moon preventing romantic reflections off the water, their arrival was masked in darkness.

Again, worry with the voice of SallyAnn resurfaced. *"The perfect setting for a murder."*

Michele had to agree that the setting exhibited the hallmarks of a Stephen King thriller, dark and isolated, with the requisite icy chill in the air. Yet for her, it wasn't the scene's menacing connotations but its gentle serenity that spoke to her. It calmed her doubts while heightening her anticipation of the impending liaison. She glanced up at her first-ever one-night stand and the gentle curl of his lips extinguished the last of any negative mental chatter.

After paying the cabbie, he escorted her down a gangway through the many shimmering yachts to the last vessel moored at the jetty's end. Inscribed across her bow was Michele's omen, the *Lady Diana*, the huntress, a goddess in the purest of feminine forms, on a quest to never marry, the vanquisher of men and animals all. The *Lady Diana* floated atop the water like one hundred feet of ancient Roman art, all sleek lines and beautiful curves.

This is sex on water, she thought, awestruck.

"Let's hope so," chimed in her sex goddess.

"Sorry, you'll have to take off those come-fuck-me boots. No high heels on the deck."

"You're kidding me, aren't you? Dancers don't ever take their high heels off." She was aghast at the thought of removing her boots. They were part of her costume for tonight's performance.

"Okay then." Without missing a beat, he swept her up into his arms, as if lifting a toddler across a puddle. He strode up the gangway, carried her on board across the deck and deposited her in the carpeted cabin. Her breath hitched in her throat like a lolly fragment swallowed too quickly. No man does that, at least not to her. Her years of fantasy were turning into a night of reality. Perhaps Walt was right after all?

"I thought there was something more to you. The way you were grinding at that bar was something else. I've got just the music for you." He strode to the audio cabinet in search of his preferred disc.

As Michele willed her lungs to resume normal function, she surveyed her surroundings while the sexual rhythms of *Essential Yello* filled the cabin.

"Drink? Same as before?" His warm voice harmonized with the music, and she wondered how many other women he'd had on this yacht, mixing drinks for them before having wild abandoned sex. A flush of anticipation warmed her cheeks, and she slid into the rich leather lounge, into a world she'd only dreamed of. The cabin oozed wealth with its teak furniture, plush beige carpet, and luxurious cream leather, all customized and fitted into every conceivable space. The sheer elegance of the warm, neutral colour palette was testament to the interior designer's disregard for the constant cleaning this vessel demanded. Nestling into the coolness of the leather, she noted the mirror sheen and craftsmanship of the full-sized teak table opposite. Everywhere, polished surfaces shone with a sensuous, soft glow.

Forwards of the main cabin were stairs leading down to what she assumed were the bedrooms while the flybridge atop was where the captain would command safe passage. She wondered if she'd encounter safe passage this night or whether she was to become tomorrow's headline in the local newspaper. "Woman Found Murdered at Marina." The night's inkiness enveloped the cabin, cocooning it in a shroud of secrecy, reinforcing her latest apprehensions.

Who is he? Is he the captain? Does he own the yacht? Too many questions swirled in her mind matching the speed with which he swizzled their drinks. "Enough," she scolded herself in a whisper.

With a deep breath of renewed conviction, she focused on the way his shoulders rolled mimicking the slight pitch of the yacht and forced herself to stop thinking of her soon-to-be lover as the Grim Reaper. After all, this was her time, she was the huntress, not the prey.

Handing her the drink and easing himself beside her, he continued his previous conversation. "So why were you wasting your time with that bartender? He'd have had no idea how to please a woman like you."

"Old habits die hard, I guess."

Curiosity creased his face.

"Long story. Let's not go there," she said.

"Everyone has secrets they don't want revealed, Michele. None of my business. I get it." There was no injury in his voice at her abrupt termination of the conversation, just understanding.

While she tried to think of a clever answer to lighten the mood, he placed his drink behind them on the window ledge, freeing his hand to stroke her face, unaware his tender touch breathed life back into her lonely skin. She lost her footing in his touch, any thoughts of her past or future gone. Gently he set her drink aside. She suspected Disney might just have been telling the truth after all for her body seemed to fill with hundreds of butterflies, her face blushed baby pink and her lips parted, waiting to be awakened with a kiss.

He reached over and lifted her onto his lap where she melted like hot chocolate. Clasping her face between his hands, her softness at the mercy of his strength, he leaned in, kissing her with tender yet passionate desire. His tongue caressed hers, snaking its introduction in her mouth. She was spellbound.

Gift-wrapping herself in his embrace, she gave up everything, the years of longing, frustration, and rejection. Her passion found a stage on which to shine as the music enlivened her dancer's body, giving art to her performance. With eager fingers, she began to unbutton his shirt, exposing his tight chest and abs which he displayed with quiet confidence. Like Poseidon, he was master of his domain, and she wanted to venerate at his feet. Following the tempo of the music, she bent forwards, licking and sucking at his flesh. He tasted delicious and he wanted her, his desire unmistakable. She was moist and ready, but he softly pushed her away. "Dance for me. Please?"

Without hesitation, she uncoiled herself and stepped back, her eyes never leaving his. Preparing for a command performance she drew a controlled inhale and abandoned herself to the erotic rhythms filling the cabin. Her body transmuted the music into subtle shades of movement and stillness, motion morphed into emotion, connecting the dancer and the audience in an inseparable coupling. Grinding her hips against an imaginary dance partner, she knew how to make herself irresistible to her new lover, and like an elastic band, she stretched their desire to breaking point with every move she made.

Trailing her hands over her body she danced without restraint, rubbing her fingers between her legs with deep fluid strokes. As an appreciative smile etched his face, she tossed back her hair, challenging him with an unspoken promise of the sex-play to come. Then dragging her hand from her warm place, she waved her pheromones under his nose, tempting him with an aromatic appetizer. He inhaled deeply, obviously delighting in her scent and performance. He was the embodiment of her perfect audience, a man who enjoyed watching her get off on the dance.

In a torturous slow peel of her top, she exposed her tanned, taut belly, extending her arms upward like vines crawling to the canopy. On tempo, she discarded the garment, arched her body and slipped her hand down into her jeans to her sex. Wet with juice she removed her fingers then brushed them across his lips. His tongue curled around each digit in delight, savouring and seducing her fingers to remain in his hot mouth where they could be sucked to climax. Although tempted, she maneuvered her hand to freedom on a crescendo and with a peacock flourish, she turned to expose her sculptured back, unclipping her bra yet not allowing it to fall.

Every time he drank a little more of his drink, she stripped a little more, shedding fragments of her past with each piece of clothing puddling at her feet. Rivers of relief began to surge through her body as she flowed headlong into her new reality.

Straddling him, she slithered from her bra and cupped her plump breasts, offering each for his caress. He obliged with warm, wet kisses while their bodies steamed and his manhood raged. Feeling little pity for his cock trapped in the prison of his *Levi's*, she slipped from his lap. Then with meticulous timing, she unzipped her jeans and peeled them down to her boots, turned, and bent in a full forwards fold to expose her naked arse and slippery sex. When his greedy fingers stretched out to stroke her wetness, she unzipped and removed her boots for the final reveal. At last, she was naked, dancing untamed, empowered by the music and her emancipated sexuality.

He pulled her to him and licked her navel in a slow, fluid stroke. Glancing down at her naked feet he said, "What about the boots? You said that dancers never take off their high heels?"

"True . . ." She reclined on the lounge and pulled her boots back on in an equally provocative reverse strip. With a languorous *développé,* she straddled him, settling her weight onto his lap. Her faultless tousled hairstyle now dripped with perspiration which trickled down her body, coursing an uninterrupted path to her fully waxed mons. His eyes followed the tiny rivulets as his hands crept up her thighs, like desert snakes retreating to a cool cave.

She blocked his advance. "You got what you wanted. Now it's my turn."

Your wish is my command." He began to shrug his shirt off, but she slipped off his lap.

"Another drink please, no ice."

He twitched a smile before collecting her glass and returning to his duty at the bar. While he mixed more drinks, she encircled him with her arms, grinding her yearning nakedness against his clothed back. He turned with his offering, and she took a couple of steps back and positioned herself prone on the elegant teak table.

"Drink me."

With a layer of perspiration glistening over her body like crystallized sand, she lay on display, nude except for the boots. Her jagged breathing invited him to begin and with the taste and smell of her still on his face, he advanced.

"My pleasure." His voice was low and promising.

Like a doctor measuring a potent tonic, he drizzled a few drops from the glass into her mouth then reclaimed them with his own. She wanted more of his mouth, but instead, he poured the icy mixture down her throat, and when she flinched, he caressed her skin dry. Then as if in blessing, he drizzled the sticky syrup in the shape of a cross from breast to breast, licking the remnants before they made a hasty escape from her body. She shuddered with anticipation. The ache of anticipation amassed in her body as he laved his tongue along her pantie line, not venturing lower until she whimpered for more. With his steady hand held high, he released the last drops from the glass to flow down to her steaming sex. The frosty chill scorched as it seeped further into the folds of her flesh, and he knelt with reverence, at the holy altar of her body.

He parted her thighs, and she surrendered. Completely. Gentle kisses followed by deeper probing with his tongue sent her into the first throes of passion where she became oblivious to the outside world. He teased and nibbled, opening her up little by little. Her body responded without restraint, arching toward his face for more. *Eat me. Eat me.* As he buried his tongue ever deeper, she held herself wide open for his feasting. He teased her without mercy, and she longed to be satiated, straining herself into his face. Pain and pleasure merged when he sucked her clit hard, tugging as if punishing it for not giving up its secrets. She'd never experienced such exquisite anguish. She wanted it to go on forever and yet couldn't bear the ecstasy any longer. With his mouth ravishing her sex and his forceful fingers working their magic inside her, she lost all sensibility and orgasmed in a shower of release.

Her primal scream splintered the cabin as a secret valve opened in her loins, liberating her from years of frustration. Awakened from a long dark sleep, her body, mind, and soul reunited with shattering force, her sex goddess now fulfilled.

Time stopped. While waves of crashing energy threatened to consume every cell of her body, she lingered on the edge of bliss, giving her nervous system time to recalibrate. She never imagined sex could be that amazing. That mind-numbing. Once the energy subsided and reality returned, she shimmied off the table, shaken, shocked and euphoric.

"That's never happened to me before." She glanced at the puddle spreading across the table. "Oh, God. Look what I've done."

"That's okay, baby. That's the point of the exercise. Not many women can do that. I love it. It's great." His chin glistened with sweat and female ejaculate. "It tastes like spring water. Here, taste." He pulled her close, kissing her with the taste of her pleasure, and her body shuddered before collapsing into his arms.

He lifted her onto the table where she lay unable to move from sheer delight and exhaustion. Removing his clothing, he revealed a body ripped with the results of hard work and discipline. Bit by bit, her eyes drifted down his taut, tanned physique until she spied his straining penis.

"Oh, yes, please," she said.

"Trust me, baby. You're gonna love this."

Michele lost herself in the arctic colours of his eyes, longing for him to start. But he drew the moment out into an excruciating wait. A small muscle clenched in his jaw and his lips curved upward in a bemused smile. Everything about him remained in control, his hair, his muscles, his cock and most of all, his command of her body.

Pulling her apart, he mounted her, taking his time, penetrating her. With every thrust forwards, he then withdrew a little, teasing her, making her ache for more. She loved and loathed the torment. When he enfolded her in his arms, she latched on, willing him to rock deeper and deeper inside her. She could feel his impatience wedged within her, throbbing to make her his own. She wanted to be his, badly. She wanted him to plunge deep inside her, to take her, to fuck her forever.

Unable to take his teasing any longer, she locked her gaze on him and dug her nails hard into his buttocks. And like a well-trained thoroughbred horse under the whip, he championed the pace. Untamed, she equalled his unrelenting rhythm, revelling in her power, her newfound freedom and him. At last, a man, a real man.

CHAPTER TWO

SATURDAY

PERCHED ATOP BURLEIGH BEACH, Divinities had morphed into a local institution over many decades. With its rich history and original spirit founded on the 1960s rock 'n' roll beach party culture, the café's mission of everyone being welcomed, regardless of clothing, status, money or sand between the toes remained intact. Today, it was abuzz with the usual Saturday afternoon crowd of hip young people, professional couples and arty singles reading newspapers or deliberating on their weekend activities.

Having listened to Michele's narration of her previous night's escapades for the past twenty minutes, Cindy finished her peppermint tea with a definitive placement of cup to saucer. "Sweetie, you're literally glowing. I'm so happy for you."

"I can't believe how fabulous he was. I feel so alive, so feminine. God, to think what I've been missing all this time . . ." Michele felt a yearning build in her groin at the memory.

"I know. It's really something isn't it, when you find someone sexually compatible? I've only found a couple of partners like that and the sex was unbelievable. Tell me more, what does he do?"

"You mean aside from giving great sex?"

"Stop right there. What have I missed?" Julie, looking ever young in a tight tangerine pantsuit and matching shoes, slid into the booth next to Cindy. "Sorry I couldn't get here earlier but I had a couple of things to finish off. Catch me up."

Michele retold her story a second time to her new audience.

"By God girl, he sounds perfect. So, what does he do? Is the yacht his? Does he have money?"

"I don't really know much else about him except sadly, the yacht isn't his. He motors yachts from place to place for various owners. He lives in Sydney. He'll be here for about a week, and I can't wait to see him again."

"So more than a one-night stand then?" Julie asked.

"Yes. I'm seeing him tonight."

"As I suspected." She wagged her finger at Michele. "Although you say you want the life of a single girl with lots of casual sex, underneath you're still looking for love, for the big happy-ever-after ending. Am I right?"

"I don't know, but at the moment I intend to explore the first option with the hope the second option may be on offer."

"I understand, sweetie. Have your cake and eat it too." Highlighting her point, Cindy waved her last forkful of black forest cake before plunging it into her mouth.

"I trust he's being the gentleman and paying for everything?" Julie's arched eyebrow lifted for emphasis.

"Yes, he's paying for everything and tonight he's offered to take me to dinner to any restaurant I want."

"Good to hear. As long as he appreciates what you're giving him."

"However, it's not food I'm hungry for," Michele quipped, and they giggled at the obviousness of her statement.

"How was your Friday night?" Cindy asked.

Julie stretched back into the booth, a predatory smirk on her face. "Well, I was so intrigued by our young waiter yesterday, I returned last night and found he was on the dessert menu."

Cindy's and Michele's eyes widened then crinkled with laughter as they realized it was inevitable Julie would pursue yesterday's flirtation. Regardless of Julie's on-again-off-again long-term relationship with Tom, everyone, including Tom, knew Julie's sexual appetite craved variety. Cindy glanced around the room to see if the young Adonis was on shift today.

"No good looking for him. I just finished him off before coming here, sweet, delicious and moreish." Julie licked her finger at the sides of her mouth for added effect. "He's not back on shift until tomorrow. Poor darling will need the remainder of today to recover from what I put him through, the pretty young thing that he is."

"Seriously, Julie, you're too much," Michele said.

"I agree, but I'm also mightily jealous," Cindy added, eager to hear more.

Julie abstained from further details with a skilful redirect to Cindy. "How was your night?"

"I finally met up with that guy I've been talking to at the gym. That police officer."

"And?"

"He seems nice enough. We're catching up again tomorrow for lunch. After all these years of being single, I wouldn't mind a happy-ever-after myself. Find Mr Right like SallyAnn did and settle down. Who knows? *Que sera sera.*"

"Speaking of SallyAnn, where is she?" Julie asked, glancing at her watch.

"She can't make it today. Richie's working so she's chauffeuring the kids to ballet classes and football training. Ah, the simple joys of motherhood," Michele said. With no regrets at being childless, the three of them ordered lunch with a good Sav Blanc to wash it down.

On her way home, while Michele made a pitstop at the supermarket, she mulled over the afternoon's conversations. In particular, Cindy's reference to the song lyrics, "Que Sera, Sera," what will be will be. That encapsulated how Michele felt about her situation. No matter how things turned out, it would be okay by her. She was having fun with a seemingly decent guy, even though he was a little mysterious. No harm was being done and her sex goddess was, at last, being satisfied, so life was good. *Que sera sera.*

~ ♥ ~

THE BAR'S OPULENT CHOCOLATE marble and dark leather furniture reminded Michele of a traditional gentlemen's club in an old British movie, very grand and conservative. She loved its splendour and dark moodiness and, as she couldn't afford to come here since her divorce, it was the obvious choice for tonight's rendezvous. With only a few other couples there already, she settled herself on the barstool when she noticed him arrive.

Mark claimed the foyer with long nonchalant strides, his powerful frame creating an unseen aura that made people give him a wide berth. A sly smile crept across her face as she remembered his rock-hard body that belied the forty-something years she suspected he was. Dressed in blue jeans and a plain white T-shirt, he reminded her of a Calvin Klein advertisement. His clothes clung to him as if infatuated with his body, a feeling with which she empathized. In some ways, he looked more handsome than she remembered, or was it because she was falling for him? His fresh, open smile greeted her on his approach. Sliding onto a barstool beside her, he squeezed her waist and planted a kiss to her cheek.

"Baby, you look hot. How are you?"

She was pleased he noticed. She'd chosen a pair of strappy silver heels to complement her slinky blue cocktail dress, and she was sans underwear. When his hand skimmed her hips, he registered the unbroken line of cloth with a carnal gleam that set his eyes alight. His aftershave mingled with his own natural musk, triggering Michele's memories of the previous night's events and caused her sex goddess to stir from a restless slumber.

"I'm fabulous, and you?"

"Good to hear you're no longer fine," he said.

"Very funny."

"Have you ordered drinks?"

"Not yet. I'll have a vodka martini, please."

"New poison? Sounds promising." He ordered the martinis, which arrived with three olives in each.

"Did you get some sleep?" His hand was on her thigh sending shivers to her groin.

"A little. And you?"

"Not a lot. But that's okay I don't need much sleep." His fingers scrunched up the fabric of her hem until they slipped under her dress to make a tentative exploration.

Her skin ignited. She couldn't believe the effect this man had on her. His touch, his smell, his taste and even the slight growl to his voice all conspired to unlock forbidden desires she never knew she possessed. His presence unravelled her while escalating her need for instant gratification.

"I missed you, baby." He breathed fire into her ear.

Placing her hand on his thigh, Michele shifted forwards a little, allowing him easier access. He found his target and urged it open. Although farcical, she attempted not to succumb to his touch by continuing the conversation.

"This martini is perfect. It's hard to find someone who can make a good dry martini."

"That may be so, but it's also hard to find someone who can be this wet this quick." He removed his hand and dipping his finger into his martini said, "Stirred, not shaken."

"Put it back!" her sex goddess screamed.

Sensing some of the other guests at the bar had witnessed their scandalous sexual aperitif, Mark said, "Come on, baby. Let's eat."

More unsteady on her feet than she expected, she leaned into him, and he guided her off the stool. She directed him a demure smile and said, "Mmm. I like being eaten."

"I know you do. But let's try to get a little food into you first, shall we?"

"If you insist."

Michele chose this restaurant because of its romantic atmosphere and the view of the city's skyline through the oversized window beside their table added that extra touch. Though conversation with Mark flowed easily if the topic was sex, he became elusive if the subject deviated. She wanted him to open up, but he played listener to her history rather than be forthcoming about his own. She decided to deal the family card, hopeful of it eliciting a more even two-way conversation.

"What about your parents?"

"I was adopted," he said with indifference.

"Really? So was I."

"I guess that explains why we're such a good fit." He reached over and squeezed her hand, sending a needle of affection through her heart.

That they had both started their lives in the same way, alone, rejected and unwanted, caught her off guard. She toyed with the ring on his hand again as if trying to piece together a puzzle.

"Yeah. I never thought much about it really." He withdrew his hand and gazed out into the night. "I spent my first few years as a kid in a foster home. That wasn't much chop. My foster father was a bit of a bastard and got his jollies by beating me with a belt. His wife just ignored me really and let it all happen." With an almost imperceptible snarl, he paused to let the memory pass, like an irate driver waiting for a deliberate loiterer to cross a busy street. "Anyway, when I was six another couple adopted me. They were good people. Dad was a police officer and Mum worked in retail. Not much money but lots of love. I could've gone either way. I could've been a real bad motherfucker or turned into the loveable bloke sitting before you today."

Closing the door to the dark emotions of his past, he returned his attention to Michele, flashing his killer smile. Beneath his brash indifference to his damaged childhood, she suspected there lay a deep wound, one that no matter how protected or ignored still festered with unresolved heartache.

"Oh, that's so sad," she said, feeling her own anxiety partner his buried hurt.

Although she'd not suffered such cruelty, she understood the self-reliance a child builds too soon when left without a parent's love in the early stages of life. With no identity, no one to protect you, no place where you belong, the world holds little promise. She'd learnt to be resilient and independent as her own protection against abandonment and it was obvious, so too had he.

"Have you ever thought of tracking down your biological parents?" she asked.

"Nope. I figure if they gave me up, they didn't want me. Why bother them now." He reached for his drink, draining its contents in one gulp.

"Yeah. What's the point of digging up the past? I never bothered either. Life has a way of working out, don't you think?"

"Yeah, I guess. Anyway, shit happens. And you?"

"I was fortunate enough to be adopted when I was a toddler by a wonderful couple. I couldn't have hoped for better parents really. We didn't have much money either but there was lots of love to go around. My Mum's still alive at seventy-eight, but Dad died when I was thirty."

"Twelve years ago."

She paused. "How do you know how old I am? I never told you." A crease wrinkled her brow as the first sign of something not-being-what-it-seemed wriggled in her stomach.

"I have my ways," he said with an impish wink, squeezing shut the small crevice into his psyche and along with it, any hope of finding out how he knew her age.

Despite that, she secretly delighted at their similarities, their shared parallel beginnings. More than just sexually, she felt certain he was her match.

Although the food was delicious, they both picked at their fine French cuisine, their appetites elsewhere.

Added to this was Michele's sex goddess's frequent grizzling. "*Come on. Come on. We can eat anytime. We can talk anytime. Let's get down to it.*"

"Baby, would you like some dessert?"

"I've brought my own." She tapped her tote bag, piquing his interest.

"Will I like it?"

"I'm sure you will."

"Well let's go then, if that's okay with you?"

"Absolutely."

As they left the restaurant, she hooked her arm through his. "Thanks for dinner." She snuggled into him, matching him stride for stride. A warm, contented feeling enveloped her. She'd never felt so safe in a man's presence.

"Will you dance for me again tonight?" he whispered.

"Of course I will . . ." She bit off the term of endearment she wanted to say, reminding herself this was supposed to be casual sex not the beginning of a romance. Yet after tonight's adoption revelation, her emotions began to construct a different outcome from her original game plan.

~ ♥ ~

THEY SOON ARRIVED AT the marina, where once more he played the role of the quintessential man and carried her across the deck and tended bar.

"Martini?" He was already chilling the glasses.

"Great, thanks."

"Stirred, not shaken." He glanced over his shoulder, sucked his index finger and winked. She returned his unspoken promise with a lick of her lips and settled into her surroundings as if they were her own. Tonight she was prepared. Having brought some of her own favourite CDs, she inserted k.d lang's *Ingénue* into the player, releasing Kathryn's sultry voice to curl around the cabin in smoke rings. With drinks in hand, he stepped in kissing her neck.

"Here you go, baby."

They sipped, chatted and danced for a while allowing k.d to inspire them in finding a synchronistic rhythm together. With their well-matched bodies interwoven in a slow erotic dance, she slithered up and down on his thigh, her sex wanting to devour him whole, like a snake with a mouse.

After finishing her martini, and unable to bear the wait any longer, she took charge. "Time for the show, gorgeous."

This time, she didn't bite back her expression of affection. Curious to see if her words had unsettled him, she was relieved to see an unflinching primal gleam in his eyes, signalling another night of unrestrained pleasure.

Mark took his front-row seat for another performance, and she unveiled not only her body but also her soul. This man had breathed life back into her, had helped her become a real woman. He'd been the turning point in her life she'd so long wanted. She would dance and dance for him, she would do anything for him.

She'd become so lost in the music, her writhing nakedness, and the dance, she hadn't noticed he was sprinkling white powder from a small plastic bag onto a plate. With expert precision, he chopped and rearranged the cocaine into lines of exact lengths with his credit card.

"Baby, have you ever tried this before?"

A little surprised she replied, "No, I don't really do drugs. I smoke a bit of pot, but I've never done anything stronger."

"Believe me, once you do sex on this stuff, you will love it." He paused and smiled. "It's just a little bit of stardust for my star. Come sit beside me."

His affectionate patting of the cushion accompanied by his flashing smile quelled some of her anxiety. Clothed only in a layer of perspiration and her silver high heels, she knelt beside this man who had just removed another veil from her former cloistered life.

"Trust me, baby. I wouldn't do anything to hurt you."

"I know, but I can't seem to get the Cheech and Chong scene out of my head where the cocaine is actually Ajax cleaner."

Her gentle giant roared with laughter. "Yeah, I love that scene too. You don't have to worry about its purity. I get this stuff direct from the best source in the country. Just a little is all you need. Here, I'll show you."

Demonstrating, he leaned in with a rolled-up hundred-dollar bill and sucked the white powder deep into each nostril.

Trying to buy time so she could process that the man she was beginning to fall for, had a dark illegal side, she asked,

"Who are you exactly? You haven't really told me. For all I know, you operate a drug-running business up and down the eastern seaboard of Australia."

A good-humoured belly laugh prefixed his reply. "I can assure you, I don't operate a drug-running business. Here . . ." He held out the note.

Fending off the offer once more she said, "You know sex and rock 'n' roll are fine for a dancing divorcee, but illicit drugs?"

Another full-throated laugh filled the cabin.

"Frustrated. Insecure. Neurotic. Emotional. Baby, that's exactly how you sound. Live a little. Relax." His eyes danced an unspoken dare.

Normally she would have declined the offer. But she considered her previous life, her past choices, so predictable, so unadventurous.

"Perhaps good girls can only enjoy good times with bad boys?" she said.

"Not a truer word's been spoken. And I'm the best bad boy you can find. I'll look after you, baby."

She sighed.

Choosing adventure, she gripped the rolled-up note, leaned forwards and sniffed. The fine powder fluttered up her nostril biting into her virgin flesh. She rubbed her nose to stop the tingle.

"And now the other side, baby . . ." With gentle reassurance, he guided her in the technique, and she followed his instruction to assault her other nostril.

"Good girl. I'll fix you another drink. Why don't you move around a little and see how you feel?"

"Okay," she said, uncertain of what might happen. "Can you put that song back on for me, please?"

MARK HIT REPLAY FOLDED his arms and watched her in rapt appreciation. Within moments, she was gliding around the cabin, arms wind-milling leisurely in time with the music. She sang every chorus with k.d. as if knowing what it was like to live outside herself, with every feeling close to gone. It was the same emotional state he knew too well. Until Michele had appeared, his life had been a battlefield, his body battered, his heart broken and cold. Because of her, he felt a slow thaw moving from the inside, out. Hope was returning to his soul. All because of a sexy dancer who was living her life with the same wicked abandon he used to do many years before. And now the coke he'd persuaded her to take was awakening new sensations in her beautiful body and spirit. He smiled and watched his lover's innocence float away. She reminded him of an angel falling from heaven as her invisible wings caressed his heart.

Michele broke his reverie. "It seems I spend all my time naked on this yacht, and you still have your clothes on."

"That's easily fixed." Reciprocating her performance, he undressed to the music while she swayed sipping her martini, drinking him in with her eyes. Circling her from behind, he ground his bare hips into her buttocks, and she swooned. He wrapped her in his arms, and she leaned back offering up her neck for more affection.

Warmed by his body, his scent shrouding her, she felt her pheromones going into overdrive.

"Do you feel any different, baby?" he purred into her ear, as his demanding cock joined the party.

"Yes. This stuff's wonderful. Everything's more alive. I feel like I could dance forever." A tingling sensation clothed her skin.

"That's just how you should feel. I told you you'd be okay." He turned her around to face him. His erection pressed up hard against her stomach stirring her to respond. She reached up to kiss him, but he stopped her. "Now, what about this dessert you said you had?"

Even through rapidly firing synapses, she remembered her plan. She rummaged around in her bag and presented a small cool pack like it was a major lottery prize.

"Sir, dessert is about to be served. Please take your place."

He motioned to slide into the dining booth.

"No, sir, not at the table, on the table."

With more laughter and in full compliance, he reversed roles to lie back on the table, propped up on his elbows.

"Tonight, sir, we have a delicious blend of yogurt and strawberries, whipped lovingly together and sweetened with desire." She held up a carton of fruit yogurt while her other hand performed the requisite flourish of a TV hostess.

"Sounds good to me," he said.

As a taste test, she offered him a spoonful and kissed it into his mouth. "Now if sir would kindly fully recline, dessert is served."

With extra care, she ladled small dollops of yogurt on his nipples, licking them in kittenish style, before returning her passion to his mouth. Coating her own breasts in the creamy treat, she rubbed them across his mouth in slow arcs while his tongue partnered with each in an erotic tug-o-war, until they glistened clean. Down his body she travelled, taking her time to taste every nuance of his masculinity. After rolling over each ridge of his six-pack, her tongue arrived at the base of his neatly trimmed shaft. Here she crowned the head of his penis with a melting soft swirl then proceeded to devour his large member with gusto. With every generous stroke, she elevated him closer to orgasm. Punctuated by appreciative groans his body responded, but she just couldn't bring him to climax.

"Is something wrong?"

"No, everything's perfect. You give great head jobs, baby."

"Then why don't you come?"

"I rarely do. It's just the way I am. But the coke keeps me hard all night."

"I see." She gave his cock a good tug. "Well, if that's the case I think it must be time for me to have some dessert too."

With a change of tempo, she dragged him to his feet then assumed the position on the table. Throwing her legs apart in a dancer's second split, she poured the last of the yogurt all over her best bits.

"Please, sir, may I have some more?" She giggled out loud at the use of her theatrical quote, knowing this was not what Oliver had meant when he asked for more gruel.

Needing no further encouragement, Mark buried his face between her legs obviously relishing the yogurt and the taste of her. By now the cocaine had kicked in giving the sex a frenetic pace, making every touch and experience electrified.

Obsessed with sex and oblivious to time, Michele fucked herself stupid through that night and the next day, eventually descending from her euphoria by late Sunday afternoon.

CHAPTER THREE

SUNDAY

"I REALLY NEED TO GO. I've got work tomorrow, and I need to get some sleep." Michele started to dress, but because every muscle in her body ached from the best workout she'd had in a long time, it required more effort than normal.

Mark lay on the bed with a Cheshire Cat smile on his face, his body pumped and flushed. "But, baby, I still got more to give you." He jiggled his swollen cock around for effect.

She so enjoyed the look and feel of him. This mountain of a man with his strong, well-defined limbs and cheeky nature captivated her. She fell back on the bed and kissed him. "Not now. Some of us have to work you know. By the way, what is it you actually do?"

"Not a great deal really. I freelance motoring yachts around for wealthy clients whenever I want. Mainly just party and have fun."

"You sure you're not some sort of drug lord?"

"No. I just like drugs. I don't deal them."

"I notice no wedding ring, so not married? No kids?" She stroked his left ring finger, holding her breath for fear of the answer.

He rolled her onto her back and stared down into her eyes. "Baby, what can I tell you? You know the story. I'm just a guy on the make." This time the kiss was deep with conviction, it lingered, warm and soft.

Extricating herself from under his body, she sat on the side of the bed and fastened her shoes. "Well, I think you must've been a prize fighter."

"Why's that, baby?"

"Because you're bloody good at ducking and weaving." She shot him a sharp glance over her dress just before it slid down her body. Wriggling it into place, she said, "Okay then. I really do have to go."

"So tomorrow, can I see you?" He was sliding into his jeans, his muscles stripped lean from the previous hours of sex.

She let his question hang like a kite caught in a tree. She wanted to be with him every moment, but this was becoming serious and not what she'd expected. Her plan was to enjoy her singledom and not get attached to a man so soon. She needed some space to digest all the new feelings and emotions she was experiencing.

"Let's give it a rest for tomorrow."

Screaming in defiance, her sex goddess rattled the chains at the horror of one day without sex. Snubbing the protest Michele stood firm on her decision.

"Not a problem, baby. I'll call you on Tuesday. I'll plan something you'll like."

"I have what I like." She took his hand, leading him up to the cabin. "Okay, gorgeous. Do your job."

Once more, he swept her up to carry her across the deck, placing her on the marina gangway. "I'll see you Tuesday, baby."

The moment lingered. Michele knew she should go, or she'd end up in his bed again.

Mark wrapped a finger in her hair, as the late afternoon sun highlighted its strawberry blonde tint. "I love long hair. I love your hair." He traced his thumb across her lips. "Thank you."

She smiled up at him. "The feeling's mutual."

She turned and sashayed away, hopeful that a new, exciting future lay before her. One in which Mark featured in a lead role.

CHAPTER FOUR

MONDAY

MONDAYS WERE TOUGH AT the best of times, but today was arduous. Michele's major client demanded an inordinate amount of detail for their awards ball that she was managing, and deadlines were being moved almost hourly. Spending so much time in front of her computer on an ergonomic chair was also becoming a little uncomfortable due to all the recent horizontal dancing she'd been doing with Mark. Her mind wandered to him throughout the day, his smell, his strength, his power and of course, his expertise in lovemaking. Normally, she thrived on busy days full of event details, phone calls and emails. But she was more than relieved when she could at last shut down her home office, take a well-deserved bath and drive to the O'Brien's for dinner.

"DARLIN', HOW YA GOING?" Richie hugged Michele in his familiar Irish way. Although he'd been long gone from his mother country, his lyrical accent persisted. "Come in, come in." Richie had been a special services marksman in the army many years before and remained a straight shooter, metaphorically, in his personal life and professional career. No one knew of his past except SallyAnn and Michele, so when it came to keeping secrets, this was the place to be.

Having just finished dinner, Samantha and Jason, ran over for welcome hugs from Aunty Michele, before Richie took them upstairs to watch television. Already on her second glass of white wine, SallyAnn fussed around the kitchen stirring pots for her husband.

"Hi, Sal', smells great." Michele dipped her finger into the saucepan for a taste test.

"Yes, it's Richie's masterpiece, one of his famous curries. I'm just assisting and trying to look busy."

"Glass of wine, darlin'?" With his usual stealth, Richie had slipped back into the kitchen and held a glass of white out to his guest.

"Thank you. If only I could find a man like you."

"Ay, we're a handsome, loyal lot, we Irish." Releasing Michele's waist from a swift squeeze he took his position at the cooktop.

While Richie and SallyAnn bickered about the level of salt in the curry, Michele reflected on how SallyAnn had made the smoothest transition to civilian life, after the stage. The O'Brien's appeared so Disney perfect, it gave Michele hope a happy-ever-after ending could be possible for her. Being here was life-affirming, a second home of sorts. Somewhere her fear of rejection never found traction.

By the time they were devouring Richie's curry, with beads of perspiration on their foreheads, the conversation turned to Michele's latest exploits.

"So darlin', I hear you've been kicking your heels up a bit?" He broached the subject with his usual insouciance warmed by his Irish lilt.

"Yes. It's a whole new world out there. I had no idea." Michele dabbed her napkin to her face, trying to cool the burn from biting into a large chilli.

Richie passed some naan bread to anesthetize her fiery tongue. "Ay, you do look grand, though."

SallyAnn pushed the red culprits to the outer limits of her bowl and studied her friend. "What's happening then?"

"Well, I met this guy."

Michele proceeded to retell her experiences with Mark over the past few days; how he'd picked her up at the club, about the *Lady Diana* and the motoring of yachts for private clients. She left out the salacious details, preferring to cover the topic with the simple explanation of the sex being great. "And then on Saturday night, he starts cutting up cocaine."

"And?" SallyAnn's familiar tone of concern arrived right on cue.

"Well, I did say I was going to get out and live, so I tried it. It certainly kept us up and at it for hours."

"Aye, it'll do that. But what was his story about having it?" Richie asked.

Michele explained Mark's version of the coke and how he wasn't really involved in dealing drugs. She volunteered as much relevant information as she could recall while Richie listened without interrupting.

Finally settling in for liqueurs and dessert, Richie leaned back in his chair, hands clasped behind his head.

"Well, I have to say, you've got yourself a curly one. This Mark fella is someone who's not who he says he is. I'm certain of that. My gut tells me he's either bad through and through or he's playing a game that maybe you're unknowingly part of. I'd be very careful darlin'. There's something amiss here."

"Great. Just what I need, intrigue, mystery, and suspense. I feel like I'm living in an Agatha Christie novel."

"Just be careful, 'Chele. You're not seeing him again, are you?"

"Yes, tomorrow." She took a good shot of *Baileys* to avoid SallyAnn's persistent frown. "Anyway, it won't last long. He leaves at the end of the week and that'll be the last I see of him, I expect."

"Maybe that'll be for the best." Richie's loosely cloaked warning hung in the air but did little to squelch Michele's curiosity.

"I guess so . . ."

"But?" SallyAnn knew Michele too well to let her unconvincing answer slip past.

"I don't know. There's just something about him. Maybe he's the one for me?"

"For God's sake, 'Chele. Listen to Richie. He's seldom wrong when it comes to assessing tricky situations. If you must, have fun with this Mark fellow and then let him go. Okay?"

"Okay, okay," Michele conceded, fanning her hands at SallyAnn.

But as the conversation turned to less heated topics, Michele knew she'd have to discover more about her mystery man. She believed they'd been brought together for some reason and it was up to her to find out.

CHAPTER FIVE

TUESDAY

GROGGY FROM TOO LITTLE sleep and too much alcohol, Michele dragged herself from bed and shuffled to the bathroom. She scolded herself for having had that second *Baileys* while thankful that Richie had driven her car home last night. She assessed her shabby morning reflection wondering if this casual sex game was worth the roller-coaster of emotions.

"Don't be silly, girl. You'll scrub up really well and tonight he has something special planned."

With this encouragement from her sex goddess, Michele managed to slap on her makeup, throw on some clothes and be on her way to rehearsals within the hour. Lots of water, several cups of coffee and numerous run-throughs created a time warp. By late afternoon, she realized she'd been a dynamo for nine hours directing a spectacular event which she felt certain would please her clients.

As she packed up, she thought about Mark. He hadn't called, nor had he sent a text. Perhaps tonight was off? Perhaps he'd lost interest? No matter, she was exhausted and needed an early night. She threw her dance bag over her shoulder and strode out of the hotel ballroom. A long hot bath, maybe some food, a DVD and bed were now the order of the day's end. Even the drive home was surprisingly pleasant. Since there weren't any inconsiderate drivers on the road to ruin her mood, the familiar end-of-show-come-down made its slow descent over her tired body. She drove her faithful old convertible into the garage, switched on the lights, entered the kitchen and dropped her bag on the floor. Not wasting any time, she stripped off where she stood, grabbed an ice-cold beer from the fridge and climbed the stairs to the bathroom.

Her bath was her sanctuary, her favourite place aside from bed. Many happy memories had been created over the years as she immersed herself in the hot waters that transformed her both physically and mentally. With steam enveloping her bathroom in a pea-soup fog, she lit candles and incense in preparation for a long quiet soak.

She cringed when she dipped her toe in the hot water, trying to avoid the first assault of heat, but her body knew the drill and acclimatized to the temperature. After she poured the bubble bath under the running tap she slid deeper into the perfumed lacy foam. Within minutes, nothingness embraced her. Like the hush after the last curtain call when the velvet proscenium curtain settles, her mental chatter quieted. Her breathing slowed and deepened as she let go of external stimuli to meditate.

"You are loved, Michele. There is nothing to fear. You can do no wrong, Heaven is all around you, and you are free." The familiar mantra of the Goddess greeted her like an old friend calling from afar. Michele ascended into higher consciousness, dissolving into her multi-dimensional dreamscape. She had many questions that required answers this evening.

Rap, rap, rap.

What's that noise? It was nothing, just her nerves resisting the call to peace. She shook herself free of the interruption. Once more, she drifted.

Rap, rap, rap. Again, the noise.

"Who on earth is knocking at my front door at this time of night?" The decision to ignore whoever it was, momentarily released her from any further anxiety until she heard the voice. This time it wasn't the voice of the Goddess. It was Mark. Stepping out onto the damp tiles, she wrapped her sudsy body in a thick robe and padded downstairs.

How does he know where I live? Before she could ponder the thought longer, she reached the door and opened it.

"Surprise, baby." His dazzling eyes melted her suspicion like ice under the summer sun, while his body and what he could do with it awakened her sex goddess.

"What are you doing here?" she asked, not hiding her astonishment to find him standing at her front door.

"I thought I'd surprise you, baby. Instead of you having to run around town to be with me, I decided I'd come to you." He wrapped his arms around her, sweeping her off her feet as he turned full circle. "Can I come in?"

"Yeah, of course, I guess so. Come in." She shimmied down from his grip, closed the door then led him into her home. She bent down to collect her discarded clothes from the kitchen floor. "I assumed we wouldn't be catching up tonight?"

"As I said, I wanted to surprise you." His cheery tone didn't waver as he met her prickly gaze with a little two-step tap dance. "Ta, da." With a flourish of his hands, he presented himself like a variety contestant waiting for her to judge his act.

Unable to restrain a smile, she clucked her teeth. "Would you like a drink? I've only got beer I'm afraid."

"Sure. Sounds great." He hovered on the spot waiting for a further invitation.

She tossed her clothes into the laundry then retrieved a beer from the fridge.

He eyed her wet body. "I've disturbed you. I'm sorry. Not a very good surprise."

"I was just taking a bath. I had a big day and since I hadn't heard from you, I decided to come home to chill out." She shot him a sharp glance.

Not blinking, he dodged her well-aimed jibe. "Sounds like a good plan. Would you like some company? I make a really good water boy, you know." He pulled a large mouthful of beer as his eyes danced with mischief.

"Really? Water boy? Is that what we're calling it now?" The game was on. Allowing her initial suspicion and irritation to subside, she grinned. "Follow me, water boy, my bath is getting cold. And grab another couple of *Coronas* on the way."

"Yes, mistress. Your wish is my command."

With a quick pit stop at the fridge and extra supplies in hand, Mark followed her up the stairs. While Michele led the way, she didn't see his well-honed skills of scouting his surroundings kick in. He made mental notes of her townhouse. Lower level — kitchen, laundry, garage and living room with large sliding doors, two separate entrances, one internal staircase only. Fifteen steps to the upstairs level — a bathroom, separate toilet, and two bedrooms at opposite ends of the staircase. As he suspected, she kept her home neat, clean and highly organized, with photos on display and an assortment of sentimental knick-knacks. Although her furniture and furnishings weren't new, they were well-made quality products. As he watched her tempting arse sashay in front of him onto the second-floor landing, he calculated there were two limited, but workable escape routes in her home, if he needed them. Unlikely, but still.

Although the steam had evaporated, the bathroom was still warm and misty when they entered.

"Mistress likes the heat, I see." He placed the beers on the vanity bench and waited.

"Yes, she does. However, it needs to be hotter. Turn on the hot water, water boy."

As a director, choreographer and event manager, telling people what to do came easily to Michele. But nothing compared to the excitement of ordering such a delicious, virile specimen such as Mark to do as she willed. The thrill of command burned between her legs as he obeyed. On finishing the task, he stepped toward her, and she disrobed. She glanced down, pleased to see his cock straining to escape.

"You may join me, water boy. Undress."

He peeled off his clothes and reached out a polite hand to help her into the tub. While she slipped deeper into her steamy, sudsy retreat, he knelt beside the bath.

"Your water boy has brought you a gift, mistress. A small treat to make your night special." He reached into his jeans pocket and extracted two small tablets that nestled into the palm of his hand like precious gems.

Not again, she thought. Tomorrow was an important day, and she needed a clear head, so sleep was a priority tonight.

"Sleep?" her sex goddess screamed, "*You are kidding me? With a man like that beside you and you want to sleep. Plenty of time for sleep, sweetheart, when you're old and grey!"*

She smiled to herself, which Mark took as her willingness to try the proffered pills.

"What are they?" She was no longer playing the mistress.

"This is ecstasy, baby. It'll make you feel full of love, totally relaxed and chilled out, just like you want to be."

Her body tensed as she drew herself upright in the bath. "How did you know where I live?"

"I've got some friends in the police force who owed me a favour. You mentioned at dinner on Saturday about your car, so the guys pieced together where you lived based on that and a couple of other things I told them."

"So, you take all kinds of drugs, yet you have friends in the police force who can track down whoever you want? Sounds very suspicious to me."

"Not really. If you recall, I did say my dad had been in the force? Anyway, you'd be surprised what goes on with the boys in blue."

"It seems so," she said, unconvinced.

"Here, baby, I brought you a special treat. Have an E. It'll help you relax." On swallowing one, he offered the other to her with a flattering smile.

"I was relaxing before you turned up unannounced."

"But I'm your surprise, and I brought this as an extra surprise. You're safe, baby. It's okay."

"Will I be able to sleep if I take this? I have a big day of rehearsals and the show tomorrow so I can't be up screwing all night."

"Well, I can promise the screwing will definitely happen, for how long, who knows? The sleep will depend on how satisfied I make you. I'll do my best."

"Go on. Let's not waste any more time." Her inner sex goddess played turncoat once more and danced around on Michele's better judgment.

He lifted his hand to her mouth until she surrendered to his persuasions, and with a sip of beer, the tablet was gone.

"I will now bathe my mistress."

Shelving her suspicions, she slipped back under the foam and allowed Mark to ease her tensions. He massaged her upper body, rubbing the length of her arms to her fingertips before returning to her neck and shoulders. She let go of the pressures of the day and relaxed into her well-known space of quiet contemplation. While he continued his platonic kneading of her body, moving to her feet and lower legs, she drifted into the silence. It wasn't until the water turned tepid, he roused her from her introspection with a soft touch on her inner thigh. Her eyelids flickered, but she didn't open them. Brushing her other thigh with a feathery touch, he opened her legs to continue his massage.

Leaning close to her face, he whispered, "If mistress will allow, I'd like to please her?"

She barely opened her eyes, nodded, then reverted to the pleasure of her real-life fantasy. His hands began to press a little stronger, opening the soft firm flesh of her inner thighs, fingers brushing her sex, making it engorge as her yearning took hold.

"Your water boy is going to take his time. He's going to make mistress ache for him until she can't stand it any longer." The whispered promise tortured her with both anticipation and apprehension.

His fingers drummed an incessant rhythm, until her clit emerged from its enclosing lips, peeping out for more. Then he stopped.

"Mistress, your impatience is tantalizing, but we mustn't rush. Slowly, slowly."

Not delighted with the 'go slow' instruction, her genitalia ached. His lips danced around her nipples as they peeked up from under the suds, while his hand continued its teasing beneath. Normally the cooling water would have disturbed Michele however, her increasing core temperature more than compensated. Nevertheless, the restriction of the bath made her impatient, and she squirmed to give him easier access. But he didn't oblige, preferring to build her desire with tentative touching. By now she throbbed. She needed release, a firmer touch, so she decided to take matters into her own hands.

He grabbed her hand, stopping its downward journey. "No, mistress. You must let me please you."

"Then do it," she moaned with a yearning in her voice she'd not heard before.

"Soon. Soon." He pulled the plug, allowing the tub to empty. Standing at the end of the bath, he grabbed her body and slid her down into the tub until she was lying flat on her back. He opened her legs over the sides exposing her snatch, hot, pink and glistening. He straddled the bath and supported his weight with his arms, then lowered his face toward her gaping mound. She smelt fragrant and musky. She tasted of sudsy water and female juice.

Michele stretched herself toward him, willing him to penetrate her with his tongue. Yet he refrained. Instead, he flicked and nibbled her clitoris, assaulting her with his expertise until she cried out for relief. She thrust her hips higher and higher toward him demanding closure. Yet each time she did, he pushed himself up and away until she quelled her insistence, lowering herself once more. Only then did he return to his torment on her aching, swollen slit. Throughout this pleasurable agony, his enormous cock hung above her face, just out of reach. She longed to consume him but couldn't reach. Every time she strained upward to taste him, he grabbed her buttocks and thrust them back toward his face so he could rake her bud once more with his wicked tongue. She was trapped in a sexual stalemate; unable to give and unable to receive, unsure how much longer she could stand this erotic torture.

"Would mistress like some penetration now?" His words oozed like hot wax with the promise of pleasure and pain.

"Oh, yes please," she gasped, begging to be put out of her misery.

He leapt over the bath and jammed his fingers deep inside her. He spun them around to find her G-spot, pumping hard against it until she ejaculated within moments. He kept hammering away at her while she shuddered, screaming in ecstasy. He climaxed her again, pounding at her body until she collapsed from delighted exhaustion. As she lay panting, he said, "Would mistress like some other penetration now?"

Unsure whether her body could take any more, she still nodded with wanton desire. Waiting for him to make his move she remained still with her eyes closed, her legs splayed. Slowly he slid into her. But it wasn't his warm hard cock he inserted. It was the Corona bottle. Her eyes snapped open, staring at him in shock.

"You're safe, baby. Go with it. I promise." With the bottle slipped tight within her, he teased her G-spot.

Surrendering to his persuasion, the effect of the ecstasy pill and the illicit debauchery of the act, Michele allowed him to work his sex toy deep within her, spinning around and around. She leaned back in the bath, pulling herself open for him. The bottle was cool, slick and in the hands of a master sex partner like Mark, surprisingly satisfying. He worked on her for a few minutes and she surrendered to his wickedness, her muscles relaxing to take more of the bottle than she thought possible. When he flat tongued her swollen clit and extricated the bottle, she opened her eyes, disappointed. But he lifted her out of the bath and carried her to the bedroom, where he placed her damp, limp body onto the bed.

"God that was good," she moaned.

"Mistress is a very good girl and will now be rewarded with what she's waited for."

In one movement, he was on top of her, deep inside, pummelling her, until he rammed all breath out of her. She was in bliss, or was she in love? She didn't know or care. When she glanced up at him, she caught him staring down at her. Until now, his eyes had remained closed during sex. However, this time he fixed on her and drove deeper with a determination to deplete himself. Yet he didn't come.

With stamina spent, he rolled off and encircled her in his arms. Michele thought she heard him say "I love you." But she couldn't be sure. "I love you too, gorgeous," she said without hesitation and cuddled into him and fell into a deep sleep.

It was the first time she'd dreamed in ages. There were two young children, a boy and a girl, sitting on a beach playing, laughing and building sandcastles. A picture postcard moment, a typical summer's day with blue skies, rolling waves lapping at the sand and not another person in sight except the children. It was a happy dream. Then it was gone. No fade to black, just gone.

THEY'D FALLEN ASLEEP WITH the curtains open, so it was the sun that woke Michele at a quarter to five in the morning. Since Mark wasn't in bed, she shuffled off to the bathroom to find him. The only sign of him was the Corona bottle and the smell of him on the towels. God, she loved that smell. Otherwise, the bathroom was neat as a pin.

"Bless him. He's cleaned up." She picked up the bottle and put it in the bin. This souvenir she didn't need. Expecting to find him in the kitchen, she sprang down the stairs to emptiness. He was gone. However, there was a note stuck to the fridge door beside her shopping list.

Good morning, mistress.
Had to go early.
Hope you had a good night.
I did. Will call later.
Your Water Boy

No kisses, no hugs. It lacked any real affection. It could have been another shopping list.

Her hope slinked out the door. The nagging whisper that had haunted her over the past couple of days now found its full voice. She was falling in love, and he'd fallen in lust. The typical female-male relationship dynamics were at play here. Her first casual sex encounter was turning into something much more than she imagined. The sharp contrast of a one-way love affair slapped with a sting, and she felt like a silly, love-struck teenager. Rising indignation became her new morning emotion.

Flying into a disciplined routine of cleaning, rearranging and divesting her home of any proof of her stupidity, she seethed. She criticized herself for taking the drugs, allowing him to have his way with her whenever and however he wanted, permitting him into her house when she didn't know how he had found out where she lived or even who he was. How could she be such a fool? She stomped and fumed, cursed and vented until within the hour, she'd bleached, swept and washed away any evidence he'd been there. Except for one hand towel. She couldn't wash him away entirely, not yet. Surely, she could allow herself just one final reminder of their tempestuous love affair? With fresh linen on the bed and the hand towel in a zip lock bag tucked under her pillow, she showered, dressed and drove off. Regardless of her mixed emotions, she was ready to move on.

CHAPTER SIX

WEDNESDAY

Despite, or maybe because of the previous night's sexcapade, Michele charged through the dress rehearsals. After giving her cast and crew final notes, she called Cindy for a little pre-show support.

"Hi, sweetie. You ready for the awards ball tonight?" Cindy's voice worked like a shot of sugar when your body needed a quick fix.

"Yeah. Rehearsals went really well. I'm sure all will be okay."

"Good to hear. How's Mark?"

"Too much to tell over the phone. He leaves on Saturday so I may need a shoulder to cry on then. What's happening with you and your police officer?"

"Graham? Actually, he's really lovely but he works in narcotics so I'm not sure if I want to get too serious with him. I don't think I need all that danger in my life."

"I know how you feel." Michele thought about her recent drug experiences, which at the time she hadn't thought were dangerous, but now she wasn't so sure.

"Yes. He was telling me about some of the drug busts he's done and the officers involved and what they went through. Pretty messed up, if you ask me."

"Do you think you'll see him again?"

"I'm not sure, anyway enough about that. You have a great night, sweetie. Chookas."

Meaning 'good luck' or 'break a leg,' 'chookas' was an old theatre term, wishing you'd play to a full house and thus be assured of affording a chicken dinner that night.

"Thanks, Cindy. See you soon."

Michele threw the remainder of her coffee away, checked her watch and went to the dressing room. In keeping with the black-tie event, she dressed in a black tailored satin pantsuit, embodying a 1940s hostess-with-the-mostest. She greeted guests, managed staff and juggled the unexpected with ease, so by the time the gala dinner was served, her clients were ebullient, which meant her invoice would be paid on time.

FINANCIALLY STARTING OVER AGAIN after the divorce had proved harder than she'd expected. Living hand to mouth each week with the associated stresses was why she relied so heavily on the Goddess's counsel. Feeling too proud and ashamed to tell her friends the whole truth, Michele had struggled to pay her rent, at times forsaking food. She chose to remain positive and found comfort in the belief that her slimmer self was healthier and more appealing. Eating was overrated anyway. As she grappled with her loss after the divorce, she'd grown to depend more and more on her meditations and discussions with the Goddess.

"You are loved, Michele. There is nothing to fear. You can do no wrong, Heaven is all around you and you are free," was the constant mantra playing in her mind. To date, she'd had no reason not to believe it. And since she'd chosen to explore her sexual freedom, her life seemed to be improving, regardless of how confused she felt about Mark.

JUST BEFORE CURTAIN-UP, she made a quick dash to the ladies' room and switched on her phone to see two messages.

"Chookas for the show tonight. Call me. Love SallyAnn xxx"

Michele softened at the memory of their dancing days when they'd wait together in the wings for curtain-up. Each of the girls would give the other a quick kiss on the cheek and a chookas before launching onto the stage. These sweetest of memories returned as she typed out a quick thank you message to SallyAnn and hit send.

"Hey baby. 11 P.M. tonight at Sugar Roll Club. Look fabulous like always. Mark xxx"

"Now he sends me kisses. Seriously? He drives me crazy." She flipped off her phone and dashed out to take her place at the back of the ballroom, waiting on her creative vision to come to life.

The next few hours sped past without a glitch, leaving Michele, her management of the awards ball and her gala show the toast of the town. When the guests and winners took to the dance floor, Michele's clients invited her to their table. The effusive praise of the Coast's movers and shakers as they cracked open the French fizz, made her confident more work would flow.

Before succumbing to the giggle juice, she excused herself from the party and caught a taxi to the Sugar Roll Club. This would be their third-to-last night together before Mark set off in the *Lady Diana* back to southern waters. Despite her early morning convictions, she wanted to spend as much time as she could with him. Aside from his elusiveness and the suspicions of others, he filled a hole in her life. He made her feel safe somehow, and her sex goddess within was restless.

FASHIONED ON A 1930s theme and dominated by black marble, art deco mirrors, plush carpet and private booths, the Sugar Roll Club featured modern, edgy styling that blended the wealthy and the wannabes who congregated there every night.

Wednesday nights, euphemistically known as hump night, were notorious for the 'suits.' The city's professional young men in their designer suits would stalk their prey at

Sugar Roll, hunting in packs and anxious for their next sexual 'kill' while pretty young things arrived in the hope of finding a respectable suitor. Often, the naïve girls ended up like frightened gazelle wandering into the lion's den.

Looking more like a cougar than a gazelle, Michele padded down the stairs into the club on a high of natural endorphins from a successful show and the quality champagne. It'd been a while since she'd been to the club but scanning the room, she noticed not much had changed. The girls and guys vied for attention, checking their reflections in the art deco mirrors whenever they cruised past. This was the bewitching hour and the room began to swell with more clientele, adding that distinctive buzz every club needs to be successful.

Stepping onto the main floor, she smelt him before she saw him. He slipped his powerful arm around her waist and bent down to kiss her.

"Hello, baby. How did the show go?"

"Fabulous, couldn't have gone better. The clients loved it, so that's a bonus."

"I've got a booth just over here. Come with me."

He ushered her through the mob of salivating, hungry suits. "Baby, you certainly look hot in whatever it is you're almost wearing."

She winked and curved her mouth in a wicked smile. She knew the fabric of her pantsuit clung to her body in all the right places, and she noticed not only Mark but the other predators trying to catch peek-a-boo glimpses of her breasts as she sauntered past.

"I've gotta be the luckiest bastard here," he said, a wide smile lighting up his face as his chest inflated.

He stopped at the furthest booth in the back corner and allowed her to slide in. "What do you want to drink, baby?"

"I've been drinking Moet so more of the same, please."

"French champagne for the lady who gives the best French." He planted an affectionate kiss on her forehead and departed to the bar.

Within minutes, he returned and placed an ice bucket on the table. "French champagne for the lady." He poured two glasses and slipped in beside her.

"A toast, to you, baby. You've made my trip very special." They touched glasses and when he leaned in to kiss her, she pulled back a little. "What's wrong?"

"I'm just sad to think you're leaving on Saturday." Reality had hit. She'd fallen for him and there was no denying her feelings.

"Listen. We've had a great time, and we still have two more nights together. You're like an angel from heaven who found me. I can't explain it any other way. I've got to leave, but I'm sure I'll be back."

"I know there were no promises made. It's just I know nothing about you except you take drugs, motor yachts around and give me great sex."

"There really isn't much else I can tell you at the moment."

"Why? Who are you? Why all the mystery?"

He began to slide back out of the booth, offering his hand. "Let's dance. Then we'll talk."

Tamping her growing annoyance, she followed him through the crowd and onto the dance floor. It took a few minutes but eventually, the music and atmosphere buoyed her spirits. Dancing with Mark had happy memories already attached, and he seemed transported by a natural rhythm, as if an intrinsic tempo sustained him. Her mood lightened. Two songs later, and they turned up the sexual heat, grinding at each other on the crowded floor.

"LET'S SIT DOWN, BABY," he said and led her from the dance floor. He'd made the decision to tell her. In normal circumstances, he wouldn't divulge anything, but his investigations had proved she was who she presented herself to be. It was time.

On their way back she excused herself to freshen up in the ladies' room while he continued to the booth. Sitting with his back to the wall, his customary position in any room, he studied the faces around him. It'd been a few years since he'd been here. He'd lost the beard and some weight since then so it was unlikely anyone would recognize him. But he was only alive because he didn't take chances, and tonight wasn't any different.

Then he saw Michele stop at the bar. A large Chinese man was talking to her, trying to pick her up no doubt. But it wasn't the sexual approach that bothered Mark, it was the man himself. Mark looked at the surrounding people in this tableau, and there they were. Two gorillas in suits, watching the room, looking out for their Chinese boss with guns likely stuffed into their belts under their jackets. Motionless, Mark willed himself to disappear into the back of the booth, never taking his eyes off Michele. She was handling herself well, although the Chinese man seemed quite insistent she join him. Flashing a sweet smile, she made her departure and weaved her way through the crowd back to their booth.

"God! Some people just can't take no for an answer. Did you see that guy trying to pick me up? This place has really gone to the dogs." She slurped down some champagne without even registering Mark's tension.

"That's because he's the biggest drug dealer in the country, and he's used to getting his own way."

She stiffened.

His attention remained on the Chinese triad. "Okay. It's time to go. We can't stay." He was out of the booth in one deft movement, holding his hand out for her to follow. Not taking his eyes off the Chinese delegation he felt her hand squeeze his. Hoping her dancing skills included following a partner, he wrapped her into his arm and took the lead. Steady and brisk he set the pace as she shadowed his urgency through the crowded club. None of the thugs seemed to register their departure and with a final glance over his shoulder, Mark ushered her up the stairs and out the door.

His body was strung tight, adrenalin pumping. Not a word was spoken. Outside they jumped into a taxi and disappeared into the night. For a few minutes, he kept glancing in the driver's rear-view mirror to check they weren't being followed. Once certain they were safe, his muscles relaxed. With Michele's head resting on his shoulder, he knew this episode had changed things. She deserved an explanation, but not now. Not in a cab. She'd have to wait until they were alone. It was going to be a long night.

IT WASN'T UNTIL THEY were on board the *Lady Diana* that Mark broke the silence. He handed Michele a martini and sat down beside her.

"I'm an ex-undercover narcotics cop. I was lead detective in a major drug bust-up here a few years ago and the Chinese boss, whose business I shut down, has a contract out on me."

She sat speechless while questions swarmed her mind like angry bees threatening to sting.

"I don't think I was recognized. I've changed a bit since then, but I didn't want to take any chances, especially since he became interested in you at the club. You're too hot for your own good, you know that." Mischief lit up his face as he brushed off the revelation about his dangerous life with little more than a casual explanation.

"But if you've been an undercover narcotics cop, why are you taking drugs?"

"Because that's what we do. We had to take them as part of our cover. We're all hooked on the stuff and we're pretty much fucked-up, part and parcel of the job." And with his smile broadening, he added, "That's why I can get the best gear in the country."

"Okay," she said, still struggling to piece the puzzle together, "so what happens now?"

"Nothing happens now. Nothing changes. We have two more nights left. Let's make the most of them."

Stunned by this unexpected disclosure of his identity, Michele took a few moments to process. "I knew there was something different about you. But I didn't expect this. Sorry, I'm not sure what to say."

"That's all right. There isn't anything really to say. No big deal."

While he collected the glasses, her mind began to connect the dots. The mystery, the evasive behaviour, how he knew her age and where she lived, the variety of drugs he had on hand, his subtle desperation to squeeze every last bit out of life. He was used to living a dangerous life with deadly consequences. The damage ran deep yet the scars remained fresh.

Michele joined him at the sink. "Thanks for telling me. Everything makes a little more sense now."

"I thought you should know. You've changed my life. You've shown me there's a lot more to life than living on a knife's edge all the time. With you, I can forget."

He lowered the tea towel and pulled her close, consuming her through his skin. She slipped her fingers through his silky hair, moulding her body to his. His lips pressed hers with a tender, lingering kiss which she returned with deepening affection.

Without a word, they descended into the cabin to spend another night together, this time without the drugs, without the role-playing, and without the cheerleading of Michele's sex goddess. They simply made love, au naturel, in the silence.

WITH ONE OF MARK'S arms angled under his head and the other curling her into his shoulder, they lay in the stillness as the water lapped a lullaby on the hull.

"Do you want to talk about it?" she whispered.

"Basically, I'm fucked. The police force fucked me over."

She held her breath, longing for some answers, hopeful he'd let her in. Moonlight shimmered across his beaten face, highlighting both his silent pain and inner strength. While his gaze searched the shadows, Michele sensed the bravado that acted as his camouflage fracture.

"I worked for years as an undercover operative infiltrating major bikie gangs and shit like that. I set up major busts and deals, negotiating large quantities of every sort of drug available on the market. Hash, speed, coke, dope, anything you can snort, shoot, swallow or fuck yourself up with." His chest swelled with a long slow breath, stoking his buried anger.

"I remember this one time when the bust went wrong, and I nearly got killed because my back-up went screeching down the wrong fucking driveway to the house next door. I was standing there with my dick in my hands, so to speak, before the silly bastards got the right house. Then there were other days I'd drive to three different Sydney suburbs on the force's Harley, firstly to buy speed, then to buy coke and then to buy heroin. I had to keep reminding myself which undercover identity I was playing at each fucking buy. Each stop I'd have to smoke a couple of joints, scull a few beers, sometimes taste the gear. And all the while, I'd be wondering if my fucking cover was going to be blown."

She remained silent while her heart wept.

"Then there were the eighteen months I worked as a go-between for the triads doing a complex deal with the Chinese mafia, which ended in a major bust and convictions. It was a big fucking win for the New South Wales Police Force. But I got shoved in the witness protection program. Not much fun there, I can tell you. All those fucking years I spent in a deadly intelligence game played out in clubs and pubs, masquerading as a crook, getting hooked on drugs, losing touch with who I was. Then once I was totally fucked in the head, I got royally screwed by the force. That's when I left the department as a suicidal mess. They gave me no assistance, no counselling, no retraining. Nothing."

Bitterness and injustice leached from his body.

"My life was on the line every minute I was fuckin' out there. They just used and abused me. And if I didn't do the job, some other big copper was waiting in line to take my place and my promotion. The department just hung me out to dry. Bastards!"

Speechless, she traced the muscles on his chest, unable to fathom how anyone could live through a life of such extremes and survive. He'd been the hero, an absolute champion. It seemed so unfair. Reaching up, she brushed her lips across his mouth knowing her words of sympathy could do little. Determined to ease his pain, her body enfolded his once more. And as much as she offered herself as the receptacle into which he could unburden his past, his damaged survival instincts refused him that pleasure.

~ ♥ ~

THE DREAM RETURNED THAT night; the boy and the girl, on the beach, playing, laughing. The children seemed to have known one another for a long time, they belonged together, and their joy caused Michele to smile in her sleep.

Pulling herself out of the dream, she blinked in the morning light that crept into the cabin like a skulking child. Naked, Mark's magnificent form filled all the space in the en suite as he shaved, unaware she was awake and relishing the view he afforded.

"Good morning, gorgeous." She stretched on the bed in a graceful pose.

"Morning, baby. Stay right where you are, I'm nearly finished." Splashing on his signature scent which leapt out to seduce her, he strolled back to sit on the side of the bed.

He gazed down at her. "God you're beautiful, you know that?"

"You're pretty damned gorgeous yourself." Her fingers slid up and down his muscular arms while he remained motionless. The moment dragged, and she sensed his hesitation. "What is it?"

"I'm married."

She couldn't breathe. "You can't be. I asked if you were married. On Sunday morning."

Her heart raced, while her mind jockeyed back in time, realizing he'd not answered the question about his marital status. He'd fobbed it off with one of his Rhett Butler moves and a kiss.

"No." Her hands flew to her face in a lame attempt to shield herself from the truth.

"I'm sorry, baby. I'm just so used to being undercover. I don't know what else to be. I'm fucked-up. I told you that last night. But then you came along, and everything changed. You weren't supposed to happen to me."

"I wasn't supposed to happen to you?" The pitch of her voice jumped an octave. "What about me? I went out to get laid and instead you sweet-talked me into your bed and promptly lied to me."

"I never lied. I just didn't tell you everything. Until now."

"Well, thanks for that!" She hurled her legs over his head and began collecting her strewn clothes.

"Please wait." He grabbed both her hands and, despite her struggling, refused to concede. He pushed her to sit on the bed before kneeling in front of her. "I'll be honest with you. When I saw you last Friday night, I thought we'd have crazy wild sex for the week I was here, and that's all."

"And?" She clenched her fists and set her jaw.

"Fuck it, Michele, what can I say. You've changed me, and I don't know what the fuck is going on." Releasing her hands, he dragged his fingers through his hair and dropped to the floor, his back against the bed.

Her gut churned with unspoken words and dashed hopes. Technically he hadn't lied to her, but he hadn't been forthcoming either. After Mark's revelations last night of his past and the pain he'd suffered, she could understand why. But understanding his logic didn't stop her rejection raising its ugly head, ready to feast on her hostile emotions.

Tempering her rage, she slid down beside him and landed with a thud. On a synchronistic sigh, they cast a sideways glance at each other. With their knees scrunched under their chins and scowls on their faces, they looked like bickering children.

"I don't know what the fuck is going on either," she said. "You were meant to be nothing more to me than my first one-night stand. And here we are. Dare I say it, feeling much more for each other than either of us intended."

He ventured a soft smile across at her which she reciprocated.

"Ironic, huh?" she said, with no fight left in her.

"Fucking hilarious," he replied, not in the least amused.

She hauled her body off the floor and began getting dressed. "Okay. You're married. I don't even know what to do with that piece of information yet. But I'm damned sure I'm not here to be your Mother Confessor."

"I didn't tell you to unburden myself. I told you because you have a right to know."

He stood and pulled on his jeans. This sensual barrel-chested tower of a man seemed such a contradiction to the boyish innocence begging from his clear blue eyes. She struggled not to throw her arms around his neck, ruffle his hair and lavish him with kisses.

He reached out, and she allowed him to hold her hands. "I'm leaving on Saturday. Can we spend the rest of my time together? Please?"

"I'm not sure. I need some time to think."

She kissed him on the cheek, picked up her shoes and left the yacht. This time, on her own.

CHAPTER SEVEN

THURSDAY

THE DAY AFTER STAGING a big event was always a bit of a downer, but now compounded with Mark's damaged history and marital status, Michele felt herself slipping into a blue funk. Knowing a bath, some quiet contemplation and a chat with the Goddess were her best solace, she settled into her watery sanctuary.

The familiar blackness elevated her beyond her chattering emotions into the stillness of her mind where the Goddess greeted her.

"You are loved, Michele. There is nothing to fear. You can do no wrong, Heaven is all around you and you are free."

"What am I to do with Mark?"

"You are close yet not close enough."

"I don't understand?"

"He is not who you want him to be, but you are close yet not close enough."

Just as she asked for clarification, Michele felt the connection sever, leaving her with more unanswered questions. Too much emotion jangled her nerves.

After luxuriating in the tranquillity for another twenty minutes, Michele towelled dry then slipped in between her bedsheets hoping sleep would bring her clarity. As she settled down, a text message from Julie provided a glimmer of light at the end of her darkening tunnel.

"Divinities 4 P.M. today. I have news. Julie xxx"

Michele texted back she'd be there then switched off her phone. She snuggled into her pillow and her hand touched the forgotten reminder she'd put there yesterday. It was the plastic bag with the hand towel steeped in Mark's aftershave. She removed the cloth and placed it under her cheek, hoping there might be a chance for them. Maybe he'd leave his wife. However, her last thought was the Goddess's cryptic message whispered into her consciousness, *"He is not who you want him to be, but you are close yet not close enough."*

THE VIBE AT DIVINITIES on Thursday afternoons was low key. Just a few casually dressed regulars sharing the latest office or neighbourhood gossip, teenage kids hanging out on their way home from school and mums with their children in tow on their way to or from the supermarket. Finding Julie in her designer business suit propped at a quiet corner table proved easy.

"First things first, how did the awards ball go?" Julie asked, and Michele gave a full account while they ordered coffees.

"Fabulous. I'm pleased it went well for you. I wouldn't expect otherwise. Now tell me about Mark. What's happening with him?"

"You mean aside from the great sex and that I think I've fallen in love with him?"

"Well, it's understandable you think you've fallen in love with him. You haven't had any sex in years, let alone good sex. He's unlocked the floodgates, so to speak. Of course, you've fallen for him. But aside from that, what else have you found out about him?"

"He's married."

Julie fixed her with a questioning gaze. "Really? And how do you know that?"

"He told me yesterday. I'm gutted of course. I thought maybe there could've been a future with him, but not now."

"And how do you feel about having an affair with a married man?" Julie vocalized the question that'd been lurking in Michele's mind.

"I'm not sure. I mean I don't like being the 'other woman' in his marriage. After all, I know what that feels like since I had to deal with the 'other men' in my marriage. But at the same time, I figure it's his choice to be with me while he's here. It's obviously going to remain just a casual affair and that's exactly what I was looking for. All things taken into consideration, it really is a win-win. If he's not with me, then he'll be off with someone else. Hell, it's not my job to feel guilty and worry about his wife back home. That's his job." She realized her rising defensiveness made her disregard for his wife sound meaner than she meant.

Julie held her bejewelled hands up in mock self-defence. "Okay. Don't get yourself all worked up. No need to preach to me. If you recall, I've had my fair share of married men. My absolution isn't necessary. Has he told you anything else about what he does or who he is?"

"Wait a minute. You texted me to say you have news but until now all you've done is play Twenty Questions. Come on. Spill it. What is it you know?"

"Well, after you told us about him, I've been doing a little investigation of my own. The yacht he's motoring — the *Lady Diana* — it's registered to a local import company that brings in goods from China. Not sure if that helps but I found it interesting."

"From China?"

"Yes. Why? Does that mean anything?"

Michele summarized the previous night's events, Mark's history in the police force as an undercover detective in narcotics, his subsequent drug addiction and the Chinese drug dealer who had a contract out on him.

"Shit, girlfriend. What have you got yourself into?" Julie rubbed the nape of her neck.

"I don't know. It gets more confusing by the minute. He told me he was an ex-undercover narcs cop and now you tell me the *Lady Diana* is registered to a Chinese import business? Maybe he's still in the force? Maybe he's still not telling me everything?"

"Or maybe the Chinese connection with the yacht is nothing. After all, there are a lot of Chinese in the world. It doesn't mean the drug boss has anything to do with the Chinese import company that owns the *Lady Diana*, a coincidence maybe?"

Michele shrugged. "Who knows?"

They both sat in silence for a moment drinking their coffees, trying to piece together the ever-growing puzzle that was becoming Michele's love life.

"Hang on. What about the police officer Cindy's been seeing? Graham's his name, I think. He was involved in drug busts here as well. Maybe he's told her something? Let me get her on the phone." Michele called Cindy and gave her a quick recap of the past twenty-four hours' events before placing her on hands-free.

"Oh, sweetie, I don't know what else to say. Graham only talked in general about his work. He didn't go into any details. What do you want me to do?"

"Will you go out with him again?"

"Yes, not a problem. He's been calling for another date, so that's easy."

"When you do out with him again, see if you can find out as much as you can about his work, previous busts, cop's names, anything, particularly any information about a Chinese drug gang who got busted a few years ago. See if you can find out if it's true."

"Okay. Can do. But I'm now officially worried about you. What are you going to do?"

"Don't worry about me. I just want to corroborate Mark's story somehow. I need to know for sure."

"I understand your curiosity," Julie said, "but is all of this worth it? He'll be gone in a couple of days. Why not just notch it up to a week of fabulously hot sex and a little mystery?"

"That'd be the logical thing to do but for some reason, I can't let this go. There's some connection between Mark and me that I can't put my finger on, and I need to find out what it is. I need to know the truth. Help me out on this one, girls?"

"You can count on me, sweetie."

"Me too, whatever you need. Just keep me posted," Julie said.

"Great. I better let SallyAnn know or we'll all cop a lecture."

~ ♥ ~

By the time she arrived, the children were in their rooms doing homework and SallyAnn and Richie were sitting at the kitchen bench sipping chilled Sav Blanc.

"Hello, darlin'." He gave her a cheek kiss and extended a welcome glass of wine. "I gather things have taken a bit of a turn?" His eyes twinkled as he settled back onto his stool awaiting the next instalment of his wife's best friend's current adventure.

"Thanks." Michele took a good mouthful before continuing. "Yes, things have definitely progressed since last time. It's all very exciting, this being single game. I think aside from falling in love, I'm quite enjoying the mystery of it all."

"Aye, but be careful what you wish for."

"What's all this talk about falling in love, 'Chele? I thought you were having great sex and that was it?"

"Maybe, but the plot thickens." Michele launched into her second performance of the previous day's revelations, ensuring no details were omitted because she knew Richie needed every piece of information to form a considered opinion.

"So, what do you think?" She posed the question to Richie, as she already knew what SallyAnn's reply would be.

He sat in silence for a few moments, piecing together various scenarios in his mind. With slow, modulated phrasing, he began. "There are a number of options here. The first option is that Mark is an ex-cop, as he says he is, and the Chinese thing with the yacht and the drug boss is a coincidence. Not likely, though. Option two is that he's still an active undercover operative and is partially lying to you to protect you or to use you as cover in his operation. Possible. Or option three is he's fuckin' bad news, and he could be totally lying to you to gain your trust for whatever ends he has in store for you. There's any number of options but regardless of anything, my advice is to leave it alone."

"For God's sake, 'Chele, what have you got yourself into? Only four days ago you were going out to have your first one-night stand and now we're talking about undercover narcotics cops, drug busts, Chinese hitmen, a mystery man you now say you've fallen in love with who says he's married, and you want to know the truth? Seriously! I love you, but this whole affair is getting out of hand."

"Aye, Michele, and there is option four . . . He could be a fuckin' assassin working for a rival Chinese drug boss and you're caught in the middle of a hit. I would call it quits girlie and not see him again."

"I know this sounds stupid, but I feel I know him. He's not the bad guy here. But there's something else he's not telling me, and I need to know what it is."

"Very well, 'Chele, but if anything happens, we wouldn't know. We don't even know this Mark. We haven't even seen him. You could disappear and what good would any of us be in the investigation?"

"I'm sure I'm safe. Don't ask me how but I do. Don't worry. I'll be fine. I just need to know what else is going on."

"Aye, darlin', but be careful. Don't take any chances with this one. At least get a photo of him."

Complying with Richie's request, Michele agreed on a risk management strategy for herself. Once her friends were somewhat satisfied that she could look after herself, she bid them goodnight then headed home to change for her next performance with her mystery man. By the time she arrived home, her phone was flashing with a text.

"Hey, baby. Can't see you tonight. Will call you in the morning. Sorry. Xxx"

Although thrilled by the inclusion of kisses in his text, she felt disappointment welling up within her.

"Call him anyway. See what he has to say," her sex goddess prompted.

Michele obeyed, but Mark's phone rang out and with it so did her prospect of another night with him. She was wide awake now with nowhere to go, no answers to her many questions and no immediate opportunity of finding them. A text was her only option.

"Was so looking forwards to being with you tonight. See you tomorrow. Call me. Xxx"

She hit send, realizing the best she could do now was wait. Patience wasn't one of her strongest virtues.

She was too wound up to eat so deciding on an early night she climbed the stairs to her bedroom. When she switched on the red bedside lamps, her bedroom smouldered with a subtle pink glow which highlighted the Toulouse Lautrec posters scattered around the walls. She loved these posters of the Moulin Rouge dancers from the late 1800s, as they were a constant reminder of the happy years she'd spent as a dancer there in Paris. She drew back her bed linen, printed with the Eifel tower, stripped off her clothes and climbed in. Reaching under the pillow, she retrieved the towel from its plastic bag and drew in a deep breath of him.

"I know there's something more to this," she whispered to a painted dancer in a can-can poster kicking up her leg.

"He is not who you want him to be, but you are close yet not close enough."

"This doesn't help me much, because I think I've fallen in love with him."

Michele slipped into a dreamless sleep with the smell of him lingering on her pillow.

CHAPTER EIGHT

FRIDAY

"**GOD, SWEETIE, JUST BECAUSE** you're having great sex doesn't mean you have to dance me into the ground." Cindy was doubled over panting hard trying to get her breath back. "You know I love these classes and God knows they're the only thing staving off middle age, but, Michele, you're killing me today."

"Cindy, it's a small price to pay. What's a little pain, aching muscles, and burning lungs? As dancers, we can't get much better than this except under a spotlight. Come on. You can do better than that."

Michele flicked her friend on the butt and cued the track again. The music bounced off the walls in the dance studio demanding they rise to the occasion. She picked up the tempo and threw herself solidly into the routine, sweat spinning off her body as she executed the first *pirouette*. It took Cindy a couple of moments longer until she joined in the dance, her breathing still laboured.

Their Friday morning dance class had become a ritual years before. Regardless of work, sickness or even injury, the two friends met each week at the studio, choreographing to their favourite pieces of music, pushing themselves and each other to kick higher, leap further, bend deeper, extend stronger and in all ways better their performance. They'd grown up together at their first studio dancing under the tutelage of an iconic ballet mistress, who was a dragon to learn from but because of her highly disciplined teaching methods, she'd wrung every ounce of talent, strength, and determination from her young charges, creating women in her own image.

"Seriously, you're going to kill me if you play that track again. Enough for today." With her head buried in her towel, Cindy pleaded for mercy.

"Are you wimping out on me? We've only done an hour. Cindy, you need to get out more, build up your stamina with some virile young man. Careful, girlfriend, you're getting old."

The challenge of the 'o' word was obviously too much to bear. Cindy threw her towel on the chair like the gauntlet of an aggrieved knight, stomped over to the player and hit 'play.' The two of them danced their hearts out in a duel of ferocious fitness and technique, at the end of which they collapsed on the floor, gasping for air.

"Now. We're. Done." Cindy spat each word out on jagged exhales.

They lay still for a few moments, struggling to bring their breathing under control.

"I think you're right this time." Michele lifted her leg up to her face for the final minutes of stretching and recovery and grinned at her long-time friend. "Another great class, well done to us. We've still got it."

Moving around on the floor like oddly shaped puppets, they stretched and pulled their limbs in all directions. Honouring their bodies in a ten-minute cooldown, they knew this last part of the class was as important as the dance. With faces the colour of beetroots just plucked from a pressure cooker, they threw their dance bags over their shoulders and shuffled off to the showers. Because the water did little to dissipate their red faces, they never applied makeup. So, with wet hair pulled back in ponytails and faces a la natural, they left the studio for the short walk to a nearby café for their second Friday morning ritual.

~ ♥ ~

MICHELE'S CAPPUCINO AND CINDY'S peppermint tea arrived accompanied by a piece each of hazelnut torte. Cindy loved sugar and savoured the first mouthful of her sinful delight. "My date with Graham went well yesterday. He's a lovely fellow. It's such a shame his work is so dangerous."

"But if you like him so much why not explore where this might lead?"

"I'm not sure. We'll see. Anyway, I was really there to find out more about your mystery man."

"So?"

"Okay. Here's what I've got. Graham was an officer in a special task force a couple of years back. They'd been watching some suspected drug smugglers for nearly a year until they had enough evidence to make the bust and the arrests. He said the group was based in China, but the task force got most of the Australian arm of the operation."

"Really?"

Cindy nodded then took another couple of mouthfuls before continuing through creamy lips. "He also said there was an undercover detective involved who'd infiltrated the gang. Because of him, they were able to make the bust and the charges stuck. The bad guys were convicted recently and are serving pretty hefty sentences."

"Did you find out anything about this undercover detective? His name? What he looked like? If he's still on the force?" Michele had to wait a little longer for a reply while Cindy swallowed the last of her torte.

"Graham was very cagey about saying anything about him. Says he was quite the hero, though."

"That's it?" Michele was disappointed the storyline ended so abruptly. She was also a little upset that she'd been so engrossed in Cindy's report she hadn't touched her torte, permitting her friend to claim it for herself.

"I'm afraid so. That was all I could get out of him. What do you think? Does it match with Mark's story?"

"Well, it appears to. But if they busted the guys here in Australia, who's the Chinese guy in the club who tried to crack onto me and who Mark reckons has a contract out on him?"

"Maybe he's the big boss from China? Who knows? By the way, the torte was delicious." Cindy put down her fork on Michele's plate with a tentative grin. Michele smiled at her friend of over three decades who'd just polished off two pieces of hazelnut torte in record time, yet was still as slim as a twenty-something-year-old dancer.

"Great. Thanks. You obviously enjoyed them both. I don't know how you do it."

"Sorry. You know I have a sweet tooth and since you didn't seem interested in eating yours, I couldn't resist.

"That's all right, my shout anyway today. You did good with Graham. Thanks. At least there seems to be some validation to Mark's story." Michele gave her friend a squeeze of affection. "Tonight is Mark's last night here. He leaves tomorrow if the weather's good. I'll have to see what more I can find out. Regardless of anything, though, I'll miss him."

"I know, sweetie. He's certainly brightened up your life. And that's a good thing. Your life needed brightening up. I'm sure everything will work out for the best. It always does. You'll see. Now tell me about the awards ball. You've been so involved with Mark you haven't told me about the really important things in your life, you and your career."

"So, baby, what would you like to do for our last night together?" Mark's cheery voice sang down the phone.

"Why don't you come over to my place and I'll cook dinner."

"Are you nuts? He's about to leave tomorrow and you're thinking about having a romantic dinner for two." Michele's sex goddess tap-danced in her mind with the proficiency of Gregory Hines.

"Sounds good. What time?"

"Come early, say six o'clock."

"You know I don't come, baby. But I'll be there at six. See you then." He was gone with a quick chuckle, leaving Michele to plan, shop and prepare for the night.

~ ♥ ~

BY FIVE-THIRTY THE scene was set, the lasagne was in the oven, and Michele was zipping herself into a hot-pink short strappy dress with matching lingerie and towering pink high heels. She'd even found time to paint her nails, adding extra drama. With a final glance in the bathroom mirror and a touch-up of fuchsia lipstick, she looked flushed and ready for action.

"Research says red is the colour of passion and that it attracts the male of the species. Well, we certainly look the part."

Michele had to agree with her sex goddess on this point. She was giving off all the right signals with this outfit. Earlier that afternoon she'd decided to play this evening cool and confident, not clingy or needy. She planned to remain resolute and in charge, and to get the answers she needed. When the doorbell rang at six, it was curtain-up and she was in the lead.

"Hi, gorgeous. Come in."

"God, how good do you look? You just get better and better." He bent down to kiss her, then he circled her, relishing the sight.

With a curtsey, she asked, "You like?" knowing full well he did.

"Very much. I love that colour. Very sexy."

"See I told you. The colour of passion . . . and you want to eat."

Michele shook her internal nuisance away and turned back to Mark as she moved to the fridge. "I have beer and wine. What would you like?"

"Champagne." He offered up an ice-cold bottle of Moet he'd hidden behind his back.

"Excellent. A guest who doesn't come empty-handed," she said, taking the bottle.

"Nor empty in other ways." He reached out, lifted her onto the counter and stepped between her legs. "You're so beautiful. I just have to kiss you."

She offered her lips to him, which he honoured with a deep long kiss that smouldered with desire. He then leaned back and lifted her dress, revealing her pink lacy panties.

"Well, this is a change. Underwear tonight? I like it." His fingers swirled under the elastic, making a direct advance on his target.

"I'm pleased you approve but remember this was a dinner invitation. We'll see what happens after that, shall we?" She removed his hand and slid back onto the floor although not before he had touched her wetness. Her unconvincing reproach had no impact on her dinner guest as he put his finger into his mouth and sucked with wickedness in his eyes.

"Not only do you look good, you taste good too."

To cover up the slight blush creeping across her face, she turned to reach up for two champagne glasses. Within a moment, she felt his tongue licking up under her dress following the course of her G-string.

"As I said, forget about the food." Her sex goddess charged forwards, commanding Michele on the game plan.

Unable to resist the enemy advance, Michele leaned further across the countertop, exposing her buttocks for more. A slow, appreciative moan escaped her throat.

"As I said, you taste good all over." He pulled her G-string aside and lapped his tongue underneath at her engorging sex, then licked the pathway to the base of her spine. With resolution fading fast, Michele shivered at his expertise and unashamed exploration of her arse.

Leaving her wanting more, he repositioned her panties, kissed both buttocks and whispered in her ear, "More of this later, my private dancer."

"Mmm. That was good." She was still stretched across the counter with her buttocks hoisted as a little of her female juice trickled down her inner leg. "You missed a bit, gorgeous, on my right thigh."

Mark bent down to lick up her yearning, his large hands pinning her hips to the counter.

His hot tongue dragged up her thigh then tried to wriggle under her panties like a determined sperm. "Have I got it now?"

"Yes, thank you," she slurred, every inch of her body screaming for more.

Battling to resume control, she managed to straighten. With quivering sex and unsteady hands, she stretched to the overhead cupboard and retrieved two glasses. She realized that if her body continued its traitorous behaviour, the truth mightn't be her reward as hoped. Pondering how best to proceed, she was brought back to the present by the pop of the cork and Mark pouring the bubbly.

He handed her a glass. "You've been my golden-haired angel. Another time, another place, things could've been different." Affection filled his eyes as he tapped her glass.

She chose not to venture onto the path he was paving. "Yes, it's been a big week, hasn't it?"

She swallowed hard to cover the sadness of his impending departure swirling up in her throat, trying instead to focus on the joy of the past week. However, she couldn't quite shake the feeling the whole affair had been a conspiracy masterminded by the universe. Like an innocent puppy being teased by a naughty boy, she'd had the treat of Mark dangled in front of her with the promise of satiety, only to discover he wasn't to be hers, and he was soon to be whisked back to his previous life.

"Are you okay, baby?"

"Yes, I'll be okay. Just a bit sad to see you go. That's all. Another time, another place, do you really mean that?" She bit her tongue for being so weak to even ask the question.

"Yes. I do. My life is too complicated and there are things I can't change. But if you want, we can still see each other when I come up again. Or the next time you come to Sydney?"

"I'm not so sure that's a good idea. I want to but . . ."

He lifted her hand, and she spun the now-familiar ring on his right forefinger.

"It's not a dress ring, is it?"

"No. It's my police badge ring."

"I see." She lowered his hand and turned to the oven. Tonight wasn't working out the way she'd planned. Her body was too willing to be taken. Her emotions were too raw, as evidenced by the hot tears pricking her eyes. She swallowed hard, summoning up all her years of dancer discipline. The adage of "the show must go on" echoed in her mind. She mustn't falter. She mustn't morph into a hysterical woman blaming him for letting her fall in love with him, for not telling her he was married from the very first moment. She could feel him looking at her, uncertain of how she'd react. The choice was hers, then as now. She gathered her strength and courage one more time.

"I hope you like Italian. I made lasagne. It should be ready soon."

"Sounds terrific. Come sit with me a while then."

By silent consensus, they agreed not to broach the topic of his departure, his unavailability and her disappointment as they settled onto the couch.

"I see you have my favourite music playing." With his head reclining on the couch, he listened to *Yello* while finishing his champagne.

"Yes. I'm a convert now, thanks to you."

"In more ways than one." Her sex goddess always knew how to lighten a mood.

"I'm pleased I've been of assistance." He patted Michele's knee with his usual cheeky wickedness.

"Rest assured. You've definitely been of assistance." With glasses in hand, she flounced back to the kitchen for a refill.

"Well, then. It's been a win-win all around."

When she lifted her gaze, her breath caught for a prolonged beat. There he was, just like their very first night on the yacht. Sprawling back on the couch, his shirt open, abs exposed, jeans straining against the bulge in his pants, looking at once relaxed, powerful and ready to pounce.

"What's with the shirt?" Although she tried for a casual jibe, her comment contained a little too much admiration.

"I'm just feeling a bit hot in here. I'm used to the sea breeze. You know how it is?"

There was nothing for it but to surrender. To allow herself to keep loving him and let the chips fall where they may. All she could do was to trust the Goddess had brought them together for some reason that might one day become clear. Shaking her head and smiling at her roguish lover, she returned with the glasses effervescing with as much delight as was bubbling up within her.

"Here you go, gorgeous. You know you drive me crazy, don't you?" She leaned down with the glass, brushing a kiss across his lips.

"Likewise." His tongue flicked up toward her for more, but she was gone.

Back in the kitchen, Michele attended to dinner and they chatted about each other's day as new lovers do. Her dance class, his yacht maintenance, shopping, cruising, topics of no real consequence but enjoying each other's company. Seated at the table and with dinner served, she began her planned investigation for the truth. "Do you like the lasagne?"

"It's great. Best I've had," he said with full cheeks.

"I bet you say that to all the girls you meet when you go cruising."

"Nope. None of them offer to cook for me."

"I wonder why that is?"

"Couldn't really tell you . . ."

"What happened to you last night?"

"I was called in for a debrief."

"Excuse me? You said you were an ex-cop. Who did you have to do a debrief with?"

"I am an ex-cop. But I do a little private consulting on the side now and again for a special unit. And after all this hoo-ha with the Chinese boss at the club on Wednesday night, I needed to get on the blower and give everyone a heads-up. Really great lasagne, by the way. Just in case you missed it the first time." He wiped the plate with the last of the pane di casa bread and replaced his cutlery. A big contented smile creased his face.

"Oh, glad you liked it." Feeling somewhat stunned, which had become a familiar feeling whenever she was around him, she returned to her meal with a final question. "Since you don't own the yacht, who does?"

"It's registered under an international company's name. But I can't tell you any more than that. It's got to do with the special unit." He finished the last of his red wine and reached for the bottle to top up their glasses. "That was a terrific meal. Thanks."

"There's more if you want?"

"No thanks. If I eat any more, I'll be too full for the rest of the night I've planned for you." The twinkle returned to his eyes. "So, do you have all your questions answered yet?"

She caught him looking up at her as he poured the wine. Interrogation was his area of expertise, not hers.

Without much conviction, she said, "I guess so, inasmuch as you're willing to tell me." She nibbled at a piece of bread then took a slug of wine. "On another note, how does your wife cope with all this secrecy and stuff?" The question appeared as if by accident, like a naked dancer unexpectedly seen by the audience in the wings during a costume change.

But there was no quick cover-up, no shock, no averted glance, just a casual reply. "She was in the force too."

The curtain came crashing down on the final tragic scene to thunderous applause. The show was over. Any hope of his leaving his wife was dashed in that one sentence. Their shared lives were intrinsically intertwined. Nothing was going to change that.

"Oh, I see," she said without seeing him at all.

"Yeah. It's been as tough for her as it's been for me. But the worst of it's over now. Mostly."

Michele pushed her chair away from the table. She cleared the plates, stacked the dishwasher, tied the garbage bag, rubbed benchtops as if contaminated by E. coli, swept the crumbs from the table and poured more wine, without uttering a word. Silent minutes slipped away, as her past week's life flashed before her eyes. Like someone dying, she longed for what used to be, but she couldn't go back. The only option was forwards.

Resolute, she returned her cleaning props to the cupboard and resumed her seat at the table. "I see. I guess that explains a lot of things. Thank you."

"And?"

"And," she took a breath, "a week ago, I made a decision to go out and have some great casual sex. I did, thanks to you, and I don't regret any of it. I don't regret meeting you, and I don't regret feeling the way I do. Fuck it! I'm forty-two and it's about time I enjoyed myself without guilt and all the other negative emotions women are conditioned to believe. If you and I were men, we wouldn't even be having this conversation. We met, we have a connection, whatever it is, we have great sex and if you're married that's not my problem, it's yours." Pausing only to have another slurp of wine, she held the floor.

"We've one final night together, tonight. I refuse to play the poor little princess who can't have her Prince Charming. I also refuse to dwell on your returning to your wife, whether she exists or not." She shot him a quick look for emphasis. "I've had playing the good girl, the guilt and the doubt. I intend to make the most of tonight and of the rest of my life, whether you're in it or not."

"Okay, baby. Would you like your surprise now?" His smile wove its spell around her.

"Absolutely. You. Me. Now."

"Time to party then. Call a cab and let's get out of here."

WHILE WAITING FOR THE taxi, Michele reapplied her lipstick in her bathroom mirror. Just as she'd opened herself up to a week's worth of great sex with Mark, her epiphany after dinner had opened something else within her. Gone was the guilt, the repression, the expectation of behaving in a socially acceptable manner. She felt free.

"So, a surprise? This sounds like fun." Her sex goddess chirped in her head like a canary, unable to contain her enthusiasm any longer.

"Right. Let's go then." She tossed her lipstick into her bag, gave her dress a quick shrug and bounced out of the bathroom, down the stairs.

THE TRIP INTO THE city was punctuated by smiles, squeezes, and cuddles. By the time Mark paid the fare, Michele stood waiting on the same spot she'd stood on one week ago, looking for her first casual sexual encounter. She never could've imagined that in seven days her life would change in so many ways. Aside from unleashing her sexuality, she'd experimented with party drugs, engaged in a range of sexual activities that had previously been taboo or unknown to her, savoured the freedom of being single, and suffered the anguish of falling in love with a married man. More than all of this, she'd discovered who she was at an authentic level. She liked who she'd found, and she knew this was just the beginning. Epiphanies and empowerment were fast becoming her favourite things.

"Okay, baby. Which club do you want to go to?" Mark's expression was filled with anticipation.

"A club? Is that the surprise?" She did nothing to cover her disappointment.

"Not a night club. Which strip club do you want?"

"Oh. Really? I've never been much into strip clubs. As a professional dancer we never really thought much of . . ." Her voice trailed off as she looked at him. His expression reminded her of a patient, loving father waiting for his daughter to piece together a simple jigsaw puzzle.

"Oh. Got it. I'm slipping back into the 'good girl' again." She smiled up at her protector. Although the epiphanies might be on the rise, remaining in an awakened state was proving a little harder to master.

"Only for a moment. Now, which one takes your fancy?"

The street glowed with neon signs; their brilliance only surpassed by the promises on offer. Girls on Girls, Best Lap Dancers, Big Bold Boys, Pole Dancing . . . the list of sexually exciting offerings was emblazoned on every shop front. Although Michele had walked this street many times, she'd never noticed how many strip clubs there were. Scantily clad men and women behind tawdry facades vied for the attention and money of the punters. Promotional girls in long slinky dresses cajoled customers on the street into entering, competing with one another when passers-by gave even a cursory glance toward their doorways.

"That one." She extended her finger with its long pink-painted talon to the third club on the right. Girls on Girls. If she was going to enter the forbidden forest, she might as well go right to the top of the variety tree.

"Good choice. One of my favourites."

"I bet it is," Michele's sex goddess chimed.

They climbed the Hollywood-style red-carpeted stairs. With Michele looking as hot as her fuchsia dress, Mark guided her before him, conducting the normal reconnaissance long entrenched in his psyche. He paid the exorbitant entrance fee and they each offered up their wrists for the tacky proof of payment ink stamp.

Once their eyes adjusted to the darkness, the scene before them unfolded more clearly. Great music was pumping while two women with extraordinary bodies were dancing on the stage and the customers, a mix of mostly men and a few women, wore grins so big their faces seemed ready to split. Scurrying around the room the wait staff could've been mistaken for strippers too, their clothing not quite enough for modesty. The male staff had bare, buff chests and wore only black neck bow ties and tight black trousers, while the female staff's derrieres peeped out from under frilly skirts and their breasts burst from push-up bras barely able to contain their contents. Michele fell in love with the place.

"There's a table over there," Mark yelled and began walking toward the stage with Michele in tow. Although not large, the venue was designed with compact booths skirting the walls and free-standing bar tables scattered throughout the room. The red and black décor reminded her of the Moulin Rouge, although contemporary rather than Parisian in style. General low-level lighting in the room kept the customers' focus toward the stage where the spotlights and specials accentuated the muscle tone of the girls performing.

"Vodka and tonic?" he called into her ear.

"Sounds great. Thanks."

As Mark swathed a path to the bar, she placed her bag on the table turning her attention to the stage. The strippers had the proverbial bodies of death. Long lean legs balanced on skyscraper high heels, breasts buoyed by bags of plastic skilfully implanted by top surgeons, strong, tireless arms that supported their body weight as they twirled upside down around the poles, eight-pack abs that any bodybuilder would be proud to own and faces made up with such expertise no one could tell if they were pretty or not. To finish off their perfection, these flawless specimens of the female form shone with the golden glow of a Gold Coast all-over tan. No strap marks on these bodies. Michele felt nothing but admiration and respect for these girls. They obviously trained hard to keep their bodies in top condition and although they didn't have any real dance technique, they moved with a certain poise and style of their own.

"Here you go," Mark hollered over the music, handing Michele her drink.

Leaning in so he could hear her, she said, "Good idea. I really like this place."

"Baby, you chose it. It's the perfect place for you." He smiled then turned his attention to the girls on stage. As soon as the new song started and the catch cry "Y'all ready" roared through the speakers there was no denying it was George Michael's classic "Too Funky." Four new strippers clad in bejewelled G-strings, bras, boots and elaborate headgear strutted onto the stage. Each girl was dressed in a different colour theme, much like the supermodels wore in the original music clip. The stripper in white even looked a little like Linda Evangelista. While the other girls didn't resemble Nadja, Tyra or Emma, they looked just as sexy in their black, green and orange costumes.

Mark moved closer to Michele as the music pervaded the room, his hand resting on her buttocks, his eyes glued to the strippers. After all the emotion of the evening, she was grateful for the diversion of the classic 1992 hit and the casual touch of his hand.

"These girls are good," she called up to him.

"Yeah," he said, smiling down at her before returning his gaze to the stage.

With the bass all but blowing out the sub-woofers, the beat carried Michele to her favourite place, her safe place. Her body began its ascent to freedom, hips swaying, testing the floor of the club — the surface, grip and slip factor — in her high heels. By the time they'd finished their first round of drinks, the girls had stripped to transparent thongs and were exiting to enthusiastic applause.

"Time for a quick break," the announcer informed the crowd as other sexy background music filled the room, the volume turned lower so customers could speak rather than shout.

"You want another?" Mark asked, holding his empty glass aloft.

"Yes, please."

By the time he returned with new drinks, the club was at capacity, no tables, booths or much standing room left.

"Doesn't take long for this place to fill up," Michele said.

"No. It's one of the better clubs so the crowd's good and usually well-behaved." "Cheers." He tapped his glass to hers and took a hefty mouthful. "Do you like your surprise?"

"Yes, I do. And I really like the music."

"I knew you would. This is exactly your type of place, baby." He leaned in, hugging her to him, grinding his thigh into her groin.

"I think the surprise wasn't just for me. You seem to be thoroughly enjoying it yourself." She hooked her fingers into his belt, giving him a sharp thrust of her hips.

"Of course I'm enjoying it but not as much as I enjoy having my own private dancer." He reached for his drink to take a sip while his other arm squeezed her closer. She noticed his eyes roaming the room, checking out the new partygoers, matching their faces to his memory files. Once he'd confirmed the room was devoid of danger, she felt his body unwind. Only when he returned his attention to her did she continue with cheeky sarcasm.

"That's very sweet of you. But I'm sure you'd prefer one of those pole dancers to be your private dancer."

"I can pay for one of them to give me a private dance, but I'd much prefer you to be my private dancer."

Michele tilted her head in feigned disbelief, but his sincerity seemed genuine.

"Baby, I mean it. You're my private dancer, my golden-haired angel, and you always will be. You changed my life." And for the first time, he let his guard down. He lowered his drink to the table and cupped her face in his hands. Then he kissed her, openly and passionately in public. This was it. The different time and the different place, in which he was hers for an instant. Another dimension surrounded them, where they were free to be together. In that moment, she was transported into a parallel lifetime.

When he released her, she looked for any tell-tale signs of regret on his face. His smile and the love in his eyes assured her there was none.

"I wish this could be different," he said.

"And now please welcome back to the stage . . ." the announcer's shrill voice shattered the illusion, and the world returned.

He reached for her drink. "Here, baby, have a drink."

She accepted the offer and sipped as the music began in the background. For that brief time, she'd felt what it would've been like to have him as her own. A glimpse of what could've been, and she hungered for more.

On the stage strode two girls in black mesh stockings, bras, and feather boas, dragging black cabaret chairs behind them, every dancer's standard wardrobe and prop. They positioned the chairs in front of the poles then straddled them, waiting for the music to cue. Recognizing the opening piano riffs, Michele's hunger for more, fuelled by the week-long awakening of her sexuality pushed her into testing Mark's resolve one last time.

Switching to performance mode she reached out to him and began unfastening his belt, sliding it inch by inch from around his waist to Janet Jackson's provocative plea in "Rope Burn" to be tied up. With the performance on stage as her backdrop, Michele wanted to give him what he'd just given her, a glimpse into the reality of their being together as a couple. She was going to reciprocate his passion by being his private dancer, in public.

With Janet's insistent request to be tied up as her own soundtrack, Michele spun his belt around her wrists as her hips embodied the snaking moves of a seductress. Stretching her tied hands overhead, she shimmied her dress upward, exposing her upper thighs, buttocks and the pretty pink triangle of her panties. She fixed him with her eyes, burning fire into his soul, demanding him to pay attention. At last, the strength of her body was matched by her new empowered attitude and sexuality, giving her performance added burn. His belt provided the perfect prop for her pleasure. She dragged it between her legs, creating just the right image to accompany the title of the song. Oblivious to the crowd now relishing her performance, Michele strutted over to a nearby railing where she lunged, twirled, arched and bent her body over, giving everyone glimpses of her panties and buttocks. Never taking her eyes off him she danced for him, only him. With little outward response, Mark rode the waves of her scorching tribute, all the time sipping his drink, in command.

When Michele struck a final rope burn pose, her body glistening with perspiration, the crowd went wild. She strode back to Mark, holding his belt aloft. He lifted his T-shirt for her to rethread it back into his jeans and like a good submissive, she obliged while the crowd's attention returned to the stage where the girls had begun another routine. With her chest heaving and her dress clinging to her from perspiration, she looked as raw as her emotions. But no matter her dishevelled appearance, her performance had had the desired effect on the only audience she was interested in. Still holding eye contact, he handed her the half-finished drink which she threw back in one gulp. With his cock all but bursting from his jeans, he pulled her to him. "It's time you strapped a mattress to your back. Let's get out of here."

Snatching up her bag, Michele tucked herself tight into his body while he shoved their way through the crowd, which converged to congratulate her on her performance. She accepted the compliments with a smile, clinging close to her protector as he steamrolled them out of the doors.

The chill of the night air assaulted her heated skin, sending steam off her body and giving her shivers. Mark hailed a cab and they scurried into the back.

"Thank you. I'll never forget that. You're one helluva woman." He bent in and kissed her on the cheek.

"Thank you too." She snuggled into his rock-hard shoulder.

"I have another surprise if you're up to it?"

"Absolutely. The night's still young."

"Venezia Palazzo Hotel, please, driver."

"Ooh, nice."

Extricating herself from him, she rummaged around in her purse for the necessary tools to bring her makeup and appearance back to face-fairy perfection. Ten minutes later no one would've suspected she'd all but sweated off her original makeup while performing a clothed striptease for her lover. With a skilfully applied second paint job, her face now glowed, and her delinquent hair was tamed high on her head by determined pins. After her transformation, she looked every inch the part of a glitzy guest stepping out of the cab for an elegant night at the famous hotel. She waited for Mark to join her kerbside then together they glided through the vast glass doors and across the hewn marble floors.

In the foyer, they entered an Aladdin's cave of blossoming flowers, ornate furnishings, and marble columns. Despite the extravagance, Michele's attention remained on Mark and she hugged his arm close to her. One of the things she'd miss about him was the space his physical presence and aura filled. It caused people to move out of his way and reminded her of a bodyguard repelling unwelcome advances, scouting the room for trouble and protecting her like Frank Farmer did for Rachael Marron in the movie, *Bodyguard.* Instead of proceeding to the bar, he guided her to reception and stopped.

"Good evening, sir, how may I help you?" The young, smartly uniformed front-of-house staff recited her signature greeting with a smile.

"I have a reservation under the name of Miller, Mark Miller."

"Of course, Mr Miller, the Imperial Suite, sir." The receptionist's eyes glanced up to see what type of man was paying for the hotel's most expensive room. Dressed in blue jeans and a Brando T-shirt, Mark looked more like the average punter, not the owner of the bank balance typically associated with this room. "Would you like one or two key cards, sir?"

"Just one, I think." He winked down at Michele.

"Very good, sir, your suite is on the fourth floor. Elevators are to your left. Have a nice stay, Mr Miller."

As they continued toward the lifts, Michele whispered, "The Imperial Suite? Are you sure you're not running drugs? This must be costing a fortune."

"Nothing for you to worry about." He ushered her into the elevator and hit four.

She then realized the impracticality of the situation. "I don't have any clothes or anything. If only you'd told me, I could've packed an overnight bag."

"Then it wouldn't have been a surprise. Anyway, with what I've got in mind you won't need any clothes." He glanced down at her with a wicked smile as the elevator doors opened.

Walking down the deserted hallway for their last night together, Michele knew she'd store this final scene in her mind forever. She'd file away all these precious moments with Mark, knowing that in her old age she'd carefully unwrap them from her fragile webs of memory and blow off the dust of dementia to relive them time and again as proof that she'd had an adventure in lust and love.

When they stepped onto the intricately patterned marble floor leading into the suite's foyer, she caught her breath. In the middle stood a circular Venetian parquet table with an enormous vase of ballooning fresh pink hydrangeas that reached toward the ceiling.

"Oh my God, this is amazing." She ran her fingers along the table then touched the hydrangeas to see if they were real. Of course, they were.

Yet, for all its beauty, the foyer was overshadowed by the richly decorated living room that opened before them, welcoming them into its luxury. With its three, oversized brocade lounges atop an antique Persian rug, vaulted ceilings hand-detailed in gold, and hand-carved tables on which stood exquisite side lamps, the room oozed sophistication, to such an extent Michele considered licking the walls to taste its magnificence.

"Not too shabby at all," Mark said, flopping into one of the plush lounges.

"Shabby definitely doesn't describe this place." She snuggled into the lounge opposite, scrunching the cushions into her lap. Laid out before them on an antique coffee table was a sumptuous late-night supper resplendent with silver cutlery, Venezia Palazzo crockery and crystal glassware.

"Let's see what this tastes like," he said, popping the cork on the Dom Perignon.

"Well, Mr Miller. It seems only the best will do."

"What can I say, I'm the last of the high rollers, baby."

With glasses struggling to contain the froth and foam, they sipped the crisp chilled fruits of France.

"Delicious. Dom is now officially my favourite," she said.

"Not a bad drop if I say so myself." He rose to take her hand so they could continue their tour. To their right was the dining room where a grand table reigned supreme in the centre of the room. Above it hung an enormous Baccarat crystal chandelier glowing like a thousand fireflies. Michele felt like Pollyanna, mesmerized by her first experience of light refracting through cut crystal. She'd dreamed of living this Disney magic since childhood and here she was. They retraced their steps through the living room to the bedroom suite with its impressive custom-made king-size bed, spa, and walk-in wardrobe that would delight any fashionista. Frosted in shimmering yellow walls and royal blue furnishings, the entire Imperial Suite epitomized a grand nineteenth-century European hotel. A fairy-tale setting for a final performance.

"And you get a twenty-four-hour private butler for service throughout your stay, madam." Mark mimicked the receptionist while he led her back to the overstuffed lounges.

"Really? A butler, all night? Does he look like Brad Pitt?"

"I can't guarantee that, but we can call him up if you like and you can give him the once-over." His eyes twinkled with mischief.

"Mmm, maybe not. I think I've enough man for one night." She freed her hand to tweak his butt.

Mark poured more champagne then led her out to the balcony. "Can you see her? Down there on the third arm? The *Lady Diana*." He pointed out the glistening craft moored below, awaiting departure. "I motored her here today so I can leave early in the morning. The forecast is all clear so it should be easy cruising back home." He leaned on the balcony, looking down at the marina with the Broadwater and the Surfers Paradise high-rise lights dancing in the background.

"Don't you dare start feeling sorry for yourself. Tonight is the last night, so get with the program." Her inner sex goddess brought Michele back from the brink with a thud.

"I'm pleased the weather will be with you tomorrow." Rubbing her hand over his strong shoulders, Michele longed for him not to go.

He turned his head, perhaps sensing her mounting melancholy. Then he flashed his killer smile and changed pace. "I'll be leaving at first light so that gives us about six hours. No sleep for you tonight, beautiful." He grabbed her hand, twirled her around and led her back into the dining room. "And since there's no sleeping on the agenda, I think we need a little white angel to help keep us awake."

"While you do what you need to, I'm going to freshen up," she called over her shoulder as she headed to the bathroom.

She strolled past the spa bath and turned on the gold-plated tap, readjusting it to achieve just the right temperature and flow. Upending the bubble bath under the cascading water gave rise to a flood of rich, fragrant foam. Its expensive perfume intensified as the heat steamed and swirled, layering mist throughout the room. Fluffing her hair in the mirror, she wished for some sexy lingerie to make the evening complete.

"You wouldn't be in it for very long anyway," her sex goddess reminded her.

"I know. But still, it would've been nice." She turned back to the spa and flipped off the tap. Feeling as pretty as the pink hydrangeas in the foyer, she drifted back to the dining room to the sensuous sounds of k.d lang filtering through the suite.

"Bless him. He's brought my favourite CD."

Against a backdrop of elegant vintage wallpaper, there he stood — the corded muscles of his arms and back straining against his T-shirt, his taut buttocks and thighs waging war in his *Levi's*, a mountain of muscle, primal sex and playfulness. He was the personification of temptation and forbidden fruits, one of which he was holding in his hand in the form of a rolled-up hundred-dollar note.

"Baby, this place suits you. You look like a princess or a goddess or something."

"Thank you. Pity you couldn't be my prince." Although the words were spoken with deliberate humour, she silently reprimanded herself, enough with the Prince Charming fantasy.

"Here, baby, have some." He offered her the note to snort a line of cocaine.

"Not tonight, gorgeous. Since this is our last night together, I want to remember it. But you go ahead."

"Okay. But it's here if you change your mind," he said, giving in to his addiction.

"I've run the spa. Come join me." She turned back toward the bedroom, her body moving to her favourite music. She floated on her feet, her weight shifting from hip to hip in an erotic figure eight, hands weaving like the wings of an eagle.

"Pity we didn't taste all this glorious food," she said as she drifted past the coffee table.

"We will. I promise. And if it's no good by the time we get to it, we'll call for the butler."

She turned with an expectant smile. "That's right. The butler. What was his name again?"

"Brad. His name's Brad."

"Correct. Brad. Yes, I think we'll ring for Brad a little later."

"Good idea. But first the spa."

By now, Michele had sashayed into the bedroom where the steam from the spa was *pirouetting* lazy circles in the room.

"Let's get some fresh air in here." Mark walked to the balcony doors and flung them open to the balmy night. By the time he returned, she'd peeled off her clothes and was dipping her toes in the water.

"Mmm, hot," she said with delight.

"I reckon. But it's you that's hot."

"Stop," she said with a girlish giggle and a flutter of eyelashes.

"Fuck it. You are. I've never had any woman who's so free of inhibitions that they happily run around nude, particularly with all the lights on. I fuckin' love it. Look at you. You're like that painting I've seen . . . of the woman with the long, red hair and the wind blowing through it. She was standing in some sort of shell, I think."

"You mean Botticelli's painting of Venus?" Michele placed her left hand on her pubis and the right across her breast, struck the right body angle and cocked her right foot on its big toe.

"That's the one. That's how she stood." With his smile broadening, Mark strode across the room, and Michele stepped into the tub with a full-throated laugh. She enjoyed making him this eager. Like a kid in a candy store, he stood salivating and grinning down at her in the tub, as she splashed about doing her best impersonation of Venus in a frothy clamshell.

"So, are you coming or not?" She was chin deep in bubbles and squirming with anticipation.

"You know the answer. I don't come" he said.

"You know what I mean. Are you getting in or not?"

"You sure you don't want a water boy again?"

"Absolutely not. The only toy currently available is a Dom bottle and that'd be sacrilege." She giggled at the thought.

"Very well then, but if you change your mind, all you need do is ask."

He removed his T-shirt, all controlled movement and muscle. Michele hoped she wasn't overtly drooling but the way Mark approached the zipper of his jeans and dragged it down with the calculated precision of a surgeon, made her snatch flutter. She tried to act nonchalant, but she couldn't tear her eyes away from him. He flicked her a sideways glance and a wry smile.

Damn! he'd caught her perving. She averted her eyes with a casual shrug and slipped deeper into the water, rubbing foam over her breasts.

"How long is this going to take?" she asked.

"How long is a piece of string?"

"Who cares about bloody string! Get in the damn spa."

Slithering out of his so tight jeans and bulging underpants, his eager cock signalled the beginning of the game. He stepped into the spa and asked, "How are you feeling, princess?"

"Like a goddess."

Before the banter could continue, she lifted her mouth to engulf his manhood in one deft movement, making him gasp with delight.

Perfect, she thought, *now I've got you.*

She set about performing her signature fellatio while he teetered on the edge of surrender. Controlling the event with her usual precision and intuitive timing, she knew she could bring him to a standing ovation like any good showgirl.

With his hand on her head, he murmured, "You're so good at this."

"I know," came the muffled response as her tongue and lips worked overtime. Sensing his resolve fade, she increased the pace. His grip tightened on her hair and his buttocks clenched. He was losing control. She continued her assault until with a final moan for mercy, he shuddered and ejaculated into her mouth. Victory was hers. Michele swallowed hard and fast, and after tiding up any spillage with a quick lick of her tongue, she smiled coyly up at her conquest.

"Game set and match on that one, girlfriend," her inner sex goddess cheered.

"Fuck, you're amazing," he said, sliding down the side of the spa like a landed trout.

Luxuriating in the bubbles, he leaned his head on the edge of the tub, sipping the last of his champagne. Michele finished her French fizz, feeling pleased with herself.

"Oh my, we're all out of champagne. Is there any more, or do I need to ring Brad?" she asked.

"Don't you worry your pretty little head about it. I'll call and get some sent up." Mark plucked the phone from its cradle beside the spa and requested butler service. Within minutes, a knock at the door signalled 'Brad's' arrival.

"Come in," Mark yelled out.

The butler wheeled in a trolley dressed in white service linen with another bottle of Dom in a crystal ice bucket and two chilled glasses. He maneuvered it into the bedroom and stopped next to the spa.

"Shall I pour, sir?" he asked, eyes averted, white-gloved hands at the ready.

"Absolutely, my good man."

"Excuse me, but what's your name? We were hoping it was Brad?" Michele gave the butler a modest smile.

"Sorry miss. My name is Roger, not Brad."

"Oh." Michele's affected disappointment broadened Mark's smile. "Not to worry, though. You still make a handsome Roger, the strong silent type methinks. On the surface, all cool, calm and collected but underneath a tiger, ready to pounce and devour."

Flashing a little more skin and a smouldering stare, Michele toyed with the butler, trying to penetrate his unflappable professionalism. Instead, he returned, seemingly unaffected, to his duty of popping the cork and poured fresh glasses of champagne, handed one to each of his guests and retrieved the dirty glasses to his trolley

"Will that be all, sir?"

"Will that be all, goddess?" Mark deferred to Michele.

"For the time being, yes, thank you, Roger. That will be all." With a royal swirl of her hand, she dismissed Roger from further duties. The butler bowed then departed the suite with his silent trolley and whirling imagination.

Mark slithered over and caressed her thighs with his capable hands. "I thought maybe you would've liked Roger to stay and the two of us could have pleasured you all night?" His lips and tongue were hot upon on her neck.

"A *ménage a trois*? I don't think so." While feigning disinterest, Michele's sex goddess flashed racy images in her mind of the three of them getting it off on the Persian rug. Vivid pictures of Roger lapping between her legs while Mark sat astride her with his cock plunged in her mouth riding her, as she bucked with the pleasure of giving and receiving, produced an electric tingling between her legs. She yearned for satisfaction and when Mark fingers slipped between her legs, she welcomed them. He entered her, one digit then another, widening her for yet another. Each time she let go a little more until she began to drive herself hard against his hand, which remained at an irritatingly slow and steady pace. She needed him to take her hard, bring her to climax, the ache that needed relief was mounting.

"Do me now. Do me hard," she begged in his ear, her teeth pulling at the lobe.

Deferring to her once more, he unleashed his powerful arm muscles, pounding her to repeated orgasms until she writhed back up the sides of the spa for escape, panting and laughing from their sex play. Reaching up, he dragged her back into the spa.

"Hard enough?" His tongue was in her mouth, dark and intense, devouring her like rich chocolate.

"Mmm, that was perfect," she purred, her yearning again beginning its upward spiral.

"Perhaps it's time to adjourn to another room?" His inquiry was rhetorical because he'd already released the plug for the water to drain. Stepping out, he turned to help her, but she was already upright. At that moment, with the breeze from the balcony catching her hair, Michele imagined she was Botticelli's Goddess Venus from his famous painting. Wild and free.

"Come here, beautiful. Let's have something to eat." He offered her his hand and wrapping the lush towel around her, patted her dry. Like a penny thief in a candy store, he loitered over her body trying to steal a touch of more flesh which she willingly allowed. Finally, with towels secured around their waists, overflowing glasses and Dom bottle in hand, they wandered back to the coffee table laden with food.

"Are you hungry?" he asked.

"I guess so," she lied. Her only appetite tonight was for sex and she intended to gorge herself.

"I am." He reached across to a platter laden with canapés, selected a bite-sized piece and popped it into his mouth. "Yum, tastes good. Why don't you lie back and relax?"

She dropped her towel onto the sofa, and he fluffed some pillows into a stack for her to rest her head. He guided her to lie backwards. "Now let's just get you comfortable."

With a delicate bedside manner, he maneuvered one of her legs high up onto the back of the sofa and opened the other wide to rest on the coffee table. She lay revealed. The coolness of the breeze assaulted her open cleft and her body tingled with desire.

"Now this is the canapé I prefer." He smacked his lips and dropped to his knees. Burying his face in her full exposure, he worked his magic with his mouth, swirling, licking, nibbling, sucking, tormenting her to anguish then stopping short of satisfaction. With a deep teasing lick, he pulled back just before bringing her to climax.

"Care for a canapé?" He proffered the silver platter to his writhing partner.

"Don't mind if I do." Paying no attention to the intense throbbing between her legs, Michele sprang to her feet and began clearing the food from the coffee table. Amused but uncertain as to the reason for this domestic flurry, Mark watched in silence. Once the table had been cleared, she selected six canapés. Positioning herself on the edge of the coffee table, she lay back and placed the tasty morsels on her own tasty morsels. One on her lips, one on each nipple, one on her belly button, one on her pantie line and one on her mount of Venus. Needing no further invitation to dine, Mark crawled over ready for the feast.

"It would seem supper is served. Mmm, a naked buffet with lots of goodies to taste. I do hope they stay in place until I get to eat them all." Seeing his challenge register in her eyes, he bent down and kissed the first canapé from her lips.

"They'll remain in place as long as you eat well and don't leave anything behind," she said, in response to his dare.

"I can assure you I'm a very tidy eater, and I won't be leaving anything behind, although that might be where dessert is served afterwards."

As his comment trailed off, his mouth made its way to her left breast where he circled the next morsel before engulfing it in one sudden swallow. Caressing her skin with his tongue, he licked his way across to her right breast. Here he spent more time nibbling at the four edges of the crouton, lifting it with his tongue, tasting it then returning it to its perilous resting place. She moaned with pleasure and impatience. Then her nipple was exposed with his abrasive chin rubbing against it, hard and insistent. It hurt, but she held firm, meeting the test.

"Good girl. Now for the entrée." Moving down to her belly button, he circled his tongue around his target. Dragging out the inevitable caused the fire in her groin to burn hotter than a fever.

"You must be the slowest eater in the world," she said through clenched lips.

"Perhaps, but I sure am enjoying my food." He gulped the morsel then curled his tongue into her navel making her gasp, nearly toppling over the last two treats.

"Careful, my goddess, you do want me to finish my supper, don't you?"

"Oh, yes please." Michele flexed her muscles to still her quivering sex and prayed the two final offerings straining skyward from her body would remain in place.

"Now let's see what this one tastes like." Nibbling at her imaginary pantie line he wasted no time and bit into her flesh and devoured the canapé.

"Only one left, baby." Balanced on her summit, his final objective trembled. He lowered his tone and slowed the pace of his voice. His eyes fixed and calculating. "I feel like a sniper. I've got the mark in my sights, taking aim, waiting for the go shot, needing command approval, then squeeze."

His hot breath scorched her mons as he hung in mid-air above her, scoping her out, not flinching. With his face so close to the target, she couldn't believe he didn't hear her sex screaming out "take the shot." There was no doubt she could hear her sex goddess shrieking out command approval in her head.

"Take the bloody shot," Michele hissed and with that he threw her legs apart, dragging her buttocks up toward his face, and assassinated her snatch with the passion of a military marksman. Even almost upside down she ejaculated within moments, spraying his face.

"God, I love the way you do that. It's like crystal rain. Fuckin' amazing."

He picked her up and carried her into the bedroom where he threw her onto the bed. Here he mounted her hard and fast, ramming his sexual frustration deep within her, spurred on by her willingness to take him no matter how hard he punished her. Fifteen minutes into this marathon he sprang off the bed, calling back over his shoulder, "So, my private dancer, want to finish what you started at the club?" He was hunting around the side of the spa for something.

"I thought that's what we were doing?"

"Ta, da!" He held his belt up like a trophy. "You wanted to be tied up, I believe? Let's make that wish come true, shall we?" He stalked over to her, wrapping the leather strap forwards and backwards around his hands. Crawling on top, he grabbed her arms in one hand and lashed the belt around her wrists with the other. It took only seconds before she was not only tied up but also leashed to the antique bedpost.

"I see your police 'subdue and surrender' skills come in handy in all sorts of situations," she said.

"Good to see you're up for the game." Her sex goddess seemed enthralled.

When he leapt off to the side of the bed, Michele rolled her body from side to side, flashing her best profiles and testing her restraints in the process. They were firm and immovable, just as expected.

"And if I had my nightstick now, you'd really know what rough sex was all about." He glowered down at his captive.

"I thought that was your nightstick?" Her gaze travelled down to his cock at full attention thrusting over the side of the mattress.

"It'll have to do," he said, "however, it doesn't get in as deep as a police baton."

The image of being fucked by a police baton was thrilling if not a little daunting. "Your nightstick gets in plenty deep enough for me," she assured him, and herself.

"Let's see, shall we." He launched himself on top of the bed, planking her body.

Bearing down into her ear, he commanded, "Open your legs."

She obeyed, and he dropped all his weight onto his knees. Without skipping a beat, he drove himself deep into her. She sucked in air. Then he grabbed both her legs and tugged them up to his ears. Thanks to her Friday morning dance class, her limbs responded, stretching rather than tearing under his weight. She adored the rough play and with her legs suspended on his shoulders, she found the position gave her more leverage. As he pounded her, penetrating her deeper, her arms and legs restrained, her competitive spirit challenged his. Moments turned into minutes, then into blocks of time, while they tested the others' body and endurance. Then he spun her around and threw her onto her elbows and knees. With his massive hands clenching her hips, he pummelled her sex from behind while she cried out in pleasure and pain, her hands still bound to the bed. Like opponents in a life or death contest neither would relinquish, both would perish in the melee. They were well matched.

DESPITE THE ROUGHHOUSING AND the frenzied effect of the cocaine on their sex play, the door to his emotions had been creaking open for most of the night, just enough to allow Michele in and his feelings out. Trusting her to this point had been a calculated move — one he'd never thought he'd consider. He'd learnt long ago about the fragility of trust, easy to lose and easy to break, yet here he was, trusting this woman with his identity and his heart.

His resolve for this to be a casual affair had been fading the more time he spent with her. Michele's liberated reaction this evening to finish their time together with "a bang and not a whimper" made it harder to conceal the depth of his admiration, respect, and feelings for her. Something was tugging at his heartstrings. Like the twitching of a fishing line with an undersized fish on the hook, a persistent nibbling at his heart unsettled him.

Despite his determination to forge forwards with his life pre-Michele and to save his marriage, he knew the rules of the game had changed. He wanted Michele so badly a deep ache gnawed at his insides, but he needed stability and security at home. No longer could he deal with the consequences of dangerous liaisons, either professionally or personally. However, he could no sooner turn Michele into collateral damage than he could stop loving her. He found himself trapped, not in a situation of life or death, but love or lie.

Unleashing Michele from his bondage, he turned her over and without a word wrapped her in his arms, lowering his face into her neck to hide any tell-tale signs of sentiment. The sense of loss increased. Even the drugs did nothing to reduce it. Sure, the sex was heightened but so too were his emotions, which wasn't normally the case. He gathered his resources, steeling himself against the inexplicable longing. Breathing her into his soul for one last time he honoured the ache in his heart. Decision made, he pulled himself back onto his arms, locked his eyes on her beautiful face and with passionate strokes he made love to her. Real love. Plunging deeper and deeper, he thrust his yearning cock into her, craving to disappear into her very soul where he'd be safe and free. His eyes drilled into hers and he prayed she could read how he felt. He loved her for the last time, giving all of himself, not holding back any longer.

Elation filled her. Here was his parting gift, something he'd withheld from her all week. He'd surrendered and impregnated her with his essence. When he rolled off, his chest rose and fell like the waves of the ocean he was about to tame. Mirroring his breathing, she lay beside him one last time.

"Thank you," she said.

"No. Thank you, baby. It's been a great week."

"I know, but I meant thank you for letting yourself come just now."

He curled his arm around her, pulling her closer to him. "There's more coke if you want some?"

"No thanks." She realized he'd gone back undercover. His emotions safely tucked away. "What time is it?"

"Four. Time to freshen up." He bounded out of the bed, grabbed Michele and tumbled her into the shower where he soaped her body with *Lux* body wash using his hands, fingers, and tongue until she cried for respite.

"Need to be saved, do we?" He threw her across his shoulder in a fireman's grip.

"Put me down, you brute," she squealed with the required damsel-in-distress voice as he marched through the suite.

"Your wish is my command." He pushed aside one of the heavy timber chairs around the dining table and dropped her onto its austere surface. "You mightn't want any angel dust, but I have to stay awake all day, so lie back and be a good girl."

Submitting, she lay sprawled on the teak table admiring the sparkling chandelier lights while he collected the remaining cocaine from the side service unit. He scraped the last two lines of coke onto her mound and proceeded to snort most of it. Then he separated her slit and licked the rest of it into her. On his exit he lingered, giving her clit a long, tempting suck.

"Yum, that tastes the best of all."

"It certainly feels good."

While k.d. lang's *Constant Craving* surged in the background, her body uncoiled like a spring and she jumped off the table to locate her high heels. Finding them strewn under an antique armoire in the living room, she knelt to drag them from their hiding place. As she did so, he dropped to his knees and clasped her hips, beginning a slow assault on her derriere with his tongue. She tried wriggling out of his grip but to no avail.

"The licking I don't mind, but if you're planning on venturing further, that's not really my thing," she said.

"That's a shame because you have the cutest arse. How about you relax a little and I promise I'll move on." Not waiting for an answer, he returned to trailing his tongue over her buttocks and crack. Pivoting her hips forwards and back he was able to drag his tongue over every inch of her cleft and arse, paying attention to her glossy clit and burgeoning lips until once more she shuddered into orgasm.

As they lay on the Persian rug, Michele studied the silent walls, thinking about how many secret liaisons the Imperial Suite would've witnessed over the years. Liaisons like hers and

Mark's, and secrets that must never be shared. Daylight lightened the room, and she knew it was time. "I wonder how they clean these rugs?" she asked, stalling.

"I couldn't tell you, but they certainly charge enough to be able to replace them after every guest if they need to." With a deep-bellied laugh, Mark pushed himself to his feet. "I gotta get ready."

"Wait. Can I at least get a picture of you? Please?"

"What? You brought a camera with you?"

"Of course. I need something to remember you by. Please?" She watched as he considered her request. Now knowing his secrets and his aversion to any possibility of discovery, she hoped he trusted her enough to give her this keepsake.

"Okay. But promise it's only for you."

"Promise." She grabbed her camera and clicked off a few images. "Great. Thanks."

"Okay, baby. I gotta get ready."

With the sunlight creeping up the suite's lemon walls, he strode into the bathroom for a shower — solo this time. Michele threw a towel around her waist and strolled out onto the balcony. Unfolding before her was a spectacular day to match the spectacular week she'd just had.

So, this is what it's all about 'Alfie,' she thought, humming the title tune from the movie. Although Mark was leaving today, she accepted deep down somewhere inside, this was the start of a new life for her.

Calling from the bathroom, his voice filtered outside, "Are you coming down to see me off?"

"Sure. Let me get dressed."

"I'll fix up the bill, but you don't have to check out until eleven, so stay, relax, get breakfast. Maybe you'll even do Roger?"

"I don't think I'll be doing Roger today. I can barely tolerate panties on my pink bits. You gave me quite the workout, you bully." She gingerly touched herself to demonstrate the point.

"That was my intention. Hammer you hard, baby, to make sure you can't walk. That way I know you won't be wrapping those fabulous legs around some other fella for at least a week."

"Very funny."

They finished dressing and bantering, playing out the last of their emotions without saying anything important.

~ ♥ ~

"Morning, folks." The marina security guard welcomed them at the gates and permitted entry once Mark proved his identity and pointed out his craft. Hand in hand, she and Mark sauntered down to the *Lady Diana* while the guard, who was probably accustomed to emotional farewells waited a discreet distance behind. And since there weren't other yachties needing his assistance in casting off this morning, he didn't appear to be in a hurry.

"Well, baby, this is it. You've been my golden-haired angel this past week. I'll miss you." He smiled down at her, and she wondered if it was the morning's brightness or were his eyes misty from emotion.

Before she could speak, Michele had to swallow her own emotion. "I can't thank you enough. I never knew sex could be that good." She reached up to kiss his cheek.

"Baby, with you, any man or woman, would have great sex." He smirked at her, obviously hoping his girlie action joke would lighten the mood.

"Stop. You're too wicked. Anyway, have a safe trip, gorgeous. Love ya heaps." She threw her arms around his neck to breathe him in one last time. She sucked his scent deep into her lungs praying for it never to be expelled, so she could remember him forever. Her heart was breaking yet she knew this was the only way. He had come into her life for a reason and now he must leave. Tears rolled down her face for the joy she'd found, the loss she now felt and for a future yet to unfold.

HE HELD HER CLOSE. He hadn't meant to feel this way, but he did. His undercover skills tried to kick in, to keep him safe from discovery. No matter how hard he denied it, he loved this woman but there was no alternative. He had to leave yet he knew they'd always remain connected somehow. He waited, like he'd done the first night he'd laid eyes on her. This time, he waited not for her to choose him, but to release him.

Looking up at the guard, Mark called, "Okay. Let's get this show on the road." Then he leaned down to her and said, "That's what you'd say, baby. Right?"

"Yes, that's what I'd say. Goodbye, gorgeous. Be safe." She stifled her crying in her hand, pivoted and walked up the arm of the marina to wave her farewells at a safe distance.

He watched her sashay up the gangway, those hips calling out to him not to go. He wondered if he could ever let her go. He doubted it.

Knowing there was no other choice, he jumped aboard. Within minutes, he kicked the engine over and executed his cast-off, reversing out of the mooring. Once he steadied the *Lady Diana* on her course, he stripped off his shirt and turned back to wave one last good-bye. Seeing Michele with her golden hair glowing in the morning light, waving him farewell, his face broke into a broad, grateful smile. Although his heart remained here with her, he was on his way home.

CHAPTER NINE

SATURDAY

As MARK SWUNG OUT of the mooring and directed the *Lady Diana* on her course, Michele watched him in the flybridge peel off his T-shirt and chug his cap onto his head. His shoulders, his waist, his buttocks, and his legs jammed into those jeans, the way he stood proud and indefatigable, everything about him made her cry out inside for him to stay. But that wasn't going to happen. When he turned around to wave goodbye, his burnished, seen-too-much-of-life face lit up with his irrepressible smile and she knew — somehow, he'd always be with her.

With a customary shrug of her dress, she turned on her heel and dragged her hand across her face, smearing the last of her makeup. There was nothing left to do except power up her best showgirl self-discipline and get on with the day.

Out on the Broadwater, and under a bright cloudless sky, early morning boaties zipped past on their way to their fishing sites. The sun's glare bounced off the churning water giving her an excuse to cover her eyes. A blessing, because she probably looked a fright after last night's sex fest and this morning's sad good-bye. Willing the magic of the day to lighten her spirits, she marched back to the hotel breathing the crisp morning air deep into her lungs. She checked her watch. Six-thirty on a Saturday morning was a little too early to call Cindy but give it thirty minutes and she'd be up and about.

By the time Michele reached the suite, all her self-control was gone. When she closed the doors behind her and viewed the chaos left by their lovemaking scattered around the room, she began to cry. Touching everywhere they'd lain, the lounges, the coffee table, the dining table, the spa and finally the sheets triggered an uprising of intense emotion. She threw herself onto the bed, and though she tried to suppress it, the emotion came rushing to the surface, spewing forth in keening howls. After all those years of not feeling good enough, of trying to be all things to all people, and then to find Mark, who made her feel truly special, only to lose him proved unbearable. Burying her head in his pillow, she breathed him in and sobbed into the expensive feather down.

"You are loved, Michele. There is nothing to fear. You can do no wrong, Heaven is all around you and you are free." Like a gentle salve, the Goddess soothed Michele's impassioned spirit.

Bereft, she remained prostrate until the heaving and heartbreak subsided. After the last of the hiccupping sobs left her throat and still cradling his pillow, she rolled over onto her back. She remembered that the last time she gazed at the ceiling was with Mark making love to her, giving every part of himself to her. Closing her eyes, she cemented the memory, breathed in and exhaled what she hoped was the last of the raw emotion from her body. Even though the anguish was fresh, somewhere deep inside she felt new-born and alive.

She leapt from the bed and hurried to the balcony to see if she could catch a final glimpse of the *Lady Diana*. There she shone, a white speck churning through the seaway. Michele squinted through the sunlight, watching the tiny dot as it made its way out to sea. She pictured Mark guiding her through a safe passage, straight and true, just as he'd done for her these last seven days. She seared the image onto the screen of her mind until at last, the dot was gone. But the memory would always remain.

~ ♥ ~

Resigned, she returned inside, found her handbag and called Cindy. "Hey, girlfriend, I hope it's not too early, but I just saw Mark off and I need that shoulder to cry on after all."

"Not a problem, sweetie. I can come over if you want?"

"I'm not at home, though. Mark organized a surprise and we spent last night at Venezia Palazzo in the Imperial Suite, which is where I am now."

"Wow! That's impressive."

"Certainly is. But I've got no clothes, makeup or anything, and I look a wreck. Can you stop by my place and pick up a few things and bring them to the hotel? We'll have breakfast then go for a swim. What do you think?"

"Sounds like a plan."

Now let's see what the other girls are doing this bright and breezy Saturday morning, Michele thought, dialling their number. Humming the tune "Never Tear Us Apart," she figured she had the best friends in the world. They'd spent many nights together over the years after a few too many wines or joints, with the four of them singing along to Michael Hutchence about how nothing could ever tear them apart. Today was again proof of that. She needed the support of her girlfriends and they were on their way.

By the time she'd tidied the room and showered Mark's smell from her body, Cindy was at the door. Looking ready for a photo shoot, she waltzed into the suite as bright as a summer flower in her daffodil printed sundress, yellow sunhat, sandals, and orange lipstick.

"Oooh, sweetie. This is fabulous." She dropped Michele's overnight bag on the floor.

"Yes. It's pretty amazing. Thanks for getting my stuff. Come into the bedroom while I get changed." Michele picked up the bag and led the way while Cindy tottered behind revelling in the suite's theatrical design.

"So how was your last night, sweetie? By the look of things, I assume it was terrific?"

"Yes, it was. Unbelievable." She regaled her friend with all the details of the night, pointing out places where certain 'activities' took place while Cindy nodded and giggled.

"Here's the breakfast menu. Order whatever you want. It comes with the room rate and a private butler, Roger."

Michele then explained how Roger featured in last night's events and her fantasy.

~ ♥ ~

With the expected efficiency of a six-star hotel, the knock at the door twenty minutes later signalled the delivery of their breakfast.

"Good morning, miss." Roger wheeled the trolley into the suite.

"Good morning, Roger. You're still on shift?" She indicated the balcony where Cindy was perched, her athletic legs crossed and showing lots of tanned thigh.

"Yes, miss. My shift concludes this morning at eleven A.M. so I'm at your disposal until then." He smiled at her with a hint of naughtiness in his eyes.

"That's wonderful. This is my friend Cindy."

"Pleased to meet you, Roger." Cindy nodded at the butler and swung her leg in a sultry manner.

"Pleased to meet you, miss."

Roger began setting breakfast for the two ladies in his well-trained manner, providing the requisite descriptions of their meals.

"Would you like me to pour tea, miss?"

"That would be lovely, thank you."

Roger poured the teas then stood to attention beside his trolley. "Will that be all, miss?"

For a moment, Cindy and Michele glanced at each other with the same thought scorching their minds. A threesome with a butler on the Imperial Suite balcony. What an exciting Dear Diary entry that would make and a first for them. Nevertheless, early morning common sense and Michele's over-worked pink bits tipped the scales.

"Thank you, Roger. That will be all." With a deliberate smile, she dismissed him while Mark's voice in her head encouraged her to, "Go on. Give him one of those great head jobs you do."

Roger nodded, snapped a turn and wheeled his trolley from the suite with the added impediment of a bulge growing in his trousers.

"Did you see that? I think darling Roger was offering other services to us aside from food," Cindy said, scraping butter onto her toast.

"It would seem so. Maybe we should've explored that a little further? What do you think?"

"Well, he did say he was on shift until eleven so there's still plenty of time." Laughing at their early morning naughtiness, the friends devoured the sumptuous breakfast.

At ten a.m. a knock at the door heralded the arrival of Julie and SallyAnn. After lots of cheek kissing and *oohing* and *aahing* about how Michele's lover had treated her on his last night, the four of them settled back on the balcony to relax. Michele gave the abridged version of the night's events then once more Roger was summoned to the room with morning tea.

Julie was delighted. "So, Roger, I'm sure you must witness a range of explicit hanky-panky in this suite? I bet you could write a book about it?" Dressed for luxury poolside flirtations in her scolding red hotpants suit, matching sandals, red striped sunhat and her mouth splashed with vermillion, Julie epitomized the scarlet temptress.

Roger held his composure as steadily as he held the teapot. "Well, miss. I'm not at liberty to say."

"Just as I thought. Discreet. Good chap." She slithered up to him, he stepped back a little.

"Would you like some scones and cream, miss?" He presented a platter of Devonshire tea delicacies to Julie, giving him a chance to step back further from her advances.

"I do love cream, Roger. What about you?" She took a bite then smacked her cream-covered lips with obvious glee.

"I guess so, miss."

He turned back to Michele. "Will that be all, miss?" Perspiration beaded on his forehead, but it wasn't the heat of the day causing his discomfort.

"Yes, Roger. That will be all. Thank you for everything."

"Thank you, miss. Good morning ladies." Roger performed his final bow and made for the door with Julie strutting behind him like an eager puppy. Blocking his escape, she whispered in his ear and slipped something into his pocket before allowing him a dignified exit.

"What have you done this time?" SallyAnn asked.

"I gave Roger my business card and told him if he likes cream as much as I do to give me a call."

"You're incorrigible." SallyAnn shook her head, and they all placed bets on whether Roger would call or not.

By the time eleven rolled around, the girls had finished morning tea, freshened their lipstick and made ready to exit. The three of them waited in the corridor while Michele gave the room a final sweep and with misty eyes, closed the door on her week of erotic adventure.

LAZING POOLSIDE IN THE private cabana gave them a chance to unwind from their busy weeks. SallyAnn had spent most of her time playing domestic goddess and chauffeuring the children to dance classes and football training. Julie had sealed a lucrative contract which she'd been working on for some time, while Cindy was planning an overseas trip to purchase costumes for her next show.

"By the way, 'Chele, did you end up getting a picture of Mark?" SallyAnn asked.

Michele nodded and fished around in her bag for the camera.

"Marvellous. Show us what this mystery man of yours looks like," Julie said.

"Yes. He's all we've heard about for the past week. Time to get a look at this champion of yours," Cindy added.

The three friends crammed in around Michele's camera as she flipped through the images.

"My. I can see what you mean. He's definitely all man and a big boy at that too." Julie scrutinized every image apparently doing the comparative math in her head about the size of hands, size of feet and length of forearm.

"I can definitely vouch for him being all man," Michele said with a cheeky grin.

"Oh, sweetie, he looks lovely."

"I must say, 'Chele, I can see why you fell for him. There's something about him that seems familiar almost." SallyAnn lingered the longest on the images obviously intrigued.

"Anyway, I had a great week and we'll see what happens from here."

By early afternoon, they all went their separate ways. Without a rendezvous with Mark, Michele did some grocery shopping, loitering at the dairy shelf with wistful amusement as she recalled the previous Saturday night's fun. She threw a token tub of yogurt and strawberries into her trolley for the night's dessert although she knew it wouldn't be nearly an enjoyable as the last time.

When she got home, she realized it'd been less than twenty-four hours since they'd been there together. He'd only left, but already she missed him. After placing the groceries on the bench, she tiptoed around her living room as if not wanting to wake the spirits from the night before. The last of his scent wafted up to her from the couch, making the memory even more poignant. She grabbed the cushion and tucked it under her chin, hoping he was safe, when her phone buzzed.

"Hey, babe. Dolphins riding with me for last hour. Wish you were here. xxx"

How awe-inspiring, she thought. To be out on the ocean with dolphins riding the bow waves would be sheer magic. She imagined standing on the flybridge, wedged under Mark's arm as the sun sets. Just the two of them and the dolphins. She heaved a sigh and text back.

"I wish I was there too. Travel safe. xxx"

CHAPTER TEN

WEEK THREE

FROM OUT AT SEA, he'd called her on Sunday afternoon sounding quite alone and miserable. In some ways, his despondency made her feel better. Then, on Monday, he'd sent a text after he left Port Stevens on his last leg to Sydney. Once he settled into his life back home, she figured future contact would be sporadic at best. However, much to her surprise, he called every night, sometimes twice, usually closer to midnight.

"My wife is asking me if I'm having an affair," he said.

"What did you say?" Michele still held a glimmer of hope that their separation might motivate him to leave and start a new life with her.

"Well, I lied of course. I can't tell Karen about you. That'd be the end of it. I can't afford to lose everything, not now."

"Well, what do you want me to do? I'm not here to be your Mother Confessor."

"I don't want you to do anything, baby. I just feel like the enemy in my own home. I can't leave Karen. She stood by me through the worst times of my life. I'm sorry. But I just can't stop thinking about you. If only we'd met earlier."

"But we didn't. It's no good wishing for something that didn't happen. Either you stay where you are and we both move on with our lives or you leave. But to be honest, these late-night calls and all this angst aren't doing you, me or your marriage any good."

Although she loved him, and she believed he loved her, love was not the issue here. Having been a police detective, Mark had been well trained in executing his duties regardless of personal pain or collateral damage. "You're right," came the clipped reply.

She felt his emotions crawl back undercover, protecting themselves against her criticism.

"I wish it was different too," she said in a softer tone, aware that tonight's conversation severed the tenuous cosmic thread of hope between them.

"A different time. A different place. I'll call you soon." His warm breath flooded down the phone smothering her with memories and regret.

She swallowed hard. "A different time. A different place. Talk soon."

She didn't sleep well that night and wondered if it was the same for him.

MARK HAD BEEN RIGHT on one count. It took her about five days to recuperate from their last night of sex together. It wasn't until the following Friday morning she no longer felt as if a football team had played a grand final game inside her.

"Now that you've been without Mark for a week, what's on the agenda, sweetie?" Cindy sat barefaced across from Michele after their dance class, enjoying a creamy slice of Mojito torte.

"Well, I don't think I've really had any casual sex yet," Michele said through her own mouthful of yumminess.

"Excuse me? What do you call all that sex you had with Mark?"

"Well casual sex is supposed to be a one-off thing, isn't it? That went on for a week and besides, there was a lot more there than just sex." Today Michele matched Cindy's eating regime mouthful for mouthful.

"Oh?" Cindy's feigned ignorance was muffled by her last mouthful of torte.

"You know perfectly well how I feel about him."

"So? What are you going to do?"

"I'm going out tonight to start all over again." Michele placed her fork on the plate.

"And Mark?"

"There's no future there, Cindy. When we last spoke, it was clear that he's back in his life and he's going to stay there even if he does want to be with me. I need to get on with my own life. Otherwise, I'll turn into one of those lonely women longing for the man she can't have. That's just not me. The best way is to get back on the horse, as they say. Tally-ho." She threw her hand in the air to call for the bill.

Though if she was honest with herself, Michele felt unenthused about the night's prospects. But she feared if she didn't verbalize her conviction, she'd remain at home eating yogurt and strawberries forever, reliving a memory and pining for a man she couldn't have.

REFLECTING HER MORE SOMBRE mood, she opted for a little black dress with matching accessories, very chic and low key. Having had success the first time at Speakeasy, she decided to return, casting a smile at the knowing expression of the bouncer.

Although the atmosphere was just as entertaining, with single men aplenty, her heart wasn't in it. After about an hour, she decided to leave.

"Please, no more strawberries and yogurt alone in front of the TV," her sex goddess pleaded.

"I know. I know," Michele muttered.

While she continued with her internal debate, she popped into the restroom to freshen up. Her phone rang with a signature tune reserved for one person.

"Hey, baby. How ya' doing?" His voice was bright and easy-going.

"Hi, gorgeous. I'm fine. How're things with you?"

"Fine? I hope you're not fine. Remember? Frustrated, insecure, neurotic and emotional?" He was smiling that big grin down the phone.

"You know what I mean. It's good to hear you sounding so upbeat."

"And you too. I've only got a few moments, so I thought I'd give you a call. What's all that noise in the background?"

"I'm out at a club looking for someone like you."

"Good girl. I knew that once you could walk again, you'd be out and about. Lucky bastard whoever he turns out to be. I wish it was me but what can I say?" He'd given his approval. He'd let her go. "Baby, I gotta go. I'll call you when I can. Take care."

"Oh. Okay. You too."

He was gone.

"Good news. Now we can go out and get laid. Sounds like a plan to me."

Disregarding her inner cheerleader, Michele felt disappointed. Her delight at hearing Mark's voice was dashed by his indifference to her sexual quest. The sad inevitability crept over her as she touched up her makeup. Perhaps he had broken free of his attachment to her? Maybe going home was a better plan. At least there she could lick her wounds in private.

As she stood on the footpath looking for a cab, a sultry voice behind her asked, "Are you alone or are you waiting for someone?"

She turned around to find herself looking at a shining tower of a man in a designer suit with gleaming shoes, polished to mirror reflection to match his ebony skin.

"Um. Ah. No, I'm not waiting for anyone. I was thinking of going home." She blinked at this exotic specimen of elegance.

"Oh goodie. We wanted one of these last week." Her sex goddess scampered around in her mind clapping her hands.

"Perhaps I can tempt you to have a drink with me?" His voice and demeanour matched his velvet skin.

She hesitated for only a moment. "Why not? That might be nice. Thank you." Michele's swift acceptance of the offer delighted her suitor and surprised her.

"Excellent. Allow me." With a gentle gesture, he assisted her from the curb to cross the street.

"My name is Benjamin."

"I'm Michele."

"Pleased to meet you, Michele. Watch your step. It's just down here." He guided her to a nearby hotel bar in silence. Filled with stylish, elegant people and with low-key café music playing in the background, the venue was relaxed and fashionable.

He escorted her to a cosy booth for two. "What would you like to drink, Michele?"

"A vodka martini, please."

With his square shoulders and trim hips accented by the crisp cut of his designer jacket, Benjamin exuded sophisticated charm. Though he tried to circumvent the crowd on his way to the bar, she noticed how women tittered and preened when he passed. She felt certain they were wondering whether the man could live up to the myth. But their obvious curiosity about taking a black man as a lover caused him little concern. For a moment, Michele questioned her own motives as to whether she'd accepted his offer for no other base reason than her own distorted bias on skin colour?

I'm not so sure about this, she thought.

"Trust me. It's all good."

With a sigh, Michele resigned herself to her pledge. At least he seemed polite and well-mannered. And after all, he'd chosen her. She'd merely accepted. Plus, his full lips were tempting.

He returned with the drinks and over the next hour they talked, laughed and got to know each other a little. He was born in America, a lawyer, based in Brisbane, first time on the Gold Coast, on business for a few days. All the hallmarks of a good one-night stand, assuming he was telling the truth. Based on her recent experience, she knew not to believe any of it.

"So, Michele, perhaps you would like to join me in my apartment upstairs on the thirty-fifth floor to look at the city lights tonight?" He was as smooth as silk.

"Why not?"

"Excellent. I can assure you the skyline will never look better than from my bedroom."

"I'll hold you to that."

"Very good. I enjoy a dare. Let's go, shall we?"

When Michele accepted his hand, his touch signalled more chemistry than she'd first suspected.

"See. I told you. We're in for a ride tonight. You know what they say about black men."

Michele silently admonished herself and her sex goddess for such a thought, but hoped the stereotype was true.

Although Benjamin's hotel room lacked the opulence of the Imperial Suite, the view from the three-hundred-and-sixty-degree panoramic balcony encircling the sub-penthouse was breathtaking. He removed his jacket and tie, and played the courteous host, while Michele wandered outside.

He joined her and offered a glass of champagne. "I'm sure this will meet with your approval."

"Thank you." She sipped the champagne which was as good as his taste in clothes. "Do you prefer, Benjamin or Ben?"

"No real preference. Whichever you choose, as long as you say it with passion." Again, he spoke with a voice that reminded her of hot lava, inescapable and unstoppable.

"That will be up to you." She flashed him a wicked smile then turned. "Now show me this view from your bedroom."

"My pleasure." He led her down the hallway, which opened onto a large master suite decorated in subdued shades of grey, with an oversized bed centred in the room.

"This is sexy," she purred.

"It's even sexier on the balcony." Benjamin slipped past her and opened the sliding glass doors. As she joined him, thousands of lights twinkled from the surrounding high-rise apartments and hotels. Late-night revellers on balconies, indoor dinner parties, and romantic trysts were evidence the high life on the Glitter Strip was in full swing.

"You're right. It's spectacular."

"Not as spectacular as it's about to be." Prowling up beside her, he reassigned their glasses to the balcony table then enveloped her in his arms, drawing her to him. Fleshy and hot with desire, his lips and mouth were as soft as their allure. His skin not only looked but felt like soft, downy velvet.

"I'd like to freshen up first?" she whispered in his ear.

"Certainly. Use the en suite bathroom just through there. I'll freshen up too and meet you back here."

In the bathroom, she removed her underwear and thought how polite Benjamin was to give her privacy, unlike Mark, who loved to show and share. Based on his understated manner, she presumed Ben would be a slow, gentle lover, a change from all the pounding sex she'd had with Mark.

"Don't be too quick to judge," her sex goddess warned.

Clothed in the plush hotel robe, her black heels, and a spray of perfume in all the right places, she returned to the bedroom balcony feeling relaxed and in control. Benjamin's naked silhouette greeted her with a compelling welcome of taut, obsidian flesh stretched over defined musculature. With his weight slung into his right hip, he resembled the Statue of David. Rock-hard muscles shone like polished marble while his long, athletic limbs were matched by an equally long appendage.

"There's a lot more going on there than what Michelangelo gave David."

Michele hoped he didn't hear her sharp intake of breath when her eyes spotted his over-endowment. Regaining her poise, she continued her approach with excitement and trepidation building in her groin. It seemed the saying about black men was correct, at least in this instance.

His long dark fingers reached out to the collar of her robe. "Now that you've seen what I can offer, perhaps it is time for you to reciprocate?"

He slid the robe off her shoulders and let it puddle at her feet. With an approving murmur, his black eyes burned into her flesh and his slender fingers explored the curves of her body. His cock grew in anticipation, brushing against her like a low-lying branch as he strolled in circles around her, examining his prize. Although a little intimidated by his lingering assessment, Michele remained firm and proud while he proceeded with his evaluation of her flesh. Succumbing to his delicate touching and intense scrutiny, her desire increased. Yet glancing down, she wondered how much of his desire she could take.

"Don't be afraid, Michele. I've learnt self-control. I'll only go as deep as you wish. I won't hurt you."

"That's good to hear. You're extremely well-endowed. But I'm sure you know that."

"Yes. But it's not a blessing. It's a curse. Many women become tense and then neither the woman nor I find pleasure."

"We'll see about that," her sex goddess refuted.

"Well, let's start off slow, shall we?" Michele reached down taking his sizeable member in her hand. As he groaned at her touch, his fingers reached around her buttocks and slid between her legs, searching for her sweet juice.

"Let's stay here on the balcony," he said with soft intensity.

"Okay. I don't mind." It was a balmy night complete with ocean breezes and clear starlit skies, a fitting backdrop for a memorable one-night stand.

Within a moment, he dropped to his knees like a cat, stealthy and flexed. His tongue slipped into her, licking her cream, enticing her to open to the delights he could offer. "You taste good," he murmured as his tongue slid in and out.

She began to buckle, so he guided her onto a sun lounge where she tucked a cushion under her buttocks, exposing herself for his delicious onslaught. But she was disappointed, for although Benjamin proved to be a good technician, licking, nibbling and tonguing her with obvious delight, he lacked the subtle art of reading her erogenous signals.

In an effort to move things along a little, she took control. "How about we change places?"

Without a word, he rose to his feet, causing her to momentarily rethink her offer.

"Girl, you're going to have to work hard on your gag reflex tonight." Face to face with his burgeoning cock, even her sex goddess was aghast.

Known to deliver on her promises, Michele steeled herself for the task. With Ben straddling her on the lounge, she began with deliberate restraint and fondled his heavy balls, while assessing his cock at close range. Not only was its length intimidating, but its girth was also comparable to a large, ripe plantain. She began slowly, by lavishing it with long, slow licks before wrapping her tongue around its head and shaft. He tasted like melted premium dark chocolate, and her initial apprehension transformed into fascination. To have a cock this size inside her would be thrilling, a challenge, a forbidden pleasure one can seldom indulge in. With eyes closed, she devoured him little by little, determined to make her treat last.

"Your lips should be bronzed, Michele. No one has been able to take so much of me."

Many years before, Michele had taken instruction from a master practitioner of deep throat, a gay male dancer who'd told her the trick was to "breathe through your eyelids." As silly as it sounded, she discovered if she focused on that, as if she could breathe through her eyelids, deep throating became a whole lot easier. Although she was grateful for Ben's compliment, there was still a lot of him being neglected and there was just no way she was able to oblige.

"Enough," he said, breathless with appreciation.

Thank goodness, she thought.

"I need to take you now." He began to slide her back down to lie on the lounge.

"This isn't the most comfortable place, you know," she said, surprised they hadn't adjourned to the bedroom.

"I know, but I do like an audience." The sheen from his face glimmered in the dark shadows of the balcony.

"Ben, I get the sex in public places thing, but maybe it's time to move inside?"

"I know it seems difficult here, but the restriction of movement is good to begin with. Believe me, let's remain here at least to start."

As a dancer, she liked an audience better than anyone, but this felt contrived and all the chit-chat had dampened the mood for her.

Keeping the pace slow and gentle, he penetrated her, urging her to take a little more of him with each measured stroke. Her body responded, stretching for his enormous cock, enjoying the sense of consuming him with her flesh.

"Mmm, that's good," she whispered into his ear.

"I'm pleased you like it." With a steady rhythm, he entered her more, picking up the tempo.

"Oh, God, Ben, that is good." Being jammed deep and full of such hot solid flesh was more arousing than she expected. She ran her hands over his rock-climbing wall of a chest, down between her legs and discovered another couple of inches at the base of his shaft. "Oh my God. There's still more?"

"There usually is. Now that you know, you're in charge. You must tell me how much more you can take and how you want it."

She now realized how restrictive Ben's sex life must be. There was going to be no wild abandoned sex happening here tonight. Feeling sorry for him and ready for a challenge, she suggested, "Why don't we go to the bedroom where we can be more comfortable?"

On the bed, she allowed him as much gain without too much pain as possible. He complied with her limitations and as they surrendered to the moment, both of them relaxed, finding more pleasure. During their sex play, Ben even tutored Michele in tantric sex. Being a yoga devotee, she played eager student to his guidance enjoying the blend of sex and yoga into a whole new lovemaking experience. Then, fulfilling his desire for more audience interaction, they returned for another balcony performance which received applause from an enthralled group of onlookers in the next building. By allowing herself to experiment, she discovered Ben had proved himself worthy of her satisfaction and she acknowledged this passion by crying out his unabridged name as she orgasmed.

~ ♥ ~

By four a.m., she looked over at her dozing dark conquest and smiled. With a soft kiss on his cheek, she whispered, "Bye, Ben. Thanks for the fun night."

He opened his bleary eyes. "Are you going? You don't have to leave, you know. Stay."

"No. It's time for me to go. It's been fun. Thanks."

"I'm still here for a few days. Can we catch up? Go to dinner maybe?"

"Sorry. This was it for me. I really have to go."

He clasped his hands behind her head, pulling her close for a farewell kiss. "I had a great time. Thank you." He reached over to his wallet on the bedside table and pulled out a business card. "Call or email me anytime. Maybe someday we'll catch up again?"

She took the card. "Maybe." But she doubted it. She threw on her dress, slipped into her high heels and waved back at him as she tip-tapped down the hall.

Out on the curb, she hailed a cab and slipped into the back seat. Knowing what the cabbie was thinking as he watched her glowing in the rear vision mirror, she returned his gaze with the widest of smiles until he averted his eyes. Even though the sex had started out stilted, Benjamin had proved to be a generous and well-equipped lover. She'd also just had her first one-night stand. She was thrilled. She'd left before daylight and was on her way home without him knowing any more than her first name. She'd graduated to the rank of femme fatale.

"Way to go," her own sex goddess commended from within. *"Finally, you're starting to experience another level of life and love."*

Michele had to agree it felt exhilarating.

By the time the birds were chirping, she was singing under her steaming shower lathering the night's adventure away. With wet hair spun up in a towel, exfoliated skin and scrubbed face, she applied a good layer of cream over her entire body. Watching herself in the mirror, she thought that somehow her reflection had changed. She looked younger, felt lighter. She glowed. Although not in the least tired she forced her mind and body to calm down. She padded into her bedroom, dragged the curtains shut and pressed play on her CD player until the sounds of the rolling waves filled the room. She crawled into bed not caring about her damp hair and grabbed her phone. No messages. It didn't matter. She'd had a terrific time without Mark. Snuggled deep into her pillow, she closed her eyes and within no time, fell asleep.

~ ♥ ~

ON THE BEACH, ANOTHER glorious day dawned with the ocean waves crashing on the sand. The little boy and girl sat together building sandcastles with buckets and spades. He ran to collect water in his blue bucket while she patted wet sand down on her fortress. They smiled and laughed; the innocent joys of childhood.

From afar, the sound of music disrupted the happy scene, getting louder and louder until Michele stirred from her dream. Her phone was clattering its Rhumba tone demanding to be answered.

"Good morning, girlfriend. It's nine A.M. Where are you?" Julie's bright insistent voice trilled down the line.

"What? What do you mean, where am I?" Michele didn't function well on four hours' sleep.

"The spa. Remember? We're doing the couples massage today. I bought it for your birthday."

"Shit. Sorry. Forgot. What time are we booked for?" She sprang out of bed and began rifling through her wardrobe for something to wear.

"Not until ten but we were having coffee first. Can you get here by ten?"

With the phone tucked under her ear, Michele hopped around on one leg while struggling the other into a pair of jeans. "Absolutely. See you soon."

"I can't wait to hear who this one was."

The last thing Michele heard was her friend's laughter before she hung up.

CHAPTER ELEVEN

WEEK THREE, SATURDAY

"**I FEEL DELICIOUS. THANKS,** Julie. That was wonderful." After spending the past few hours being pampered and perfumed, the two friends drifted from the spa, like vaporous versions of themselves.

"The perfect way to begin a weekend," Julie said in a lyrical voice. "Why don't we finish with a stroll along the beach?"

"Yes please."

Having caught up on each other's news including Michele's Friday night special with her Negro lover, they wandered to the promenade in a peaceful state of mind.

"So, where to from here?" Julie asked.

"Why don't we just walk down to the jetty and back?"

"No, Michele, what are you going to do with your life now? I know things haven't been easy for you since the divorce, and I also know you don't talk to any of us about how tough it's really been. But we worry about you."

"It's okay. Things are working out."

"I didn't ask about 'things,' I asked about you."

"I'm fine really." Michele couldn't help but hear Mark's voice in her head defining her status as frustrated, insecure, neurotic and emotional. Melancholy knocked at the door.

"Really?" Julie turned to her friend, arching her eyebrow, waiting for more.

Perhaps it was the massage, perhaps it was the reminder of Mark or perhaps it was just time to confide in someone, but

Michele felt tears well up in her eyes. "God. I hate this. I seem to spend so much time crying lately."

"Let's sit down for a minute." Julie guided her to a nearby bench overlooking the waves rolling along the beach as tears trickled down Michele's cheeks.

Michele sniffled back the threatening outburst and composed herself. "Look, the divorce was the best thing that happened to me. Really it was. I admit, it's been hard financially, but I'm making ends meet. I'm also enjoying this being single, the sex and not having to answer to anyone but myself. It's just this 'Mark' thing has really affected me, and I can't seem to get him out of my system."

"Let's not talk about Mark, or your feelings for him, let's talk about you. What do you want for you? For instance, where do you see yourself in twelve months' time?"

"God, Julie. I don't know. I only decided a week ago to have casual sex and now you want me to think about what I want in a year's time? I don't know." She gazed out to sea thinking of the dolphins cruising with Mark the previous Saturday morning. Dolphins don't have to think about what's happening in their future. They just get to have fun with Mark. She envied them.

"Well, if you've no clue as to how you want your new life to work out then all you're doing is bobbing around in the ocean like a cork." Julie motioned to the endless ocean in front of them for emphasis. "You'll go wherever the tide takes you, wherever circumstances lead you. That 'come-what-may' attitude to life may work if you're someone who never feels disappointment or doesn't care. But you do care what happens, you care deeply. You need to at least consider how you want your life to work out. I'm not a great believer in Walt Disney's plots, but I know you are. So, what's the happy-ever-after ending you're really looking for?"

"I don't know. I just want to go out and live a little. See what happens. Trust in the universe I guess."

"And how is that working out for you?" Julie asked with her usual pragmatism.

"Well, it brought Mark into my life."

"And I ask again, how's that working out for you?"

"I know. I know. He's married. But regardless of all that, I still believe we were meant to meet." Michele paused, considering how best to sum up what she was trying to say. "Therefore, I'm going to continue flying Trust Airways and see where it takes me."

"What on earth are you talking about, 'Trust Airways'?"

"It means I've no other choice but to trust things will work out exactly the way they're meant to. All I have to do is take the opportunities that come to me even if I don't know where they'll lead. Just like I trusted to go with Mark. And even though he's married, I still trust there was a reason we met. I can't explain it any better than that. But I do know it's all about trust, trusting in the Universe, trusting in my gut instincts. It's like that old saying of throwing the chips in the air and seeing where they land. My life is in the air. I can't make my life land exactly where I want it, but I can trust that it will land in the best possible place for me."

As Michele voiced her philosophy aloud, her spirits lifted. Somehow it made more sense when she heard it from her own mouth, rather than from the voice in her head.

Julie breathed a heavy sigh of resignation. "Very well then. You fly Trust Airways while I keep my feet firmly on the ground."

Michele reached over and squeezed her hard-nosed friend's perfect, manicured hand. "Thank you for worrying about me, but this time, I have to live my life the same way as I dance, without limitation. Trusting that I won't fall if I push too hard, trusting that all the hard work and training I've done will support me in my new freedom. I have to live not like there's no-one watching, but like there is someone watching over me. Who knows if there is a pot of gold at the end of the rainbow, or a Prince Charming waiting in the wings, or if this is the third act before the final curtain? I'm forty-two, I don't have many material things, and this could be my swan song. I refuse to die with regrets."

Julie reciprocated her friend's touch with a compassionate smile and loving indulgence. "Sometimes I think you are

Tinker Bell, just without the green costume and the fairy dust."

Michele screwed up her nose, just like a cheeky Tinker Bell.

"So, when it's time to bail out at thirty thousand feet because your pilot doesn't exist, you know you can count on me. Yes?" Julie said.

"I won't have to bail out. But if I do, yes I'll call you." Michele put her arms around her friend's neck and hugged her, careful not to displace her expertly tied Ferragamo scarf.

"Right then. Let's go." Julie rose to her feet, setting the pace as they returned along the promenade. "What are you doing tonight? Out for more casual sex?"

"No. I can only afford to do that once a week and last night was it for this week. Looks like a night at home in front of the telly. Do you want to join me?"

"Sorry. We're having this launch party for the new retail project I was telling you about last Saturday. We're about to start stage one and tonight is for the media, investors, company execs, that sort of thing. Would you like to come?"

"Really? Sounds like fun." Michele all but skipped at the invitation.

"Careful you don't take flight on those gossamer wings of yours."

"Come on, Julie, say it." Michele capered around her.

"Say what? Are you sure you shouldn't be on medication?"

"Say that you believe in fairies."

"Oh for goodness sake." As Julie tried to shoo her away like a nuisance fly, Michele grabbed her friend's hands and spun them both around in circles, dancing as if no one was watching.

"I'M SO PLEASED YOU enjoyed it." With a gracious smile, Michele received the compliment on how 'great the awards ball was,' from the attractive, sun-kissed woman dressed in the long gold evening gown standing beside her. Julie's launch party was filled with a similar crowd to those who'd attended the awards ball the week before. Since her arrival, Michele had spent most of the time accepting compliments on the event and being shuttled from one champagne-sipping group to another, liked a prize-winning pooch at Crofts. Finding a quiet dimly lit corner, she'd tried her best to become unseen, like Mark used to do, but she wasn't as successful. This effusive woman had glimpsed her from the other side of the room, made a beeline for her and started a conversation about Michele's recent achievement. Not that she really minded. Julie's launch party was proving an unexpected networking opportunity so she capitalized on it, handing out business cards in the hope more work would flow from this influential crowd.

"I must get my husband. I'm sure he'd love to meet you." She flounced off in search of her partner.

Julie sidled up and handed her a fresh glass of champagne. "My goodness. You're quite the hit, aren't you?"

"I'm so sorry. I had no idea your launch party would be filled with most of the audience from the awards night."

"Don't be silly. I think it's terrific. You're giving us some star power, you local celebrity you. And that certainly helps us to sell retail space to potential tenants here tonight. Just keep smiling and everyone will be happy." Julie clinked Michele's glass and while she scrutinized the 'dinner suits' for prospective lessees, Michele watched the personification of success; a reality she dreamed for herself.

"Here she is. This is Michele, the woman who created the whole event at the awards ball last week." The golden woman had returned. Holding onto her hand was a short, bald lover of good food. With his olive skin, he was of Mediterranean descent and his dark eyes smouldered with the intense ancestry of the gods of Mount Olympus. His black three-piece dinner suit was tailor-made and the fine, embossed satin stripe on his trousers matched his gleaming black shoes. On both his forefingers shone yellow-gold rings while an expensive designer watch peeped out beneath his crisp sleeve cuff.

"This is my husband, Nick Stavros," his wife said.

"Hello, Michele. I'm an avid admirer not only of your work but also of you. You're a beautiful woman."

Michele and Julie shot a simultaneous look at Nick's wife who paid no attention to her husband's intimate compliment. Michele proffered her hand. "It's a pleasure to meet you, Nick."

Nick took her hand and encircled it in the warmth of both of his. "We were actually introduced on the awards night, but it was very quick and there were lots of people all clamouring to talk to you. However, I remember you wore that very sexy black pantsuit."

As he continued to compliment her fashion sense and caress her hand, his wife seemed oblivious, but Michele's discomfort grew.

Julie stepped up with an explanation. "Nick, you're being naughty." She turned to Michele. "Nick Stavros is one of the financial partners in this new project. He fancies himself as a bit of a ladies' man. It must be all that Greek blood coursing through his veins."

Changing targets, he released Michele's hand and turned his attention to Julie. Placing his hands on her waist, he kissed her on both cheeks. "Julie, you always ruin my fun."

"Michele is a dear friend of mine, so you go easy," she warned her investor with a wagging finger, before departing to entertain more guests.

At the same time, Nick's wife said, "I'm off to talk to Helen. She's over there. I'll see you later." With a flurry of gold satin, she was gone.

"There are a couple of chairs on the balcony, Michele. Shall we sit?" With a wave of his well-manicured hand, he indicated outside.

"Very well," she said.

Once seated and with fresh glasses of champagne, Nick wielded his sonorous voice like a maestro's baton. "You look lovely, Michele. A delight to behold."

"Doesn't your wife mind you making these types of comments about other women in front of her?"

"Not at all. We've an open marriage."

"Does that mean what I think it means?"

"And what do you think it means?"

"That you have extramarital relationships, and neither of you minds what the other one does."

"That's not quite the marriage we have, but you're close." He shuffled his chair a little nearer to prove his point by proximity.

Having just dealt with the 'married man' debacle with Mark, she was determined to nip Nick's approach in the bud. "Well, Nick, let's get something clear here. I'm not interested in having sex with you, or with your wife. So, if you're happy with that, I guess we can continue talking."

"That's fine with me."

"Funny you should say that. Do you know what fine means?"

"Frustrated, insecure, neurotic and emotional," he replied without missing a beat.

"Yes," she said, not concealing her surprise, "I only know one other person who knows that."

"And who would that be?" His dark eyes twinkled.

Michele paused to sip her champagne. There was something about Nick Stavros she liked. Smart, sophisticated and successful. If Julie trusted him in business, Michele figured she'd trust him too. "His name is Mark, and we met a couple of weeks ago." For the next hour, she assailed the attentive Greek businessman with the story of Mark, how he was married, that he'd been an undercover narcotics detective, the *Lady Diana*, the great sex they'd had. Then she reached further back into her history to her marriage, her ex-husband, their divorce.

Nick became her confidante, her pseudo-Sigmund Freud, a professional stranger who appeared broad-minded, unbiased and removed from her in every possible way. All of which combined to give Michele a trusting listener with no investment in the outcome, no strings attached.

"You've certainly had quite the ride," he said.

"In more ways than one. So, Nick, what about you?"

Pulling his cuff back, he glanced down at his wristwatch and its magnificence glinted in the moonlight. "Unfortunately, I don't have time at the moment. Our car is waiting. However, I'd love to continue our conversation if you like. Why don't you join me one day for lunch?"

"But what about your wife? Are you sure she won't mind if we go to lunch, just the two of us?"

"Not at all. Do you have a business card?"

"I think so." She retrieved the last of her business cards from her evening purse.

"I must go. It's been wonderful talking with you, Michele. I'll call you." Nick leaned in and kissed her on both cheeks, then strolled off to collect his wife.

At the end of the night, Julie looped her arm through Michele's as they sauntered out to the car park. "So, what do you think of the inimitable Nick Stavros?"

"Well, he's very charming, intelligent, successful and a good listener. But his marriage seems a bit odd. He asked me to lunch and said his wife won't mind."

"Are you going?" Julie avoided making any opinion on the Stavros marriage or on the lunch invitation.

"I guess so. Mr Stavros may think himself a ladies' man, but he's not my type at all, so no harm in going to lunch with him."

"There've been many before you who thought the same way. Be careful, Tinker Bell."

CHAPTER TWELVE

WEEK THREE, SUNDAY

"**ARE YOU ALL RIGHT**, Mum?" Michele helped her mother up the stairs to the Chinese restaurant.

Although they'd spoken on the phone, it'd been a couple of weeks since Michele had last seen her mother. Her further decline into the darkness of dementia was undeniable. The muscle and flesh on her mother's frame had disappeared as if by an evil spell, while her ability to have a conversation was almost gone.

Still living alone with her treasured cat, Michele's mother refused with the stubbornness of a tantrum-throwing-two-year-old to vacate her unit in favour of residential care. Having fought on the topic many times, Michele relented and decided it was better to allow her mother the dignity to remain in her home. Even to starve herself to death if she so chose, seemed a more agreeable option than placing her into a facility against her will, where she'd live out the remainder of her days feeling patronized, hating her daughter and pining for her beloved pet. To assuage her own guilt, Michele managed her mother's affairs, ensuring she received daily in-home care including prepared meals. But Michele suspected the food ended up in the garbage because of her mother's forgetfulness.

"I'm fine, thank you," her mother said, not knowing the word ignited Michele's memory of her week-long love affair with Mark.

Once seated for yum cha, Michele did her best to have a conversation. Her mother, named after a precious gem, Pearl, had been a beautiful young model during World War II. She'd spent the first four years as a newlywed standing on a railway platform waving her new husband off to far-away places to fight in the war, wondering if he'd ever return. Michele had pictures of her mother from those days and although she was now seventy-eight years old, her mother's face still wore the smile of her youth. It was sad that her mind had deserted her, taking with it those cherished memories. Her mother's cognition now performed only basic functions, remembering to take her medication, feed the cat and trying to recall who was coming to care for her on which day of the week.

"So, everything is good for you then, Mum?" Michele leaned over to cut up the spring rolls and steamed pork buns for her mother.

She'd been the golden only child. The one her parents had wanted but had been unable to have on their own. After many years of waiting, they'd been blessed to receive Michele when she was a toddler. As older-age parents and working-class people, they'd sacrificed much to send their daughter to dance classes and Michele reciprocated their love and devotion, never wondering who her birth parents may have been.

"My event went well, Mum." She tried to remind her mother of what had been taking place in her life.

"Can I have some more crunchy food?" Pearl lifted her bowl to Michele with the innocence of a well-behaved child.

"Of course. When the next trolley comes around, I'll get some for you." Michele wiped the crumbs and sauce from her mother's lips. The familiar sadness she'd been feeling over the past few years had been replaced by the inevitability of the situation. Their roles were now reversed; the mother becomes the child and the child cares for the mother, one of life's cruellest dances, a loyal partnership to its bitter end.

"So, Mum, I see you still seem to be going all right living on your own?"

"Yes, Michele. You told me the moment I can't take my medication or look after myself I'll have to leave my home. I won't be leaving my home. What would happen to Puss

Puss?" Pearl recited the deal-breaker issues that guaranteed her independence.

"And I see you're still as determined as ever on this matter." Michele steered the conversation once more to the possibility of going into full-time care.

"Can I also have some of those nice little custard tarts?" Pearl resumed her flight of fancy, leaving Michele to attend to her mother's wishes, pay for lunch and take her home to Puss Puss.

"SEE YOU SOON, MUM." When she hugged her mother goodbye, she tried not to flinch at her thin, desiccated frame.

Pearl looked up at her with intense blue eyes moist with love.

"See you then, Michele. I love you."

"I love you too, Mum. You take care now." Michele breathed in a lungful of French perfume, a gift she'd given her mother for her birthday. Even its strong fragrance couldn't disguise the scent of decay that permeated her mother's body.

As she drove off with a knot in her stomach, waving to the frail, yet joyous woman standing on the driveway, a soft, comforting voice resounded in her mind, *"You are loved, Michele. There is nothing to fear. You can do no wrong, Heaven is all around you and you are free."*

"Possibly so, but what about Mum?"

"She too is loved. She knows there is nothing to fear and she can do no wrong. She is already in Heaven and she is free."

With tears again cleansing her eyes, Michele drove home with no music, no need for further guidance, no thoughts, just silence.

CHAPTER THIRTEEN

WEEK FOUR

LIFE BEGAN TO REVERT to its pre-Mark normality, much to Michele's disappointment. She missed the heady anticipation of being out with him every night, of doing exciting things and living on the edge of his dangerous life. Her days were filled with developing creative projects, signing a few deals and meeting prospective clients, while her nights held little promise of more than staying home or going out to 'get some strange.' Much to her surprise, the glory of casual sex had lost its glow quicker than she'd expected. With no tally-ho instructions plaguing her mind from her sex goddess, she felt quite indifferent. To make matters worse, since her encounter with Benjamin she hadn't spoken to Mark. So, when Nick's deep, sensual voice resonated down her phone, a flirtatious smile crept across her face.

"Hello, Michele. It's Nick Stavros. How are you?"

"I won't say I'm fine because we both know what that means. I'm very well, thank you. How are you, Nick?"

"Much better for hearing your lovely voice. I'm calling to invite you to a special event for a friend of mine in Brisbane. It's a celebrity sports star dinner. It's this Friday night. Are you free?"

"I am. Thank you. Where is it?"

"No need for you to concern yourself with the details. I'll send a car to collect you."

"That's very kind of you." Michele provided her address, and Nick gave her the pick-up time and event details.

"I'll see you then. I'm looking forwards to spending more time with you Michele." His rich voice seemed to drip with ambrosia, the heavenly drink of the Greek gods.

"I'll see you Friday evening, Nick." She refrained from making any further comments, determined to keep the relationship platonic.

~ ♥ ~

At Friday's après-dance-class-coffee-and-cake session, Cindy's excitement bubbled over as she broke the news.

"I decided to take your advice and see where it might lead." Having devoured her torte in record time, Cindy sipped her steaming peppermint tea.

"See what might lead where?"

"Graham, the police officer."

Michele shook her head in confusion.

"We've been seeing a lot of each other, and I think it might work. He's really quite adorable." Cindy's little finger twitched on her teacup handle.

"Really? I thought you were a little put off by his police career."

"I was hesitant, to begin with, but the more we talked about it, the less it seemed to matter. He's taking me away this weekend to Sydney." Cindy's blonde curls frothed around her face.

"Wining, dining and dancing, I assume. This Graham seems to have made quite the impact." Michele hadn't seen her friend this impassioned about a man for a long time.

"Strangely enough, he has. He's ticking a lot of the boxes. Been divorced for years, only one child, a teenage daughter who lives with her mum in Sydney and holidays with Graham. No financial issues. The ex-wife is remarried and happy. And I'm meeting the daughter this weekend."

"Ooh, sounds like he's fairly serious if he's introducing you to his daughter already. I'm happy for you. I know you've wanted a good man in your life for a while now. I hope it works out. Funny if he's the one."

"Yes, that's what I thought and even funnier if we meet up with your Mark in Sydney. Graham said he'd introduce me to some of his Sydney mates while we're down there."

The possibility of this dawned on Michele, with more negative than positive repercussions.

"God, if you do you mustn't let on that you know me."

"But, sweetie, why would your name come up? Graham hasn't met you yet. If by some chance I do end up meeting Mark, he'll just be a friend of Graham's. He certainly won't know that you and I are friends. I'm sure you never talked about me to him."

"Of course, you're right. There's no connection. Still, it'd be easier if Mark wasn't one of the buddies Graham plans on you meeting this weekend."

"Regardless, your secret is safe with me. You know that." Cindy patted Michele's hand for reassurance. "Now tell me, what are you up to this weekend? More big black men?"

"Actually no, I met this man at Julie's work party last week and he's taking me to Brisbane tonight for a celebrity dinner for a friend of his."

"That's sounds glamorous."

"He's very successful, it seems. He's an investor in Julie's latest project so she knows him. But he's not my type at all, too short for me, especially after Mark, bald and a bit too full of himself although he's very stylish. And even if I was interested, he's married."

"Oh no, not another one. Where's the wife? Why's he taking you? And why are you going with him?"

"It's all very strange if you ask me, but she doesn't seem to mind what he does. He's Greek, and I think she is too. An open marriage is what he calls it. Anyway, he's assured me that it's okay for us to go out and as I've no interest in him sexually, *c'est la vie.*" Michele flourished her hand in true French style and Cindy responded with the appropriate resigned facial expression and snooty nose. When they'd danced at the Moulin Rouge together, instead of using the English idiom, no harm no foul, they'd decided to Gallicize themselves and use *c'est la vie* instead. Complete with hand gestures, facial expressions, and dreadful French accents, it became part of the pair's repertoire.

Cindy giggled. "Oh, sweetie you're certainly living a whole new life since your divorce. First, there was Mark your perfect match, then the well-endowed Benjamin and now we have this Greek man with a seemingly accepting wife. Be careful she's not a rabbit cooker, though. Imagine what SallyAnn's going to say about this latest instalment." They burst into laughter and anticipated SallyAnn's advice. "And to think all of this has happened within the space of a few weeks."

"I know," Michele said. "They say fact is stranger than fiction and, in my case, it seems to be true."

ANSWERING THE SHARP RAP at her front door that evening, Michele was greeted by an immaculate chauffeur, trussed like a Christmas turkey in a navy-blue suit, with cap under his arm. His expression was one of absolute discretion and service.

"Good evening, miss," the chauffeur greeted then stopped abruptly.

Michele also caught her breath. Surely not, but it was. "Roger? Is that you?"

"Yes, miss. How are you this evening?" Roger, the waiter from the Imperial Suite, bowed in his customary fashion as she stepped forwards, closing the door behind her.

"My, my, my, Roger, this is most unexpected," she said, feeling a slight blush bloom on her face.

"If you will allow me, miss."

Ignoring his reciprocal blush, she allowed him to usher her to the gold stretch limousine parked on the side of the street. In her glimmering red evening gown reminiscent of the dress worn by Jessica Rabbit, she felt every bit the movie star walking to the car. Roger stepped forwards, opened the back door of the limousine and assisted her into its luxurious leather seat.

"Thank you." She smiled up at him and he closed the door, careful not to catch her dress.

After Roger eased the car away from the curb, Michele decided to break the ice. "So, Roger, tell me your story. First Venezia Palazzo and now a stretch limousine?"

"Well, miss, I own this limousine and work primarily for private clients. Then sometimes I also work as a private butler for the Venezia."

"Well, I must say it's a surprise to see you again."

"And for me, miss." Ever the consummate professional, he left the conversation at that, turning his attention to the road. "Mr Stavros is expecting you at his residence first, miss. We should be there in about ten minutes."

She smirked when she caught Roger glancing at her in the rear-view mirror. Nick hadn't made any mention of going to his place first and by the look on Roger's face, he probably knew more about Nick Stavros than she did. Not concerning herself any longer with the intrigue, she admired the interior of the limousine, noting the rich red carpet which complemented her gown, the black leather seats and the crystal champagne glasses tinkling in the bar rack during the journey. Regardless of Nick Stavros's inflated ego, he knew how to treat a woman.

THE DOUBLE GATES SWUNG open for the limousine to turn into the property. Ahead on the snaking driveway, a sprawling home languished on manicured lawns, flanked by rambling gardens. The crunch of gravel under the wheels reminded her of a historical drama set in the UK. Very *Pride and Prejudice*.

"A lady's imagination is very rapid; it jumps from admiration to love, from love to matrimony in a moment." Amazed that she remembered this line from Jane Austen's book, Michele sensed an uneasiness tickle her nerves. Thankfully, Roger brought the limousine to a halt and with it, her whimsy. Alighting from the vehicle proved the perfect reality check, forcing her to focus on remaining elegant and balanced on her needle-thin red stilettos.

"Thank you, Roger." Lifting her scarlet sequined gown, she made her way up the sandstone stairs to the front door. Just as she was about to press the buzzer, the door opened.

With an air of authority, Nick Stavros occupied the threshold to his home like a Greek god. Dressed in burgundy dinner trousers and vest and crisp white shirt, the neck of which was open revealing the requisite gold chain with two medallions, he exuded the energy of supreme ruler. The sparkle of his Fred Astaire black patent shoes was outmatched only by the flint that flickered in his dark eyes.

"So pleased you could come, Michele," he said, welcoming her into his home. "You look sensational."

She thanked him for his compliment and glided past him feeling his eyes skimming over her. Just as she was about to turn back toward him, her gaze travelled forwards through the rest of the house. But the world began to spin. The walls, the floor, and the furniture appeared to shimmer as if coming to life, just for an instant. As this unseen dance of the senses greeted her, the Goddess whispered, "*This is your house, Michele. Welcome home. Heaven is all around you and you are free.*"

She clamped her eyes shut for a moment to regain her poise and steady herself. Turning her attention to her host, she said, "You have a beautiful home."

"Thank you. Come through, please." He placed his hand on the small of her back, guiding her through his home, her home if what the Goddess had just said was correct. He escorted her into the large central entertainment space with its sparkling indoor-outdoor pool flanked by a fully stocked bar any nightclub would be proud to own. Accepting his offer, she slithered onto a bar stool while he took his place as bartender.

"Would you like champagne? Or if you prefer something else, please choose what you'd like." He brandished his arm along the rows of spirits, aperitifs, and liqueurs.

"Champagne will be wonderful. Thank you."

While he poured the French fizz into crystal flutes, his eyes remained fixed on his guest and his appreciative smile didn't leave his face.

Deflecting his apparent fascination, she said, "How long have you lived here?"

"We've been here a few years," he said and proceeded to tell the story of moving to the Coast for business.

"By the way, where's your wife tonight?"

"She's interstate for a week with friends. She says hello."

"Oh. She doesn't mind you taking me out, just the two of us?"

"Not in the least bit. She knows I need female company and that you'd accepted my invitation. You mustn't worry yourself about it. Would you like to see the rest of the house perhaps?"

Michele accepted, hoping that if she allowed him to take her on the grand tour she could nod and smile without having to converse, while she digested this strange situation. As he led her through the house talking about his renovation plans, she took the chance to study her host more closely.

Just taller than she was and a little rotund, he was drama personified. With a striking face accented by a black moustache and goatee, intelligent eyes and a large imperial nose, he carried himself as if, like Anthony Quinn, he'd break into dancing Zorba if he heard Greek music. He flowed like thick honey syrup through his home, spreading warmth and comfort. Yet beneath his clear enjoyment for life, she suspected lay a dark intensity. When they returned to the bar, he topped up their glasses and took a seat next to her.

"We'll finish this bottle then we'll set off. Did Roger introduce himself?"

"As a matter of fact, I'd already met Roger." She explained to him the connection at Venezia Palazzo.

"I see. Six degrees of separation, as they say. And how are things going with Mark?" Sipping his champagne, Nick's eyes burned hot with interest.

"He's stopped calling and texting as much, so I guess he's back in the swing of his life in Sydney. But I just can't seem to shake the feeling this relationship isn't over. I don't know. It's very confusing." She didn't try to cover her disappointment. She'd already spent hours telling him the 'Mark' saga so there was nothing for her to hide. She'd only met Nick once, but she valued his opinion.

"Well, Michele, I've always believed actions speak louder than words. Mark's words are telling you how much he misses you and cares for you, but his actions are telling you the opposite. You're a smart woman. You decide." His lips curled in an indulgent smile before he returned to sipping his champagne.

"Yes, I guess you're right," she said, more to herself than to him.

"Michele, you're a desirable, talented and intelligent woman. Any man you give yourself to needs to be your match. Not just be a great lover and fun to be around. He needs to be a king to your queen."

"But that automatically makes me his subordinate if I'm somebody's queen."

"Not in the least. It means the man, as king, worships and adores his queen, reigning only to please her." He reached toward her, wrapping his sculptured fingers around hers. An unexpected spark prickled her skin, and she withdrew her hand, giving it a brisk rub.

"That's an interesting way of looking at it, I suppose," she said, a little rattled. "I think I'll just go to the bathroom to freshen up before we go if that's all right?" She slipped down off the barstool to make her exit.

"Certainly, I'll put on my bow tie and we'll set off."

In the bathroom, she leaned against the door staring at her reflection in the mirror. "What just happened?" She took a couple of deep breaths.

"He is your match," spoke the Goddess, loud and clear.

"Not bloody likely," she said aloud, while scrounging in her evening purse for lipstick. With hands unaccustomed to shaking, she painted more crimson onto her lips, taking longer than usual.

"Oh God. And I'm wearing red as well!" Her hand froze over her mouth.

"This is your house, Michele. He is your match."

"No. He's not my type or my match. Forget it." Thrusting her lipstick back into her bag and berating herself for wearing a flaming red gown that screamed 'look at me, I'm ready for action,' she evicted the Goddess from her mind.

What was she thinking? Here she was parading around like a peacock in front of a man who wanted to play supreme ruler to her lowly serf. Much like his wife played. As Michele had just told the Goddess, 'not bloody likely.' With her restoration work complete, internally and externally, she stuck out her chin and strode back to the bar.

She decided to change the topic. "You know, Nick. I think you'd look much more handsome if you shaved off your goatee. It makes you look a little demonic, and I don't think that's really who you are." Her tone sounded more abrupt than she'd planned.

"Perhaps you're right. Maybe I should."

~ ♥ ~

At one a.m. Saturday, Roger waited at the limousine while Nick walked Michele to her front door.

"Thank you, Nick, for a lovely evening," she said, removing her keys from her purse.

"It was my pleasure." He pulled her closer, leaning in for a goodnight kiss.

She planted her hand hard against his chest. "I don't think that'd be wise, Nick. I'm not playing anyone's mistress." She smiled one of her best showgirl smiles, hoping this would give her the advantage.

"Very well then, Michele. I can quite understand your thinking. Would you have lunch with me today instead?"

"Today?"

"Yes, I'll send Roger to collect you at noon. That gives you plenty of time for sleep, doesn't it?"

Used to getting his own way, he was a hard man to refuse.

"Very well then. But just so there can be no confusion here, Nick, you're not my type. You know I like tall, strong men with a little scoundrel thrown in, so please understand that whatever you think might happen, it won't."

"I totally understand. I'm not your type. I'll send Roger for you at noon. Drinks at my place then off to Peter's Wharf for a fabulous seafood lunch." He scooped up her hand, kissing it in true European fashion. Then turning on his heel, he strode to the open back door of the limousine where Roger stood. As they drove off, Nick waved like a departing royal but his smile flashed checkmate.

Wow. What a night, she thought as she climbed the stairs to her bedroom.

Nick had been the charismatic gentleman, a role he performed with aplomb. His entire network of friends and colleagues seemed to be straight out of a television soap opera, gracious people all living the good life. While she hung her gown in the wardrobe, memories of the night's intelligent conversations and laughter swirled in her mind. She put her ruby shoes back in their box, pleased with how the night had ended and her management of Nick's attempted kiss at the front door.

Like a jack-in-the-box, her sex goddess sprang awake. "*I think you should give this one a go. He might be all right in the cot.*"

Closing the shoebox lid and shaking her head, Michele repeated, "Not my type. Not my type at all."

CHAPTER FOURTEEN

WEEK FOUR, SATURDAY

Eleven hours later, she ascended the Stavros' sandstone steps once more. When she buzzed the bell, the door cracked open just a little.

"Hello, Michele." Nick's sensuous voice laced with mischief squeezed through the small gap.

"Hi, Nick, are you going to let me in?" She pressed on the door, but it remained fixed.

"In a moment. Do you remember what we talked about last night?" His opening comment teased at her memory.

"We talked about a lot of things. Can you be a bit more specific? And why all the mystery?"

"The conversation about kings pleasing their queens," he said, leading her deeper into his web.

"Yes, I remember."

"Well, what do you think?" He threw open the door and posed for her, looking daytime elegant in cream trousers and loafers, a pale blue linen shirt, navy blue sports jacket . . . and no goatee.

Michele's hands flew to her mouth. "Oh my God. You shaved it off. I didn't expect you to do that." She was shocked he'd wasted no time acting upon her suggestion. She was also astonished at the positive difference it made to his face. Without the sinister little beard, although bald, he bore a striking resemblance to Hollywood actor, Omar Sharif.

"I did say a king's job is to please his queen. Do you like it?"

She threw her arms around his neck. "I love it. You look so much better." She kissed him on both cheeks as he closed the door, nodding to Roger to wait. "It's amazing what a difference losing that beard has made to your face." She couldn't contain her delight on their way to the bar.

"I'm pleased it meets with your approval." He began popping open the champagne. "It's amazing what delight a bare chin can bring to a woman." He chuckled and filled the glasses

"But what will your wife say?"

"She doesn't mind. I did ask her before I shaved it off."

"This is the strangest marriage I've ever come across. It's certainly not a marriage I'd want."

"Perhaps not, but it is what it is," he said. "Enough of my marriage, more about kings and queens."

Seated at a balcony table overlooking the ocean, with seagulls squawking overhead and the waves roaring below, they drank, ate and laughed like old friends. They didn't return to his place until sunset, where he whipped up a Frangelico affogato each for dessert.

"So, Michele, did you have a nice day?"

"It was wonderful, thank you. Nearly as good as this." She spooned in another mouthful of ice cream, coffee, and liqueur.

"Good. So, would you like to come to dinner with me tomorrow night then?" His eyes swam with contented curiosity.

"Tomorrow? Surely you must want to spend some time alone?"

"Every woman needs a man who'll treat her like a queen. No woman deserves a man who'll test her trust and play with her feelings. Let me be your king again tomorrow."

"Come on. You've got to give him a chance." Michele's sex goddess who'd been nudging into Michele's mind throughout the afternoon found voice.

Deciding to play along, she said, "Very well then. Be my king for another day."

"Excellent. I'll send Roger to collect you at five o'clock. Wear something comfortable and warm." He walked her to the front door where he tried to kiss her.

She pushed him away again. "Nick, thank you for shaving off your goatee. That was unexpected and it's made such a positive difference. However," she strung out the pause, "may I say your moustache is too fluffy."

"That's easily fixed. I'll trim it closer tomorrow, and you can test it then?" He smiled with the flint in his eyes igniting in anticipation.

"I can't promise I'll test it but if I do, I'll give you an honest critique."

"That's all I ask. Goodnight, Michele." He leaned in and kissed her on both cheeks.

CHAPTER FIFTEEN

WEEK FOUR, SUNDAY

AFTER ENJOYING A LIGHT lunch on Julie's high-rise balcony, SallyAnn, Michele, and Julie grooved to Michael Jackson's *HIStory* album blaring in the background. In high spirits, they debated the next instalment of Michele's adventures of singledom.

"Are you kidding me? You've gone from the superhero to a Greek god. It could only happen to you." Julie's amusing summation of the difference between Michele's two beaus seemed accurate if exaggerated.

Even SallyAnn, who was taking a break from motherhood, nodded in agreement. "However, there's one important point everyone seems to be missing here and that is they're both married." Her melodramatic emphasis on the last word made them laugh.

"So back to the saga at hand," Julie returned the conversation to Michele. "What are you going to do with Nick? I haven't said anything to date. However, he's known as a man who always gets what he wants, in business and with women. Regardless of whether he's your type or not, he's broken a few hearts in his time, you know."

"I agree he's very charming and certainly knows how to turn it on. But this whole wife thing, what's that all about?" Michele screwed up her nose.

"Not quite sure. They're very discreet whatever it is they do. But I must say they don't show any real affection toward each other at all. Maybe they're not the happy couple living an agreeable, open relationship as he likes you to think they are," Julie said.

"What are you going to do, 'Chele?" SallyAnn asked, jigging around as if desperate to leap from the balcony in a grand *jeté.*

"I'm not really sexually attracted to him, but I am attracted to his mind, to the way he thinks. He's the first man I've ever known who I can have a clever conversation with. His mind reminds me of a snowflake, really intricate with little branches of thoughts that keep growing out in all directions, changing moment by moment." She fluttered her fingers around her face symbolizing Nick's thinking processes. "I love bantering with him. He's quite the challenge. He'd make a great business partner, I think."

"Yes, in business he's a real asset. However personally? Just be careful with this one. His reputation precedes him." Julie cast a cautionary glance across to her friend.

FUSSING AROUND WITH FINAL preparations before Roger arrived, Michele realized how accustomed she'd become to the lifestyle Nick had introduced her to in the past few days. No longer awestruck by being collected by a chauffeured limousine, or being wined and dined at expensive restaurants, she'd slotted into his successful world, a world she'd visualized as her own for years. He lived life with a rich dynamism akin to the passion she felt when she danced. Perhaps the Goddess was right, and he was her match. Pity, she felt no sexual attraction to him and even if she did, he was married. However, being courted by a successful, intelligent man had its advantages.

The familiar ring broke into her thoughts.

"Hi, baby," came the cheery voice of the caller.

"Hi, gorgeous. How are you?" She couldn't contain her excitement as she welcomed Mark back into her life.

"My golden-haired angel, I've missed you. Sorry I haven't called. How did you get on that night at the club when we spoke?"

"Well, I got myself a black man," she said with pride.

"I see. A police nightstick on legs, was he?"

"Stop." Her little girl giggle bubbled up. "We had a great night and that's all I'm going to say."

"Lucky bastard. That's my girl. I do miss you, you know."

"I know. And I miss you."

"As I said, another time, another place." He chose not to broach the subject of his inability or his weakness to leave his marriage, but his voice betrayed his true feelings. Changing the subject to something less disheartening, he said, "What are you doing for Christmas and New Year. It's a big one this time around, you know."

"I haven't really planned much yet. Christmas with my mother, I guess. I don't know about New Year's Eve."

"Why don't you come to Sydney for the New Year? I think I might be able to get away."

"Really?"

"I can't promise anything but maybe. If not for New Year's Eve, then at least the couple of days following."

Michele was beyond ecstatic. "Okay. If you're sure?"

"Yes, baby. I'm sure. Talk soon. Take care."

"You too. Talk soon."

She twirled around her small townhouse, dancing and spinning like a ballerina in a music box. Mark was back. Like a prince on a white charger, he'd returned, bringing with him the possibility of a new future together. The knock at the door broke her private celebration because she'd quite forgotten her date with Nick. With Mark still galloping around in her mind, she snatched up her handbag and dashed outside.

"WHAT ARE YOU UP TO, Nick?" she asked when they alighted from the limousine at a secluded park.

He led her to a small rotunda under which was set a romantic table for two with chilled champagne nestled in the ice bucket. Roger appeared carrying a large picnic basket which he proceeded to unpack while Nick retrieved the champagne.

"I thought we'd dine casually under the stars this evening. A Greek feast of bread, olives, cold meats, cheese, and meze. Cheers." He handed her a glass of champagne.

"Cheers." Surveying the made-for-magazine scene before her, Michele thought the only thing missing was the photographer to take the pictures.

"This is lovely, Nick. Thank you." She waited while Roger laid the food and once he retired out of earshot, she said, "I'm just a little concerned this is all too much. I don't understand how your wife could possibly be okay with this?"

"Why don't we walk a little and I'll try to explain." He guided her onto the neatly trimmed grass. "Elissa and I've been married for nearly five years. She's my second wife and as I've already told you, I have two children to my first wife. Elissa and I have an arrangement. We both enjoy sexual variety however we prefer to play together with other partners wherever possible."

"I see. And I'm being groomed as one of those partners, am I?" Michele stood rigid waiting for an answer.

"No. In fact, quite the opposite."

"Meaning?" Regardless of Nick's candid denial, her suspicions persisted.

"I'd like to explore where you and I might lead, Michele. I feel very strongly about you." He turned to face her.

Michele softened. "Nick, as I've said before, I'm not going to be anyone's mistress and even if I was, I'm sorry, but I wouldn't be yours. You're a successful, intelligent and generous man, but you're not really my type."

"But he is, Michele." The Goddess beamed in as if riding on the rising moon, causing Michele to look skyward for a winged apparition.

"I understand," he yielded once more, "although I disagree with your assessment. However, can we at least be good friends? I do enjoy your company."

"Of course. But I think this being together, just the two of us, should stop."

"Very well. When Elissa returns, the three of us will become good friends. How's that?" His negotiating skills were faultless. She was left with a sense not of having won the discussion, but of acceding to Nick again.

"Okay. Let's give that a try," she said, suspecting the topic wasn't yet over.

"Excellent. However, I do have one last request. You did promise you'd give me an honest critique of my moustache. I'm not sure if you noticed, but I trimmed it as you suggested." He turned his profile to show off his grooming skills.

"Yes, I did notice. It looks much better." She cocked her head from side to side giving his upper lip her full attention.

"Any further suggestions?"

Although she had no intention of misleading him, she decided to answer his question. "Pheromones are important, and the right aftershave can make all the difference to the attractiveness of a man to a woman. Perhaps . . ."

"Very true. Do you have any suggestions for a new aftershave?" His tone remained even and compliant, showing he took no offence.

"Based on your character I think you need something that has more musk in it, something stronger, more alluring. You're an exotic man, Nick, something more like you."

"Excellent. I'll look into it."

As if summoning all the energy of the night, his dark eyes blasted her. "One day, Michele, you will be my queen, you'll see." The power of his promise sent tiny shards of light hurtling through her body. Unable to break his stare, she shivered under its intensity until he released her with a deliberate nod. Although she chose not to refute or continue the conversation, there was a distinct agreement to Nick's vow from an unseen party in their midst.

After they took their seats for dinner under the stars, she studied the enigmatic man across from her, wondering what strange power he had to charm her so. Perhaps Julie was right. Perhaps he was a Greek god.

CHAPTER SIXTEEN

WEEK FOUR, MONDAY

THE SAME DREAM OF the little boy and girl on the beach interrupted her sleep in the middle of the night. She arose muddled headed and stumbled to the toilet. Had she just spent the night with Mark or was it Nick? She flicked the light on in the bathroom and caught a fleeting image in the mirror. It looked like the little girl on the beach. Confused, she went back to bed and fell into the dream on the beach.

"SWEETIE, I CAN'T TELL you what a great weekend I had with Graham." Cindy's voice turned *pirouettes* down the phone. "We had the best time and his daughter was delightful. She seems genuinely pleased to see her father happy. I'm so happy."

Cindy's phone call had awakened Michele from a deep sleep at seven in the morning. Still a little groggy, she poured hot water into her coffee cup while Cindy chattered on about her wonderful weekend.

"I couldn't be happier for you." She took a good slug of coffee. "Tell me more."

"We had the best time . . ." Cindy gave a full account of the 'best weekend of my life. "And I met Mark."

Michele spat the coffee back into the mug. "What?"

Cindy calmed her voice. "Yes. And I met his wife Karen as well."

"Oh God," she gasped.

"He's such a character. I can see what you love about him. He's got the kindest heart and the best sense of humour. He's so self-deprecating."

"I know. I had such fun with him." Michele slurped more caffeine. "And Karen?"

Cindy paused. "She's very nice. But I can see why you made such an impact on him. How can I say it? You're the polished diamond, she's not."

Michele sighed but not because she was relieved. "Regardless of the lustre, he's with her and not with me." She wished she was still asleep.

"Anyway, sweetie, we didn't talk long so no harm, no foul, *c'est la vie.*"

"That's a blessing. So? Did you find out any more about Mark?"

"Nothing. Zip. Graham introduced them both as ex-cops and friends. That was it. However, I did ask Graham later if Mark was involved in the drug busts on the Coast."

"And?"

"All Graham would say is that he couldn't say, intimating that I was right, which in my terms is an unequivocal admission. Appears your Mark is the champion after all. Your instincts were right. Seems he is who he says he is."

Relief swam over Michele and gentle sobs wriggled up within her like tiny tadpoles straining to be free. "Thank you, darling friend. I knew he wasn't the bad guy."

"Oh, sweetie. I feel for you. You're so in love with him, aren't you?"

"I'm afraid I am." Plucking up more of her showgirl spirit, she pulled her shoulders back and said, "Anyway, he rang yesterday, first time in a while, and invited me down to Sydney for New Year's Eve."

"What are going to do?"

"My heart wants to go, but my mind says stop wasting your time."

"Which one are you going to listen to?"

"I guess I'm going to go with my heart. Maybe Julie was right. Maybe I just want a happy-ever-after ending in my life after all."

"But do you really think Mark is the one who's going to give that to you?"

"Maybe not but I still have hope. But hey, the worst that can happen is that I have some great sex. Right?"

The silence from Cindy was answer enough. "And what about this other man you met at Julie's launch party? Have you seen him again?"

"Oh Nick, yes. He's been quite the gentleman." She was about to launch into the exposition of the Stavros soap opera when Cindy interrupted.

"What's his full name?"

"Nick Stavros." The ensuing silence created another vacuum. "Why? What's wrong?"

"Fuck."

Michele knew something was wrong because Cindy rarely swore. "What?"

"If it's the same guy . . . I met a Nick Stavros back in 1988 when you and I danced in Formidable at the Moulin Rouge."

"Really? I don't remember him."

"No, you never met him. You were off that night with an ankle injury. It was when we did the Royal Performance Benefit in Paris of the show . . ." Cindy trailed off.

"Oh God no." Michele held her head in her hand.

"Oh, Michele. I'm so sorry. Maybe it's not the same Nick Stavros?"

"Greek, short, a little heavy-set, very charming, has a bit of the Omar Sharif about him, smart as a whip, bald?"

"That's him except the bald. But come to think of it, his hair was thinning back then so I guess he's bald now." Cindy affirmed Michele's fear. It was the guy Cindy had had a one-night stand with that night in his hotel suite.

"I can't fucking believe it!" Michele slammed her fist on the kitchen benchtop.

"God, I wish it wasn't the same guy, but it certainly sounds like him."

"Not your fault."

Michele told Cindy all about the Nick Stavros she knew, his open marriage, his charm, his campaign for kings and queens, his great oration on actions speaking louder than words. She vented her spleen on each event with which she felt Mr Stavros had manipulated her.

"Nick was quite the charmer that night as well. That's how I ended up in bed with him. God, that was so long ago. I can't believe now he's chasing you. What are you going to do?"

"I'm sure Mr Nick Stavros will call to invite me out again, which I will do just to give him the third degree and a piece of my mind. Him and his bloody kings and queens. And I'm going to Sydney to meet Mark for New Year to give him the same as well. Bloody wimp. But most importantly I'm going to concentrate on me and move on. Bloody men." Her lofty commitment to her continued liberation made Cindy giggle.

"You go, girl. I love it when you launch into your feminist affirmative action. See you tomorrow at eleven at the gates?"

"Okay, see you then. What a pity you and I aren't lesbians. Then we wouldn't have to deal with men and their lying, cheating ways."

"Yes, it'd make it all much easier. But we both love cock too much. See you tomorrow, sweetie."

CHAPTER SEVENTEEN

WEEK FOUR, TUESDAY

TEETERING ON SKYSCRAPER STILETTOS, Julie dazzled in her black polka dot white suit and a hat with short black and white tufted feathers. Her sparkling *Cavalli* sunglasses wrapping around her face added the requisite mystery to the glamour. While Cindy, dressed in a fitted black ensemble with a red pillbox hat cocked on a jaunty angle on her head, red gloves, shoes, and handbag looked just as dramatic as she chatted away to Julie about Graham. SallyAnn and Michele arrived within moments of each other and sashayed to the gates to join their friends. SallyAnn's long showgirl legs were draped in a striking yellow pantsuit and her blue eyes peeped out from beneath a dainty yellow fascinator under which her short platinum hair lay sleek and flat. Her smile shone matching the colour of her outfit, demonstrating how much she loved her days out with the girls.

Looking as striking as her friends, Michele wore a reworked white sheath dress from her wardrobe, dressing it up with a large white picture hat and red accessories. She was pleased with the finished product because it looked far more expensive than it had cost. What could be done with a sewing kit, some feathers, ribbons and odds and ends were limitless if you knew how to mix and match. Shooshing, as it was known in theatre, was a technique of making something out of nothing in order to look fabulous. Today she'd succeeded. The four forty-something women were show-stoppers, as evidenced by the men who slowed their pace for an appreciative glance up and down.

"God, I love Melbourne Cup. Especially with the four of us together." SallyAnn shifted her weight from one hip to the other, accentuating her lyrical gait.

"Me too," Cindy said, looking very Parisian in her black and red. "We've had such fun."

"Let's not go there," Julie said, but they still chatted and laughed about the many sexual encounters she'd had at the end of previous cup days.

"Okay. Time to get to the marquee and start making memories for this year, shall we?" Michele gathered the troops and they stepped off in sync, on the same foot as if rehearsed. They struck a perfect picture and received a couple of wolf whistles on their way to the punters' circle.

"How good is it to still get a whistle?" Michele beamed at the pair of fellas whose eyes were giving them the once-over.

Julie put extra chutzpah in her walk. "I love it. Makes me feel sexy and young still."

"Ooh, he's cute. Looks a little like Jude Law." SallyAnn eyed a tall, lean man in a grey suit studying his watch and race guide, waiting for someone.

"SallyAnn, you're married. *Tsk-tsk*," Cindy scolded.

"It's called window shopping. And if I didn't already have one at home, he'd be my pick for the day." Without any hint of discretion, the others turned around to inspect the man who'd caught SallyAnn's attention. Peering over their sunglasses they unanimously agreed with her assessment. When his piercing grey eyes lifted to meet theirs, they saw something of the naughty schoolboy in Mr Grey Suit. Obviously enjoying their attention, he smiled and nodded before returning to his race guide.

"So, where's Richie today?"

"Out with the boys, which suits me fine." SallyAnn strained her neck looking back at her race favourite.

"Girls, can you please promise me not to use the word 'fine' today. You know who that reminds me of." A chorus of "okays" affirmed Michele's request and as they were ushered to their table in the Moet Marquee, chilled champagne was served for the first toast of the day.

"Now what are we betting on in race one?" Cindy was the punter of the group. Her father had been a keen gambler who'd taught her how to study the horses, so she was already planning her betting strategy.

"Sorry, I don't have any money," Michele said. "But I'm happy to help you choose if you want?"

"Here's what we'll do." Cindy opened her race guide. "We'll box up three horses in a trifecta for six dollars in race one. I'll put the bet on with my money and if we win, we'll go halves."

"Sounds great. Okay. What do you like?" Michele pawed over the race guide with a pen at the ready.

"Choose the angels." The Goddess joined the conversation.

"You first, Michele. What do you like?" Cindy asked.

Michele looked for the angels in the field. "This horse called Seraphim looks good to me."

By now Julie and SallyAnn were intrigued and flicked their race guides to the page.

"There's another horse here called My Angel. Let's do that one as well," she said, thinking of how Mark referred to her as his golden-haired angel.

"Very well." Cindy circled the second choice. "Since we seem to be on a heavenly theme, let's go with Cupid's Bow for the third horse."

Michele ran her eye over the remaining horses in the race, and seeing no other contender with an angelic reference, she agreed.

"Righto. I'm off to place the bet. The race will start in about fifteen minutes."

"YOU KNOW, WE'VE PICKED a couple of outsiders in this trifecta? Don't get your hopes up on this one," Cindy said, rejoining the group.

"And they're racing!" trilled the caller's nasal voice over the speakers. The images of vibrant silks atop strapping horse flesh flashed across the massive television screens in the marquee as the horses jostled for position. Dashing towards the turn, the horses' hooves slammed on the track and set the tempo while the four of them jiggled along watching the race, engrossed.

"And it's Seraphim making a move," the caller cried with a hint of surprise.

"Come on, come on," Michele prayed, willing their horses onward.

"Cupid's Bow and My Angel are moving up in the field, Cupid's Bow and My Angel making their move," the caller shouted as the horses began to thunder around the turn and into the straight.

"Oh my God, Michele. We might actually win," Cindy squealed while SallyAnn and Julie jumped up and down holding onto each other as if they'd bet thousands on the race.

"Come on. Come on!" Michele screamed, her hair standing on end.

"Seraphim, Cupid's Bow and My Angel, looks like it's going to be Seraphim, Cupid's Bow and My Angel for the finish . . ." hollered the race caller as the jockeys and their horses busted a gut galloping out the final fifty metres.

Holding their breath, the women waited for the conclusive moments.

"It's Seraphim, Cupid's Bow and My Angel!" the caller confirmed with his voice at fever pitch. The marquee erupted in a cacophony of screams and cheers.

"We won. We won!" Cindy shrieked. "I can't believe it. We won."

The four of them danced around in ring-a-ring-a-rosie.

"On my God," Julie yelled. "How much will it pay?"

"I'm not sure, but it's going to be big," Cindy cried. "We had two outsiders in that race come home. I can't believe it. We have to wait until the placings are confirmed then I'll go and collect."

"Here, have some champagne." SallyAnn splashed more on the cloth than in the glass.

Thank you, thank you, Michele said in her mind, as tears welled up in her eyes.

"You are welcome," came the silent reply.

Cindy raised her glass in victory. "Well done, Michele, here's to our first win of the day."

"And the placings for race one are Seraphim first, Cupid's Bow second, My Angel third," and as the announcer continued with the rest of the placings, his voice was drowned out in the Moet Marquee by the four well-dressed women at table thirty-nine.

"Be back shortly," Cindy called, scampering off and waving the winning ticket in her hand.

Michele fixed Julie with a stare. "Fly Trust Airways."

"You're kidding me?"

"Nope."

"Well, I'll be damned."

"No, you won't. There's no such place as hell."

Throughout this strange exchange, SallyAnn followed the discourse as if watching a tennis match. "What are you two on about?"

"Let me explain." Michele retold SallyAnn the conversation she'd had recently with Julie on trusting her intuition.

"Well, if you're getting results like that, your intuition is worth listening to," SallyAnn said. They spied Cindy in the distance scurrying toward them like a mouse to cheese. She plonked a wad of money on the table. "Seven thousand dollars." More wild screams filled the marquee intoxicating the other punters to try their luck on the next race.

"You're kidding me?" Michele was stunned.

"Here you go. Let's count it out. Three and half thousand dollars each." Cindy began to divvy up the winnings while Michele, Julie, and SallyAnn looked on like eager children watching mum hand out pocket money.

"That's yours, sweetie." Cindy thrust the cash across to Michele.

"Oh my God. I've never even held this much cash before." Michele was overjoyed.

"What a start to Melbourne Cup," Julie said.

"Yes. Got any more tips, 'Chele?" SallyAnn asked.

"Not at the moment. I'm just going to sit for a while and regroup. However," — Michele waved her hand at the waiter — "the next bottle of champagne is on me."

By the time bets had to be placed for the main race a few hours later, they'd studied the form guide using all types of systems including favourite colours, names of horses beginning with a consonant, sexiest jockey names and a range of other silly criteria. The Goddess had vacated for the day after having given her one piece of spectacular advice in the morning. Michele and Cindy had kept the French fizz flowing, adding even more sparkle to their table.

"Here's what I'm doing," Cindy said. "I'm going to take another trifecta for the Cup and hopefully my three will come in first, second and third."

"Sounds like a plan." SallyAnn and Julie worked together on picking their horses.

But Michele felt an intense urge to follow Cindy's lead. "Whatever you pick, I'll have the same."

"Okay. Let's see if luck stays with us a second time."

After collecting SallyAnn's and Julie's pick, Cindy dashed to place everyone's bets before the race.

Five minutes later, when the horses crossed the finish line for the last Melbourne Cup of the twentieth century, the marquee exploded with screaming punters and thunderous applause.

"How did you go?" Cindy cried out over the noise to Julie and SallyAnn.

"Not so good. We missed one horse," Julie said. "What about you two?" Julie asked.

"We're waiting on the photo. I bet the same as Cindy." Michele's heart raced while she stared at the screen waiting for the judges' decision. This win would cover the last debts from her divorce. Her ties with Adam would be over. She could taste financial freedom on the tip of her tongue, sweeter than the champagne. The decision flashed up on the screen, sending the crowd into a frenzy. Michele and Cindy grabbed each other in hysterics. They'd won. For the second time that day the heavens aligned, raining abundance down on them.

CINDY DUMPED ANOTHER PILE of notes on the table in front of Michele. "Fourteen-thousand dollars! That's seven thousand each."

This time, Michele let the tears flow. She stared at the money unable to speak. Here was the pot of gold at the end of the rainbow stacked in front of her.

"That's ten and a half thousand dollars you've won today, 'Chele. That's wonderful." SallyAnn said.

"Congrats, girlfriend." Julie leaned over and squeezed Michele's hand. "That'll get you out of that financial hole."

Michele turned to Cindy. "Thank you. Thank you."

"Don't thank me. Today was about you. Someone was definitely watching over you today, sweetie."

Michele needed no convincing of that.

"This has been the best Melbourne Cup we've ever had," Julie said. "Time to party."

~ ♥ ~

AFTER CAROUSING FOR A few more hours with other race crowds around town, the four of them took to a nightclub for some serious dancing. Taking turns guarding the winnings, they alternated on the dance floor between more glasses of French champagne. "You ladies are obviously winners?"

Michele turned around to see a familiar face. "Tom." She leaned in to give Julie's on-again-off-again a kiss. "Julie's on the dance floor out there somewhere." She pointed to the centre of the heaving throng.

"No thanks," he said. "I'll wait 'til she's finished." And he chatted to Michele and Cindy about their good luck at the track.

"Tom, darling." Julie hugged him from behind, before planting a juicy kiss on his cheek.

"Mate, I thought it was you with these four gorgeous women." The voice wasn't familiar, but the man was. He was SallyAnn's pick-of-the-day at the track, Mr Grey Suit with the electric grey eyes. Close up he looked even more like Jude Law. The women swooned.

"Craig, how are you?" Tom slapped his mate on the shoulder, and they shook hands. "Let me introduce you." Tom explained Craig's connection as an investment stockbroker in a rival company.

"You're just the man we need at the moment," Michele said. "We've got winnings we need to invest." She and Cindy did another recital of their winning day at the races. Fuelled by more bubbles, music, and dancing, they whiled away another hour, with the delectable Craig. As the only single woman, Michele responded to his advances leaving no room for doubt of her willingness to celebrate with him.

On her way back from the toilets, she felt a slight tug on her arm. Craig was at her side. "I'm not sure what you've planned for the rest of the night, but I'm going to book a room at the Marriott under the name of Craig Kidman. I'll wait there until midnight. I'd love you to join me. If you don't, no problem. However, the offer expires at midnight." He didn't wait for a reply. He turned and left the club.

"Oh goodie. He's delicious," her sex goddess said. *"Let's not dawdle. This is an offer we don't want to miss."*

Michele agreed.

By eleven-thirty, SallyAnn surrendered. "That's it for me. I have to go home before I drop."

"Us too," Julie said.

"We'll take you home if you like," Tom offered.

"Are you sure, Tom?"

"Of course. No problem."

Cindy shot Michele a glance then asked him, "Can you drop me off too?"

"Sure," he said.

Michele grabbed Cindy and whispered, "Take my money. I'll get it tomorrow." Leaving a few notes in her purse, she turned to her fellow carousers and said, "I think I'll find myself a nightcap, if you know what I mean." She kissed her friends and they left her to her quest.

She realized the Marriott was one block away and, according to her watch, she had about five minutes to get there. Coursing through the crowd, she descended the stairs in record time and ran up the street, weaving between the Cup day revellers. Her faithful red pumps held firm as she raced to catch the pedestrian green light. With her hand holding onto her flapping hat, she pictured herself as Barbara Streisand, running after Omar Sharif in *Funny Girl* with the lyrics of "nobody's gonna rain on my parade" repeating in her head. Navigating the terrain and dodging obstacles, she galloped toward the finish line like her winning horses.

Sprinting up to the hotel's reception desk just before midnight, she fell onto the desk wheezing. "Mr Craig Kidman's room. please."

"Yes, miss. He said he was expecting you. Room 217." The hotel clerk cocked his brow in unconcealed disapproval and pointed to the elevators to which she walked at a more ladylike pace.

When the door to Room 217 opened, Michele was greeted by a half-naked Craig, standing only in his shirt. He wasn't wearing underwear, for when she glanced down, his erection peeked out to welcome her.

He's started without me, she thought with a smile.

"Hello, gorgeous." She tried to mimic Barbra Streisand's Bronx accent, but Craig cocked his head bewildered. "Your shirt, it's gorgeous, French handkerchief linen?" Michele continued her *Funny Girl* performance, as she tickled his dick.

Obviously impatient, he reached out and grabbed her, dragging her mouth to his lips. He secured her head in his hands and plundered her mouth with demand. On coming up for air, she came under the scrutiny of his ethereal eyes and a fire ignited in her belly.

"This one's going to be fun," her sex goddess said.

"You're a very naughty girl for being late for our rendezvous," he scolded.

"But I'm here now." She squirmed an apology against his hard cock enjoying the feel of it against her thigh.

"Perhaps. But naughty girls need to be punished." He held her firm, grinding himself harder against her, heightening the suspense.

"What sort of punishment?" she asked, eager for her chastisement.

"Get undressed. Leave the hat on."

Obeying him, she removed her clothes in slow, sensuous moves, peeling them off item by item, while he leaned back on the bed tugging his cock, riveted by her performance.

"Over here."

She slid to his side.

From his fine-featured face growled a rough, throaty tone. "Eat this." He thrust his eager penis upward.

Bending over, she proceeded to give him one of her signature head jobs while her white picture hat bobbed up and down on his groin.

"Is this punishment enough?" she asked with her mouth full, knowing too well who was being punished.

"God, yes." He groaned in obvious delight. "Take off that bloody hat."

With a pop release of his cock, she sprang to her feet and unpinned her hat. "I'm going to have a shower. Join me?"

"Try to stop me." Craig peeled off his shirt and followed her into the bathroom.

They ignored the bathroom's desperate need of renovation and stepped into the bath-cum-shower to get to know each other better. Soaping and kissing were interjected with sucking, licking, touching and tugging as they explored each other's bodies without restraint. Though he was tall and lean, with low-slung hips, and sinewy arms and legs, Michele suspected he possessed staying power, like a good thoroughbred. An all-night fucking machine with a long, lean cock.

Balancing on the edge of the old-fashioned bath, Michele clung to the old shower rail while he studied her private parts with his intense, grey eyes. Bending down, he curled his tongue into her, flicking her clitoris as it swelled. "You're so juicy," he muttered while producing a flutter in her snatch.

"Mmm, life is juicy, Craig. At least it's meant to be." She wrapped her legs around his neck and began to ride his face like a determined jockey.

"I knew you'd be a fuckin' great root," he mumbled, between tongue lashes.

"And I knew you'd be a fuckin' good rider. Your boyish good looks don't fool me." She ground her snatch into his face, demanding more.

"Really? But they got you here." He drove his tongue deeper into her.

"You think so?" Michele lingered on the edge of climax, hoping the old shower curtain rail would hold. "Your boyish good looks aren't what got me here. I came because you paid for the room.

"And you're going to come again."

His banter spurred her on. "I better. Think yourself lucky, Mr Grey Suit. I'm the best winner you backed all day."

"Really? Well take this. I'll show you who the winner is." Despite his apparent lack of body mass, he supported her weight. And with his mouth devouring her snatch, Michele rode his face into a screaming orgasm.

"Fuck," he said. "You're a squirter. The elusive female ejaculation. Do it again."

She hung limply from the curtain rod and tested her footing to descend. "Sorry, it doesn't happen on demand. But if you keep that great technique going and if I can get into a more comfortable position, you'll probably get an encore."

"This I gotta have." He threw her over his shoulder and marched her into the bedroom where he ravaged her again and again until the sheets were drenched from cum, sweat and sudsy water.

~ ♥ ~

BY DAWN, THEY LAY spent. Basking in the afterglow of sex, she awarded the night a nine out of ten. Beside her, Craig's lips were swollen in a satisfied smile, a perfect reflection of how her lower lips felt.

"That was fuckin' fantastic," he said.

"I have to agree. You put in a sterling performance. One of the best."

"Ditto. Whenever you want a repeat performance, let me know."

"I will." She thought he'd make a great fuck-buddy.

The two of them drifted off to an exhausted sleep with Barbra Streisand singing in Michele's head. "I'm going to live and live now."

CHAPTER EIGHTEEN

WEEK FOUR, WEDNESDAY

STRETCHED OUT ON CINDY'S bright yellow couch, she and Michele sipped their mugs of steaming hot chocolate. Michele had arrived late that afternoon with the largest box of hand-made chocolates she could buy for her friend as a thank you for the day before. In return, Cindy made them French hot chocolates complete with whipped cream and chocolate curls. Contented, they enjoyed the sinful delights, while the summer evening wrapped around them like a silk pashmina. With Whitney Houston singing in the background, the dancers' feet kept time while their blood sugar spiralled upward.

"This reminds me of that scene from *Forrest Gump*." Michele licked toffee cream from her fingers. "The one where he says life is like a box of chocolates."

"Yes, I remember. You never know what you're going to get." Cindy's hand hovered over her favourite caramel chocolate before snatching it up and popping it into her mouth.

"Looks like we've eaten the ones we don't like and now we're onto our favourites, hey Cindy?" Michele referred to more than just the chocolates.

Spying the last dark cherry liqueur, Michele's fingers crept over to claim it.

"Let's hope so, sweetie. How wonderful it'd be if the rest of our lives tasted as good as these."

While chocolate decisions occupied Cindy, Michele's gaze wandered outside contemplating where her life was headed. Still confused by her feelings for Mark, she couldn't seem to shake the connection between them. His presence hovered on the edge of her life with a murmur of hope. Then there was Nick's unwavering commitment to be with her, to please her. Perhaps this was simply one of his sexual strategies, yet deep within her echoed an urging to explore his advances, to believe he might be her match. Alongside her emotional whirlpool remained her stubborn resolution to be single, to live her life without having to share her 'chocolates' permanently with any man.

"*Remember, free will, Michele. It is your choice,*" the Goddess reminded her. "*You create your own destiny by the choices you make. Just like yesterday.*"

Yesterday. I listened to you and chose what you told me, she thought.

"*Yes, but it was still your choice. It is always your choice.*"

I just don't want to die with regrets about what I could've achieved on my own. But then I don't want to die alone either. She mulled over the same dilemma that remained unresolved.

"*Again, it is your choice. Remember, a choice made with love is more empowering than a choice made with fear.*"

I just wish you weren't so bloody cryptic.

"*You are loved, Michele. There is nothing to fear. You can do no wrong, Heaven is all around you and you are free.*"

"Yeah, yeah, yeah. As I said, too bloody cryptic."

CHAPTER NINETEEN

NOVEMBER AND DECEMBER

THE WEEKS LEADING UP to Michele's trip to Sydney for New Year's Eve were filled with work, sex, and dance. With extraordinary energy, she became a career warrior princess. Honing her skills ready for the next opportunity that lay just around the corner, she remained focused on herself and her future, whatever that may be. Craig became her part-time lover, an arrangement that proved physically and economically advantageous, with his regular booty calls appeasing her sex goddess.

Whenever he could, Mark called. It wasn't often, but his passion for and power over her guaranteed his continual presence in her life. And when she hungered for his touch, she'd remove the vestige of him from its zip-lock bag, inhale his scent and relive their tempestuous week together.

THE END OF THE year brought the requisite Christmas events and work parties and attracted clients who needed her management skills. One such client was Nick Stavros. He called Michele soon after Melbourne Cup and invited her to a dinner party to discuss organizing the Stavros's Annual Fancy Dress Christmas Party. Determined to test his motives, she snared Nick alone in the garden during the dinner party and steered the conversation to what she wanted to discuss.

"These gardens are beautiful. In some ways, they remind me so much of my time in France. Have you ever been to Paris, Nick?"

"Yes, I have. I spent some time there back in the '80s."

"Did you do anything special there?" She fiddled with a petal.

"You may be surprised to hear this, but I actually attended the Royal Performance of the Moulin Rouge's centennial show, *Formidable*," he said, flaunting his perfect French pronunciation.

"Really? That's interesting. I was a dancer in *Formidable*."

"I know."

"How do you know?"

"After you told me of your dance background, I did a little research of my own and discovered you danced at the Moulin Rouge when I was there in Paris in 1988. Michele, what is it you want to know?"

"Do you remember a dancer from the show called Cindy Whitehead?" She watched him as his steel-trap mind flicked through its memory files searching for the connection.

His face lit up like a struck match. "As a matter of fact, I do. Lovely young girl. Remarkable smile, head full of soft blonde curls, very flexible if my memory serves me correctly." He returned Michele's scrutiny, lifting his eyebrows for added meaning or perhaps just to worsen her agitation.

"You do remember?"

"Of course. Cindy and I spent a wonderful night together that night of the royal performance. She was a delightful girl and an equally delightful lover."

"Cindy is my best friend. She was then and is now."

"That's marvellous," he said, ignoring her indignation. "Please say hello from me next time you see her. Perhaps we could all catch up together?"

"Why? So, you can have a threesome with Cindy and me?" She knuckled her hands on her hips, chin out ready for battle.

"No, absolutely not. What does it matter if Cindy and I had a one-nighter all those years ago? We were both consenting adults. What happened then has no bearing on how I feel about you now."

"But you were married then, and you slept with Cindy, and God knows how many other women. And you're married now, and you want to sleep with me. It just seems the more I get to know you, the more I don't know you." She stalked off along the sandstone balcony shaking her head, unable to hide her anger and confusion.

Nick raced after her and catching her arm, turned her to face him. He waited until she calmed a little and then lifted her chin. Finally, she consented to look at him.

"And?" His voice flowed over her like thick nectar soothing the burn.

"And? I don't know. You've gone out of your way to make yourself attractive to me, and I guess it's working. But I just don't want to be with a man who wants all that sexual variety. I can't ever be with a man again I can't trust."

"Ah, so there may be hope for me yet?" His expression relaxed at the admission of her growing affection for him. "What's past is past. This is now. If I had you, I'm sure I wouldn't want or need other partners." Lifting her hands, he pressed his lips to both with a tender kiss.

"Really? How can you say that when you've lived the life you have?"

"Because, Michele, I know. I've been looking for you for a long time. You'll see."

A part of her longed to be convinced, but she knew further conversation would be futile. Resigned, she chose to forfeit the conversation and allow Nick to escort her back to the dinner party.

~ ♥ ~

TWO WEEKS LATER, SHE was busy in the Stavros house managing the final preparations for their Christmas party before the guests arrived. Nick had offered her too much money to reject the job and as Elissa seemed happy to have her manage the affair, Michele had accepted. She'd chosen Arabian Nights as the theme, with Nick hosting as the Sheik of Tweak, a similarity in persona she couldn't resist making the most of.

"Seems you have everything under control, Michele?" Nick stood behind her in the kitchen and looked over her shoulder while she completed her final checklist.

She swivelled around to face him. "Yes, all good. Now all we need are the guests."

Costumed in flowing robes of burgundy and gold with heavy chains adorning his neck, he looked the part of a middle-eastern chieftain. His ethnic features added authenticity to the role, as did his godlike manner. However, it was his scent that intrigued her most.

"You've changed your aftershave?" She sniffed the air trying to place the brand.

"I took your advice. Do you like it?" He leaned in closer, holding his cheek within kissing distance of her mouth.

Breathing him in, she nodded in approval. "Yes. I do. It's perfect for the Sheik of Tweak, very exotic."

"Excellent." He kissed her on both cheeks then nuzzled her neck. "You're my most favoured harem dancer," he said, alluding to her glittering costume that did little to conceal her bejewelled belly. "Perhaps you'll perform the Dance of the Seven Veils for your sheik later?" His hot breath glanced across her shoulder.

"Perhaps?" Reciprocal warmth rose to flush her face when he brushed a kiss on her décolletage.

"Until later then." His hand skimmed her stomach, light as a feather, and he retreated to the bar. Up until now, she'd shielded herself from his charm, yet the energy of his touch startled her skin and threatened her defences.

"I did tell you to give this one a chance." Her sex goddess twirled around doing an erotic belly dance inside her hips.

Refusing to consider her inner advice, Michele returned to the job despite the desire stirring in her groin.

~ ♥ ~

AT NIGHT'S END AND after bidding farewell to the last guests, Michele joined her clients for a quick event post-mortem at the bar.

"Well, that was a great night. Thank you, Michele. You did a terrific job." Nick clapped his hands in appreciation.

"Certainly was. Thank you so much. A wonderful job. Now if you'll both excuse me, I'm off to bed." Elissa slipped off the barstool and disappeared up the hall. Michele said goodnight to her departing form while Nick topped up their glasses.

His eyes flamed with anticipation. "Now, how about my dance of the seven veils?"

"You can't be serious. What about Elissa?"

"Michele, if Elissa didn't want anything to happen between us, she wouldn't have gone to bed. That was her way of giving her blessing."

Michele pushed her glass away and sprang off the stool ready to leave. "Sorry. All too weird for me."

"No, wait." Nick dashed around the bar and grabbed her shoulders. "Just give me a chance. You keep saying I'm not your type, but I know I'm exactly your type. Stop pining over Mark. He's not right for you. I am. I'll do everything to help you make your dreams come true. I'll take you to seventh heaven and back."

"What?" The hairs on her forearms stood to attention. "How often have you used that phrase?"

"Which phrase?" His dark eyes darted across her face.

"Seventh heaven." It was the name of a show she'd designed years before.

"I can't ever recall using it until now."

"He is your type. This is your home, Michele."

Not now, she objected silently.

"Michele, please." Nick's hands stroked her shoulders as if examining rare silk, causing tiny ripples of attraction to radiate out from her. Her head spun, and though the signs were undeniably in his favour, she hesitated. His dark, liquid eyes held her gaze, beseeching her to let go, searching her soul for permission, and she once more heard . . .

"He is your type. This is your home, Michele."

Unwilling to fight any longer, she reclined her head back, proffering her neck and bosom to receive his adoration. He lifted her back onto the stool and ruched up the layers of her gossamer skirt, exposing her thighs to the cool air. She submitted to his charm, and he lowered himself on bended knee. Taking her foot in his hands, he proceeded to kiss every toe with delight and nibble her ankle like a rare delicacy, causing the bells to tinkle on her anklet. His hands continued their exploration, massaging her lower leg, stroking her knee and then travelling to her thigh where his mouth came to rest. Her sex steamed, and she drifted forwards on the stool, granting him permission to continue. Yet, he refused her invitation and returned to her other foot, administering to it with the same indulgent attention. With such devotion being lavished upon her legs, Michele began to topple.

"Allow me." He rose to his feet and slipped his arm around her waist to steady her. She relaxed into his firm embrace, allowing him to usher her into a guest bedroom.

"So, my most favoured harem dancer, my queen, would you like your sheik to tweak you?" The warmth of his breath drizzled over her flesh, making her moist and sticky as they lay together on the bed.

"Yes please."

"Very well." He crawled back down the bed to kneel between her legs and lifted the copious folds of her skirt to expose what he'd been longing for. She could feel his eyes probing her nakedness.

"You're so perfect, Michele," he said. "Your mounee looks like it's never been opened. It's closed like a flower waiting for the first beam of sunlight." He ran his finger delicately over her sleek slit.

"I'm not going to fuck you. You know that. You're a married man." She babbled her speech onc more time while her body screamed for relief.

"Of course. But I'm going to please you with my mouth, my tongue, and my fingers so one day you will want me to be your king." His voice prowled over her body like a predator. Lifting her buttocks, he placed a pillow underneath her, raising her snatch for a closer inspection.

"What a beautiful plump peach." Edging closer he inhaled her essence.

With the tip of his tongue twisting in a slow-motion, he reached out for an exploratory taste. Long lazy licks sent shrieking pulses racing through her body to the ends of her fingers. White-knuckled, she scrunched the other bed pillows, clinging to them as if they could save her from the coming adoration. Nothing aside from his tongue touched her, tormented her, lavished her without respite.

"Mmm," he growled, "see how this beautiful peach ripens when she is tended to?"

Michele felt herself engorge and reached down to open her folds for more. "Time to taste the fruit please," she pleaded, her breathing quickening.

"No, not yet," he said in a royal tone which caused her hands to retreat. "No one can touch the fruit except me."

For a few more moments his worship remained measured until he dipped his tongue deep into her slit peeling her back from arse to clit. She squealed in delight.

"Now here is the flesh I've been longing to taste."

His mouth formed over her snatch, devouring her like the juicy peach he'd been alluding to. Working his lips and teeth, he chewed at her with just the right amount of pain to heighten her pleasure. Feasting on her folds, he curled his tongue in different actions, obviously gauging which techniques produced the most pleasure for her. Michele wanted to scream.

He repositioned himself higher, and with purposeful fingers peeled her open, burying his tongue deep within her. His timing was impeccable.

"God that is so good." She moaned, stretching her legs and pointing her toes to maximum extension while he feasted. "Finger fuck me please," she whimpered.

With expert technique, he inserted his fingers deep within, triggering her G-spot to immediate ejaculation. Though she tried to squirm away, he dragged her down toward him for more.

"Not so fast, my queen. Your peach has plenty more juice to give to me." Thrusting his face and fingers into her again, he ravished her to orgasm once more, drinking her with an unquenchable thirst. Like writhing snakes, their bodies remained joined, his face embedded between her legs, as he tried to deplete her of any lingering doubts and sexual tension until at last, she lay shattered and satisfied.

"See? I am your type," he mused, his fingers stroking her swollen mons. His face glistened, not only with her juice but with the delight of demonstrating his ability to please her.

Michele had little energy left for a rebuttal. "Maybe you're right. Perhaps you are my type after all."

With a sphinx-like smile, Nick slid down between her legs to reassure her of the fact.

CHAPTER TWENTY

CHRISTMAS EVE

IN KEEPING WITH THEIR Christmas Eve tradition, the four women donned their brightest festive garb and gathered at Julie's apartment to exchange gifts and girlie gossip. In jubilant Christmas spirit, Cindy admitted her relationship with Graham felt like a dream come true and that they'd been discussing moving in together. Being a man of action, he'd guaranteed his alpha-male status in Cindy's life by surprising her with an early Christmas present and booking them a ten-day Fijian holiday over the festive season.

"Now this one sounds like a keeper," Michele said.

"I think you may be right, sweetie. The more time we spend together, the better it gets."

SallyAnn, Richie and the children were off overseas to visit his family for a month. "I'll just be pleased to get on that bloody plane. I swear to God I've got three children, not two. Richie's left everything to me to plan for this trip and it's his family we're going to see. So help me if he doesn't pack his own bag, I'll throttle him. Then I'll put him in the bloody bag and ship him back to his mollycoddling ma in the mother country."

After the obligatory male bashing to alleviate SallyAnn's languishing spirits, Michele asked Julie what she and Tom planned to do over Christmas.

"We're having Christmas apart this year," she said in a subdued tone.

"What? Oh, sweetie, what happened?"

"Tom asked me to marry him, and I said no."

"What? Why?" Michele asked.

"I'm just not the marrying kind. I thought Tom understood that. I'm happy to keep things the way they are, but he wants more. He wants us to live together. He wants the whole man and wife fiasco." For the first time in years, Julie sounded miserable.

"But you and Tom have been together for ages and he's such a good man, why not get married? SallyAnn asked.

"You just got through telling us that Richie is your third child and you're asking me why I don't want to get married?"

"Every marriage is different. I have a husband who is a good provider but on the other hand, he's a traditional man who likes his meals on the table when he comes home from work. He suffers from man flu, bad moods and stress, so yes, at times he's the typical pain-in-the-arse male. But we've got two great kids who I love dearly and I'm certainly better off than most women. Even though I gave up my dancing career for this marriage, I don't regret it. My marriage isn't a blight on my life and marrying Tom needn't be for you either."

"I know," Julie said without conviction. "But I don't want to lose my independence, my freedom to do what I want, when I want. If I married Tom, I'd have to live with him, together. I just can't bear the thought of doing that." She spoke as if nuptial cohabitation was a scourge on the earth.

"What now?" Michele asked.

"We've decided to take a break from each other. I miss him but you know me, I'll bounce back." She smiled half-heartedly.

Ever optimistic, Cindy said, "See what happens in the New Year, Julie. Who knows?"

"True . . . Now, Michele, when are you off to Sydney to see your undercover lover?"

"I leave on the thirtieth for a week." She was anxious and excited at the thought of seeing Mark.

"And what about your other suitor? Mr Stavros?" Julie asked.

"He's a strange one, really he is." Michele proceeded to enlighten her friends on the recent events with Nick. "So since then, he's taken me to lunch a couple of times. He's very gracious, a real gentleman, but there's no way I'm going to have a full-blown affair with him."

"But what are you going to do with him? I mean he'll be expecting more of the same after your recent sheik-feasts-on-your-peach episode." Cindy giggled at her own cleverness.

"I don't know. He's still on about men being kings and women being queens and that I'm his queen blah, blah, blah. Then my Trust Airways pilot keeps telling me he's my match. But he's married, and I don't want to take it any further." Michele twirled her glass around and around, much like her thoughts on the matter.

"But didn't you say he does whatever you ask, and he goes out of his way to please you?" Cindy asked.

"Yes, he does, but all the while Elissa is hovering in the background. It's just too weird for me." Looking around at her friends' faces, she realized if she sought any clarity from them, her hope was misplaced.

"Listening to your adventures with your Greek god makes me dizzy. Backwards, forwards, volley, point, score. It's like watching Wimbledon." SallyAnn turned her head from side to side for effect.

"That's how I feel most of the time," Michele said, still spinning her glass in circles.

"Anyway, I guess all you can do is see what happens, sweetie. Sounds like the same Christmas carol for all of us this year." She held up her glass for a toast and began singing loudly, "Hark the herald angels sing, let's just see what this new year brings."

CHAPTER TWENTY-ONE

THE LAST THURSDAY OF 1999

"**So, Mum, did you** write Julie's phone number down?" Michele asked down the phone again.

"Yes, dear." Her mother's voice sounded more anxious than certain.

"Mum, I can hear you fidgeting around. Have you lost where you wrote it down?"

"Um, um, oh here it is. I found it. Here it is, dear." Pearl gave a sigh.

"Okay. Read it back to me then."

"It's um . . . um . . . Julie, 0491 570 156."

Michele worried about leaving her mother, but she also needed to have her own life. "Good. Now put that next to your phone. If you need anything while I'm away, just ring Julie. She'll come over. Okay?"

"Where are you going, dear?"

"Sydney, Mum, Sydney. I've told you every day this week. I'm going to Sydney for a week." She tried her best not to voice her exasperation but failed.

As usual, Pearl didn't register her daughter's impatience. "Oh yes, dear. That's right, Sydney. When will you be back?"

Michele sighed on the other end of the phone. "In a week's time, Mum. Next Thursday."

"Well, you have a good time, dear. Puss Puss and I will be fine. No need to worry about me."

"Okay then. I'm going now. You can call me on my phone anytime you need. Or you can call Julie. Your carers will be there every day so everything will be the same as usual."

"And what time will I see you this weekend?" Pearl's mind reverted to its fragmented state.

"No, Mum, you won't see me this weekend. I'll be in Sydney." She knew she had to get off the phone otherwise her mother would be more confused.

"That's right. I'll see you next Thursday. Bye, Michele. Have a good time. Love you." For an instant, the pieces of Michele's trip clicked into place in Pearl's mind.

"Thanks, Mum. See you then. Love you too." She hung up wondering how much longer she could leave her mother to live alone. But the time for that decision or its ensuing battle with her mother was not now. She snatched up her handbag, dragged her suitcase to the garage and said farewell to her home for seven days of hot sex with Mark.

WHEN SHE ARRIVED IN her hotel room Michele left a voice message on his mobile. "Hey, gorgeous. I'm here. Room 303 at Star Casino. Call me." Over the next hour, she unpacked and gave her room a thorough inspection before settling in to admire the great view over Darling Harbour. Another hour passed, and since she hadn't heard from him, she decided to bolster her lagging mood by wandering down to the bright lights of the casino. Here another hour sneaked past and then another slinked off to the corner taking with it the last of her optimism. The couple of martinis under her belt only added to her broken spirit. Dejected, she returned to her room around ten. There she waited one more hour until the last glimmer of hope faded. With no other alternative, she decided to undress, shower alone and go to bed. It wasn't the triumphant start to the holiday she'd planned. At midnight, just as she was drifting off to sleep her phone beeped with a text.

"Hey, baby. Sorry. Couldn't get away. See you tomorrow. Xxx"

"Really?" she said to her phone. "And it's taken six hours for you to realize it. What a waste of time." She fumed alone in her bed, too angry to reply. She switched off her phone, threw her shoulder into the pillow and knew that her first night wasn't going to render any beauty sleep.

~ ♥ ~

AT THE SOUND OF the approaching water, the little boy and girl scurried around like ants defending their sandcastles. Though they worked hard to stave off the intruding waves with buckets and spades, they eventually surrendered to the will of the ocean. Disappointed, they stood together holding hands, peering down at the destruction on the beach.

The confident little boy turned to the girl. "It'll be all right. I'm here. We can start again."

The little girl looked at him and in a tiny voice replied, "I know. We can start again." And with the sun shining in their squinting eyes, the pair set to making another sandcastle together.

~ ♥ ~

THE LIGHT FLOODING INTO Room 303 roused Michele from her dream. Unsurprisingly, she hadn't had much sleep and awoke still angry with Mark.

"Damn it," she said out loud on her way to the bathroom. "I'm not waiting around for him. I'm going out." Within the hour, she was dressed and on her way to join the throng of tourists and locals at The Rocks on Sydney Harbour's foreshore. On this last day of the twentieth century, Sydney was abuzz with New Year's Eve preparations. People staked their claims on public areas to watch the night's biggest fireworks spectacle being staged on the Sydney Harbour Bridge and surrounding buildings. Event managers and television crews busied themselves around the precinct cordoning off private corporate boxes, testing speakers, ordering staff to and fro, and taking control of as much land and air space as they could. She yearned to be part of it.

Perhaps I should move to Sydney and set up my event management business here, she thought, walking the streets and watching the set-up. *There's more work, more buzz, and more Mark.* She corrected herself on the last detail. She'd come to Sydney on his insistence, and he was nowhere to be found. Now, after a few hours walking off the previous night's wrath, she'd calmed down enough to send a brief text to her invisible man:

"Hey, Mark. Big night tonight. What time will I see you? Xxx"

She decided to add the kisses at the last moment to soften the omission of her usual term of endearment at the beginning of the message.

He responded straight away:

"Gotta work. Should finish by 2 A.M. Will come then if that's okay?"

"Fuck," she hissed aloud. "New Year's bloody Eve going into the new millennium, and he can't get here 'til after two A.M." The hard tone of her voice caught the attention of happy holidaymakers setting up their chairs for the night's festivities on the grass. They frowned at her and she made a hasty retreat. Keeping her fingers away from her phone, she strode around Circular Quay to the Opera House where she found a vacant spot way up on the highest step. With her handbag wedged between her knees, she took a breath before typing out a return message:

"Can't you make it any earlier?"

"If I can, I'll call you. See you after 2 A.M.? Xxx"

Alone on New Year's Eve 1999 in Sydney while the rest of the world celebrated an event that happened only once every thousand years. She could hear Nick's calm yet authoritative voice in her head repeating, "Actions speak louder than words."

She felt like a fool as she typed her reply:

"Okay. Try to come earlier, please. Happy New Year." No kisses.

CHAPTER TWENTY-TWO

NEW YEAR'S EVE, 1999

By THE TIME HE arrived, the new millennium was already three hours old, welcomed in by enough firepower to make the fireworks manufacturer a wealthy man. With roads still blocked to traffic, controlled chaos ruled as tens of thousands of happy revellers partied in the streets.

Wearing his trademark smile, Mark waltzed into the overcrowded bar looking his usual effortless self as people parted before him like the Red Sea. At the sight of him, Michele's forgiving nature surfaced but she'd rehearsed a righteous indignation speech and she was determined to give it.

Reaching out, he caught her up in his arms, hugging her to him. "God, I've missed you."

"Me too." She breathed him in, and her senses flooded once more with the happiest memories of her life.

"Look at you, baby." He beamed, holding her at arm's length. His eyes raced over her like a winning athlete admiring his trophy.

In keeping with the importance of this rendezvous, she'd chosen a super-short red-sequined sheath dress accessorized with red everything. "You look so hot." She'd made sure she did. "Happy New Year. Sorry, I'm so late but getting here was crazy." He pushed in beside her at the bar trying to get the bartender's attention.

"Happy New Year to you too, gorgeous. But I've got to say I'm pretty pissed off you couldn't make it earlier." She waited a beat then continued, "After all, you invited me down here saying we'd spend time together. I go to all this effort at the busiest time of the year, pay top dollar for the room and then you do your invisible man impersonation on me. I could've saved my cash and partied with my friends on the Gold Coast. They wouldn't have let me down." With her heart pounding and her skin bristling, she knew her fear of abandonment was making her lose control. Her voice quivered and tears of rejection stabbed at the back of her eyes. Just as well everyone around them continued in their raucous revelry not noticing the sexy lady in red balling out the big guy next to her.

"Baby, I'm sorry. I couldn't get here any earlier. I did text you this morning and tell you."

"Why? Why couldn't you get here earlier?" Although she had no right to demand anything, she wanted answers.

"Karen's in hospital, and I couldn't get away until now."

"But you said you had to work and now the excuse is your wife is in hospital. Which is it!" Her voice broke through the surrounding sound barrier of merriment. She was past caring about his wife or what people thought and, with blazing defiance, glared at the prying faces around them.

Mark lowered his voice in the hope she would too. "I've been working with the water police on a case and then I visited Karen in hospital. I even got the water boys to motor me across the harbour so I could get here. Otherwise, I'd still be trapped in gridlocked streets. I'm really sorry. Believe me, there was nothing I could do about it. I'm sorry." His blue eyes beseeched her to believe him, to forgive him.

To control her mounting fury, Michele marched off to a quiet corner where she'd be safe from total embarrassment and the fallout could do less damage.

Mark stood behind her, his hands resting on her shoulders. "I'm sorry, baby. I know things haven't worked out the way I promised. More than anything, I wanted to spend last night and tonight with you."

Spinning around to face him, she flung her hurt into his face. "It's just so unfair. I was so looking forwards to celebrating the new millennium with you. It was all your idea that I come down here. And now I've spent it all alone. I feel such an idiot."

"You're right. I shouldn't have asked you down unless I could guarantee to be with you. Up until a couple of days ago, I thought I could. I'm sorry. The last thing I ever wanted to do was hurt you or for you to think I was taking advantage of you. Please forgive me."

Perhaps it was because his plea seemed genuine, or that arguing over something neither of them could control didn't solve anything, or that this was all she could ever expect, she screwed up her nose and sighed with regret. "I'm sorry too. I had high hopes. Silly me."

He wrapped her under his shoulder, the place where she felt most safe and protected. He kissed the top of her head and whispered, "Another time, another place, baby. I am sorry."

"I know. Me too." She looked up at him, wondering why she couldn't stay mad at him. With weakening resolve, she reached up and kissed him on the cheek. "Come on. Let's go."

Taking his hand, she led him to the elevators and up to her room. Once inside he took her in his arms and kissed her. She returned his craving and within minutes they were undressed, at home in each other's arms.

"What else do you have for me, my golden-haired angel, aside from a fuckin' great pussy?"

"Romance, head jobs and more fucking. So bring your fabulous cock with you."

She'd planned for this trip with her usual expertise, bringing with her music, candles, and various accessories for romantic, sensual evenings together. After recovering from their initial obsession with each other, they relaxed in the foam of the spa surrounded by flickering candles with k.d. lang playing in the background.

"When do you go back?" He wiggled his toes between her thighs.

"I leave next Thursday."

"I'll try to see you as much as I can. But I can't promise anything, baby. Things are a little tense at the moment." He reached forwards and replaced his toes with his fingers. Before she could voice her disappointment, he was inside her, twisting his fingers around to assail her G-spot. She had no power or inclination to stop his insistent demand on her flesh. He knew how to please, and she surrendered to his touch.

"Come on, baby. I need to eat you."

Within moments, she was squirming on the bed as, like a sorcerer unveiling magical tricks, he surprised and delighted her to repeated orgasms. Gratified, she lay with a contented, childlike smile on her face.

"That's my girl," he said. "I can only stay another few hours." She returned his comment with a frown and a pout. "So let's make the most of it, baby—" and he dove between her legs once more.

By NINE A.M. ON the first day of the year 2000, she lay on the bed sore and satisfied, while Mark readied to leave. Admiring his broad beam of a back as he shrugged on his shirt, she asked, "So what now?"

He turned and sat on the bed beside her, his shirt open, his tight abs rippling under his tanned skin, all combining to make saying goodbye even harder. "I don't know what else to tell you, baby. This is all I can offer."

"I know. Another time, another place." Her reference to his previous excuse brought a bittersweet smile to both their faces.

"Afraid so. If you like, I won't contact you anymore. Would that make it easier for you?"

"Not really. I'm a big girl."

"If I can get away again this week do you want me to call?"

"Why not? I came down to see you. May as well make the most of it."

"Okay. But no promises." He moved to continue dressing.

"I know. No promises. If I have no expectations, then I can't be disappointed."

She knew she should be ranting about the situation but this time she felt a total disconnect. She was part of the conversation yet there was no more longing. No more gut-wrenching heartbreak. Perhaps she'd needed to go through this with Mark one last time. Perhaps, now, she'd won freedom from his influence.

He stood at the door, waiting. "Are you going to kiss me goodbye?"

Sighing, she leveraged herself off the bed. Padding over to the door, she dropped her robe on the floor so he could remember her in the state he'd seen her most, nude. She nuzzled into his body with quiet affection.

"Goodbye, gorgeous."

He kissed the top of her head. "Goodbye, baby." His hands lingered on her nakedness one last time. He turned, opened the door and didn't look back.

CHAPTER TWENTY-THREE

THE FIRST MONTH OF THE NEW MILLENNIUM

"I'M SO SORRY TO be calling you." Julie's anxious voice rushed down the phone.

"What's wrong?" Michele's worst fear wrapped its fingers around her throat.

"It's your mother. The ambulance is taking her to the hospital. It seems she's had a turn of some kind. I'm on my way there now."

"Okay. I'll come home. Call me when you know more. I'll get on the first flight back." She ended the call and picked up her pace back to the hotel.

She hadn't heard from Mark in three days. Not that she'd expected to. There'd been a finality to his leaving this time. Devoid of grief and tears, she'd accepted their destinies led in different directions. He'd come into her life at just the right time and although the passionate connection between them would always remain, there was no happy-ever-after ending in the future together. Theirs was not a Walt Disney storyline. She'd decided to enjoy her remaining days in Sydney by catching up with friends and investigating work opportunities. The change of scenery had given her the time and space she'd needed to re-evaluate her life. The Goddess had remained silent during those soul-searching hours, yet Michele's sense of being on the right path for her future had grown each day. Now with this one phone call, her world shifted again.

~ ♥ ~

"How is she?" Michele dropped her luggage at the door of her mother's hospital room.

Julie clutched her friend's hands and gave her the update. "The doctor was just here. He said she's had a pretty severe heart attack. She's resting peacefully at the moment."

"Thanks, Julie. You're a godsend. You go home now. I'll sit with her."

"Are you sure?"

"I'm sure. You go. I'll call you in the morning." Michele kissed her goodbye then tiptoed into the room. Pulling up a chair she settled in for the wait. She reached out for her mother's hand, and Pearl opened her eyes. "Michele, hello darling. You're supposed to be in Sydney, aren't you?"

"Yes, Mum. You remembered. I came home because you're sick."

"Who's looking after Puss Puss?"

"I will, Mum. She'll be fine." Again, Mark flashed into her mind. How a simple word could bring back such vivid memories still surprised her.

"Well, if anything happens to me, you have to put Puss Puss down. I don't want her going to anyone else."

"I could take her, Mum?"

"I guess that'd be okay. But if you don't take her, I don't want her going to anyone else."

"I promise. Anyway, you'll be home in no time and Puss Puss will be waiting for you."

"And what about your brother? Who's going to look after him?"

"I don't have a brother, Mum." She realized Pearl had again taken flight into the wicked world of fancy orchestrated by her dementia.

"Yes, you do, dear."

"I don't understand, Mum? I don't have a brother."

"You do, dear. I just didn't tell you. You were such a pretty baby with yellow curls. You were always smiling. We loved you so much."

"I know, Mum. I love you too." She stood and gave her mother a kiss on her forehead. Her yellowing skin felt like the paper on which her father wrote his World War II love letters to her mother, fragile and withered. "You rest now, Mum. I'll be here when you wake up."

"Okay, dear. But you must find him."

"Find who, Mum?"

"Your brother."

Michele resumed her seat, watching her mother drift. Like a contented child going to sleep, she smiled, recalling happier times. A deep sadness diffused Michele's bones, making her feel brittle, as if she'd break if she tried to leave. Long ago this wretched disease had kidnapped her mother, and permeated their relationship like a lethal virus, destroying their joyous, candid conversations. And now in these valuable, irreplaceable moments, it separated them even further with fanciful stories.

"*Much like me? So others would say? Am I a flight of fancy?*" The Goddess broke Michele's disquiet but not her focus, which stayed on her mother's laboured breathing. She had no time to decipher cryptic clues. Her mother straddled the worlds of life and death, and Michele wasn't prepared for the inevitable. The Goddess could wait.

Her mother's eyelids fluttered open and with a resolute focus Michele hadn't seen on her face for some years she said, "Michele, remember days turn into minutes, weeks into seconds, years into moments and decades flash by in an instant. Dance through your life without regret."

Words of wisdom were not Pearl's communication style, yet she uttered them with ease and intention. "It's all right, Michele. It'll be all right." Pearl drifted to sleep, her clammy, skeletal hand clasping her daughter's.

HAVING RETURNED FROM OVERSEAS, SallyAnn had offered to hold the gathering at their house while Richie played emcee, finishing with a traditional Irish poem and toast.

"And when you sit and stories tell, I'll be with you and help you recall. So, fill to me the parting glass. God bless, and joy be with you all." Richie raised his glass. "To Pearl."

"To Pearl," everyone chorused, drinking a toast to Michele's mother who'd died of a massive heart attack three days earlier.

"How are you holding up, sweetie?" Cindy squeezed Michele's hand as they sat on the couch.

"Okay, I guess. Once we finish here today, I need to start going through Mum's things."

"Why not leave it until tomorrow, and we can all come and help?" Julie sat on the other side of the couch, holding Michele's other hand. If it hadn't been such a sombre occasion, the three of them with such perfect posture would've looked like models in a little black dress photoshoot. On the periphery, SallyAnn glided past with a tray of finger sandwiches befitting a domestic goddess and loyal friend.

"Maybe I will," she said. "I knew Mum would leave soon, but I still can't quite get my head around it, you know?" She looked at her friends who nodded with sympathy. "I mean. Look at us. We three have no children. When we die who will care? Who will mourn us?"

Cindy put her arm around her grieving friend's shoulders. "Just because we don't have kids, it doesn't mean no one will care when we die. I promise I'll mourn for you, sweetie, if you go before me." Not meaning to be humorous, Cindy realized she'd made a joke and the three of them tittered quietly together.

"True," Julie said with more conviction. "We have each other, although I always wanted children."

Cindy and Michele gasped. "No."

"Yes. But my body clock never turned on. I guess I didn't find the guy with the right gene pool."

"But what about Tom? He had good genes?" Cindy said.

"No. He wasn't right somehow. I can't explain it. Anyway, too late now." Julie shrugged off her loss of motherhood and a dream unfulfilled. "Regardless of whether we have children or not, we have each other. And, it looks like you're going to end up with Graham. He's got a daughter. She can look after all of us." Julie nodded at Cindy, who then steered the conversation to a topic she'd delayed for the past couple of days.

"Sweetie" — she took both Michele's hands — "I can't find the right time to bring this up, so I guess now is as good as any."

Feeling exhausted by her mother's death and the funeral arrangements, Michele just looked at her friend with a puzzled expression.

Cindy continued with as much tact as she could. "You've told us how disappointed you were with your time in Sydney and that you didn't see Mark except for that one time."

"It's all right, though. I think I've worked through it at last. My expectations were too high. He always told me he wasn't able to leave his wife. *Que sera sera.*" She shrugged and smiled at her use of one of Cindy's favourite phrases.

"Sweetie, your expectations aren't too high for the right man. It's just that Mark isn't the right man," Cindy said.

"What are you getting at?"

Cindy gazed into Michele's swollen eyes. "Mark did visit Karen in hospital on New Year's Eve like he said, but it wasn't because she was sick." Michele shook her head, confused. "It was because she was giving birth to their son."

"What?" Michele gasped, feeling an imaginary football slam into her stomach. She reared back onto Julie, who wrapped her arm around her shoulders.

"He called Graham a couple of days ago with the news. We didn't know when to break it to you so we thought since we're all here together, now might be the best time."

Michele looked to Julie, who nodded in confirmation of Cindy's story. Then she glanced towards SallyAnn, who'd been keeping her eyes on the conversation as she played hostess, knowing what was transpiring.

"I see." Michele pieced together the events in her head, realizing this was the real reason for his lateness, his swift departure and his ongoing absence since that night.

"Are you okay?" Julie asked.

"I guess I am. He really is something, isn't he? His wife is having a baby and he still finds time to run off to be with me. I guess I should feel flattered really."

Cindy and Julie glanced at each other, obviously concerned that Michele was cracking under the pressure of recent events.

"Well, I guess you could look at it that way," Julie said, picking up pace. "I doubt anyone else could've pulled it off. He's certainly a bit of a bastard, but he's obviously smitten with you."

Cindy joined in the positive approach. "Seems you two have quite a connection, sweetie."

"Yes, we do. I just wish he'd told me, that's all." Michele was disappointed he'd hidden such an important moment of his life from her.

"It's all that undercover shit for years. He's damaged, you know that," Julie said. "Anyway, it's over now. You had great sex together and some good times. Now you can move on with a new life."

"Yes. You should feel blessed you never ended up with him. He's got too much baggage that one. I pity his poor wife," Cindy said.

"That's true. So much has happened, what with Mum's passing, life's going to be very different for me now. Time to grow up, I guess. No more Walt Disney or wishing for happy-ever-after endings. It just doesn't happen that way."

Amazed that no matter how many tears she shed, there were always more, Michele let them trickle down her face as she cried for the loss of her mother, her lover, her familiar life and her childhood dreams of finding true love. While SallyAnn delivered more food and Richie topped up everyone's glasses, the wake for Pearl Johnston, paid suitable homage to a woman who was loved, had nothing to fear, could do no wrong and was now free and in heaven.

~ ♥ ~

CURLED UP ON MICHELE'S lap, Puss Puss seemed content in her new surroundings. Probably because Michele went out of her way to ensure there was fresh water and kitty litter daily. She even responded to on-demand meowing by chopping up Puss Puss's favourite meat at dinner time. Michele didn't mind. The cat somehow made her feel closer to her mother.

With a box of love letters her mother and father had written to each other during World War II beside her, Michele stroked her new pet and read aloud some of her father's letters. "To My Flower of the Desert . . ."

A knock interrupted, and after relocating a cranky Puss Puss, Michele shuffled over and opened her front door.

Nick stood holding an enormous floral arrangement. "Hello, Michele. Sorry, I didn't call but I wanted to say how sorry I was to hear about your mother."

"Oh, Nick. These are lovely. Come in." She motioned him into her townhouse, placing the sympathy flowers on the kitchen bench. "I look awful. I'm sorry. I've spent the last few days going through Mum's things." Running a hand across her red-rimmed eyes, she glanced down at her shabby grey tracksuit pants and T-shirt accessorized with fluffy grey scuffs.

"Nonsense. You look beautiful." He wrapped his arms around her with a comforting hug, which she received without protest.

"Sit please." She walked to the couch and stacked the letters away, making a space for her guest.

"What are those?" he asked.

"These are love letters my parents wrote to each other during the war years."

"How wonderful. Would you mind if I read one?"

"I guess not. I was just reading them aloud so if you like . . .?" She held a letter aloft and continued her recital. Thirty minutes passed before she realized her rudeness. "I'm so sorry. I haven't even offered you a drink." She sprang to her feet, making for the kitchen.

When she squeezed past, he caught her hand. "No need. Sit with me, please. I've missed you. Is there anything I can do?" He held her hands, watching her lower lip tremble.

With tears rolling down her face, she began to unravel. "I don't know what I'm going to do. I have no one now. Yes, I have my friends, but I have no family. I'm exactly as I started. An orphan. I'm all alone, with no one to call my own. I don't even have someone who wants to call me their own." Intense sobs shook her body as her suffering found release. "I'm scared, Nick. I feel so abandoned."

He gently lifted her chin, his eyes scanning her reddened eyes and tear-streaked cheeks.

"Don't. I look awful." She dragged her hand across her eyes and nose, trying to wipe away the heartbreak.

"On the contrary. You look perfect." Nick took her hands in his, his stare filled with compassion. "You are even more beautiful without makeup, more beautiful in your sorrow, and more beautiful because you think you're an orphan again. But you're not. I love you, Michele. I'll be your family. I want to call you my own."

"But you're married. But more than that, I'm sorry. But I don't love you." She lowered her eyes in shame.

"But I believe you do love me. You just don't know it yet. Why not give it a chance?"

"But that doesn't change the fact that you're married."

"I can be unmarried too." His remark opened a small fissure in her heart.

"He is your match, Michele," the Goddess repeated.

"Let me help you. What do you need?" His tone changed to that of the competent businessman, used to solving problems and taking decisive action.

"Well, there is something." She explained the strange story her mother had told her about a missing brother. "I'm not sure whether it was dementia talking but I'm interested to know whether this brother exists."

"That's easy. I can organize my lawyers to do the search for you if you like."

"Thank you, but can I use my own lawyer?"

"Of course. Just get them to send the account to me when they're finished."

She threw her arms around his neck, smothering his face with grateful childlike kisses. "Thank you. I simply couldn't afford to do this by myself. Thank you. Thank you."

"My pleasure."

~ ♥ ~

THAT NIGHT WHEN SHE readied herself for bed, her hand slipped under the pillow and retrieved the plastic bag containing her nightly sleeping relaxant. Unzipping it, she smelt the faint scent of Mark drift upward like the intoxicating curl of smoke from an expensive cigar. With the facecloth in her hand, she walked downstairs into the laundry to put on a load of washing. The pungent soapy smell of the washing powder promised the load would return cleansed of any lingering unwanted evidence.

Stealing the well-known line from Shakespeare's Hamlet, she whispered to the facecloth clasped in her hand, "Goodnight sweet Prince and flights of angels sing thee to thy rest." She inhaled her last deep breath of him, then dropped the facecloth into the wash, watching it flutter to its perch on top of the load like a small bird settling onto a nest. Spinning the dial to the wash cycle, she paused then released it to commence. With this one deliberate act, she turned her past toward a clean sparkling future, yet to unfold.

CHAPTER TWENTY-FOUR

EARLY 2000

"**May I speak with** Mr Benjamin Richmond, please?" Michele fiddled with Ben's business card.

"Who may I say is calling?" the gatekeeper of his office enquired.

"Just tell him it's Michele. Michele from the Gold Coast." She prayed this would be enough.

The line went silent and then Ben's measured voice rolled down the line. "Michele, the lady with the lips that should be bronzed. Now, this is a surprise." The tone of affection in his voice brightened her mood.

"Ben, how are you? I wasn't sure you'd remember me."

"How could I forget you or that wonderful night we spent together? I often think of you when I'm alone."

"I bet he does," her sex goddess chimed in.

Remembering the taste and feel of his chocolate skin, she felt her groin twitch. "Yes, that was fun, wasn't it?" She paused. "But, Ben, this is a business call."

"What a pity. I thought it was a booty call?"

"Sorry. Not this time." Deciding not to allow him another sexual retort, she launched into the purpose of her call. Since he was a lawyer, she wanted him to conduct a search for her possible missing brother.

"Okay. I've got the details. Any idea of your biological background?" he asked, professional and confidential.

"None. I was never interested in finding out."

"Very well then. I've got a few cases on at the moment. Are you in a hurry?"

"Not at all. Whenever you have the time is good."

"Great. I'll let you know. And now that I have your contact details maybe I can call you on a personal basis?"

Ben's athletic, well-hung physique flashed back into her mind. "Maybe, but not now, Ben. I've got a few things I'm working through. Maybe in a couple of months?"

"Not a problem, Michele. It was really nice hearing from you regardless. I'll see what I can find out."

"Thanks, Ben. It's appreciated." She rang off feeling buoyed by their conversation.

"Oh, Cindy, it's beautiful."

With her left hand held up to the sunlight, Cindy's expression sparkled just as much as the two-carat princess-cut diamond in her engagement ring. "We're going to have a Spring Gala wedding, and Michele I want you to be our wedding coordinator. We'll have such fun planning it."

"I'd love too."

"And I want all of you to be my bridesmaids. I want what Julia Roberts had in *Steel Magnolias*. An extravagant garden wedding with all the trimmings."

"Okay. But let's go easy on the pink puffy dresses, please." Julie screwed up her nose just at thought of being a bridesmaid.

"Count me in. I love weddings," SallyAnn said.

"Here, I bought these bridal magazines on the way over." Cindy upended her tote bag allowing a dozen or more magazines to tumble onto the table. "Grab one and let's see if we can't find me a dress as perfect as Julia wore in the film."

~ ♥ ~

Along with planning Cindy and Graham's wedding, Michele enjoyed Nick's romantic presence in her life. He lavished her with attention, intelligent conversation and humour. Some nights he'd arrive at her townhouse with a carton of champagne, 'just in case' of emergencies. Other times, Roger would be waiting with the limousine ready to whisk her off to a surprise destination.

"You're making me fall in love with you, you know?" she said as they sat together on her couch one autumn night.

"That's always been my intention." Nick kissed her hand.

"I guess you do have a few redeeming characteristics, even if you are a tad short, bald and a bit too full of yourself."

"What can I say? I'm Greek. Blame my mother for my aversion to helping in the kitchen and tea towels. Greek men aren't created to do women's work."

"If you ever want to make love to me, you're going to have to get over your delusions of grandeur. You're not actually a Greek god. You know that, right?" She cocked her head in expectation of agreement.

"Perhaps you should join me in my delusions, as you like to call them, and be my Greek goddess instead. That way we can be a match for each other." He advanced toward her, the black depths of his eyes luring her to succumb.

"And we still have the matter of you being married to overcome."

"Indeed we do. However, if you're willing to look your fears in the face, you may see your future sitting before you." A knowing smile curled his lips as he allowed her time to consider his perspective.

Could he be right? Could her fear of losing her freedom be stopping her from finding her happy-ever-after ending?

"Dance through life without regrets, Michele," her mother had counselled.

With Pearl's advice resounding in her mind and accompanied by the Goddess's gentle assurances, she permitted the fire between them to combust. "I guess it's time we found out if we are a match then?"

Obviously startled at the unexpected timing of her consent, he followed her upstairs to consummate their relationship.

~ ♥ ~

"THAT HAS TO BE the worst sex I think I've ever had," she said, feeling as messy as she looked.

"Me too."

They lay on the bed staring at the ceiling, astounded that they hadn't been able to find a rhythm together.

"How can that be?" She remembered how she'd orgasmed when Nick went down on her, but tonight had been a disaster.

"I'm not sure, let's call it beginner's bad luck. Look, anything worth doing is worth doing well. I guess we just need a little practice." He sounded unfazed, confident that next time would be better.

"Maybe?" But she remained unconvinced, uncertain there'd be a next time.

NICK LEFT SOON AFTER their sexual debacle, and Michele opted for an early night, thinking that a good night's sleep would wipe the disappointment of their first lovemaking session from her mind. When Puss Puss's angry hissing roused her during the night, Michele struggled to consciousness. But her body was rigid, her eyes clenched shut, and she was floating above her bed. At least that's what it felt like. She knew something was wrong because Puss Puss' hissing grew louder and angrier. Praying that supernatural evil only existed in horror movies, she began to recite the Goddess's mantra in her mind. *I am loved. There is nothing to fear. I can do no wrong, Heaven is all around me and I am free.*

As she repeated it, she felt herself descend back to the bed and her eyes blinked open. She switched on the lamp to see Puss Puss glaring balefully at her from the bottom of the bed.

"Surely not? I was only dreaming." She spoke aloud to the cat, trying to reassure herself, but her logic turned to fear when she registered the temperature in her bedroom. It was freezing. She slid out of bed and pulled her gown around her shoulders. Scurrying on chilly feet, she rushed off into the guest bedroom where the normal summer temperature hung in the air. Returning to her bedroom, she shivered again as the icy chill pricked at her skin.

"This is ridiculous," she said to Puss Puss. "What's going on here?" Checking the bedroom window, she noticed it was open, yet condensation trickled down the pane on the inside. The difference in temperature was unexplainable. Instinctively, she picked up her phone and dialled. Within two rings, Nick answered.

"Michele, is everything all right?" His concern flooded down the phone.

"Okay. Time to stop the games now. Who are you?"

"What do you mean?"

"From the beginning, I thought there was something weird about you, but this proves it." Her voice began rising in pitch and strength. "I think I've just been levitating in my bedroom and now it's icy cold in here. Like it's ten degrees colder than any other room in the house. And it's your face that came to me. I figure you're somehow behind all this weird shit. So, I say again, who are you?" This was the first time any of these thoughts had surfaced and she was shocked to hear them tumble from her mouth. Was she going mad?

"Michele, I don't know what you mean? Are you all right?"

"I'm fine," she yelled down the phone. "Who the fuck are you?" The ensuing silence was chillier than the air in the bedroom.

"I'm Nick. I can't tell you what happened. I don't know. But I do know I've been searching for you all my life. We're supposed to be together."

"Oh, for God's sake. Come on. That's all you've got to say? Give me a break." The temperature in her bedroom began to warm up in direct proportion to her rising anger.

"Okay. Okay. I was thinking of you just now. Focusing on you. Perhaps that's what you felt. I've had similar experiences as well that I can't explain."

"Like what?" Her confusion shifted to curiosity.

"Weird stuff as well. Voices in my head telling me things about us. Past lives, you call it. I remember things from other places, other times. In Egypt, we were together, you were my queen. Really weird shit. Listen, do you want me to come over?"

Calming down, she declined. "No. It's all right, I guess. But can you please not focus on me again so I can get some sleep?"

"Of course. Sorry. I didn't know."

"There's something going on here that neither of us understand," she said, with no idea what it was.

"That's what I've been trying to tell you since I met you. I'm sure there's nothing for you to worry about. Just think of seventh heaven. I won't say I'll see you in my dreams otherwise you'll end up on your ceiling again. Goodnight, Michele. Sleep tight."

"Goodnight, Nick."

She slid back under the sheets, mystified by the experience. The room temperature returned to its usual warmth and Puss Puss purred in peace on the bottom of the bed like nothing had happened. Deciding it wasn't worth worrying about, Michele scrunched her pillows and readied herself for sleep.

After a few minutes, she drifted into the twilight zone before sleep and heard, "*You are loved, Michele. There is nothing to fear. You can do no wrong, Heaven is all around you and you are free. He is your match. You've been together before.*"

CHAPTER TWENTY-FIVE

WINTER 2000

Since her strange supernatural episode, Michele's attraction to Nick had grown and matured. Although both opinionated and headstrong their compatibility was evident, if at times strained. Due to his determined view on women being queens and men being kings, the battle of the reigning royals often ended in pyrrhic victories. Yet every time she readied herself to leave the relationship, the Goddess reminded her that he was the right partner for her. Sexually, the couple found their rhythm, although, at times, she yearned for Mark's rakish presence. As expected, his contact never resumed. Her quest for the holy grail of singledom had detoured to an unlikely Prince Charming in the form of Nick Stavros.

With the help of Michele's girlfriends, who arranged to look after her business and Puss Puss, Nick whisked her away on a romantic five-day holiday to Canberra. Wrapped in thick coats to ward off the winter cold, they strolled along the banks of Lake Burley Griffin watching the ducks enjoy the frosty temperatures. The past days had been fun if at times tense, as they discovered their relationship expectations fell short of ideal when they spent long periods together. At present, the chill in the air was as much a result of the lingering energy between them as the freezing climate in the nation's capital.

Nick reached to hold her gloved hand while they wandered along the lakeside path. "I'm going to ask Elissa for a divorce."

"What?"

They'd not discussed Elissa for some time now. Michele had decided it was his marriage, and he needed to be responsible for its continuation or demise. Since Elissa had never voiced any objection to their relationship, Michele took her silence as accepting, if uncomfortable, approval.

He stopped walking and turned toward her. "Michele, I love you. I want us to be together." The depth of commitment in his eyes was compelling and in some ways disconcerting. That this man was willing to give up everything for her touched her deeply.

"Nick, what can I say to the man who would be my king?"

"Just say you want us to be together too. Be my queen, Michele. Move in with me. Let's see where this goes."

"Nick, you're nothing if not persistent. Are you sure? Divorce can be so messy and expensive."

"I've no doubt things will not end up well between Elissa and me. But I remember you saying you weren't going to be anyone's mistress. And it's time I put my money where my mouth is. I love you and now, I think you love me. This is how I can best show you I'm serious about you, about us." He wrapped his arms tighter around her waist as snow began to fall.

Nick's unfettered declaration of love and his willingness to risk everything warmed her, melting away some of her apprehensions. "But isn't rushing into a divorce and moving in together too much? We've only known each other for a handful of months. You've got a lot to lose if it doesn't work out between us. To be honest, I'm not sure I want to give up my single life yet."

"I'm willing to take that chance, if you are." His eyes beseeched her to say yes.

Here was Prince Charming saying all the right things with the requisite romance of any good Disney story, yet within her, resistance remained. Or was it just the ghost of her tempestuous affair with Mark that wouldn't be put to rest? Her eyes looked over Nick's shoulder, searching into the distance to foretell the future. She waited and listened for an omen. Nothing unusual presented itself except a box of *Redhead* matches lying on the grass beside the pathway. Matches, a match, he's your match.

With a sigh, she ignored the phantom of the past, trusted her instinct and accepted.

"Okay, Nick. But it won't be easy, you know that. Neither of us is very good at giving up control, and we hate not getting our own way. And if you recall, I said from the very start that you're not my type."

"I know, I know, as you keep reminding me." He chuckled, holding her tighter.

"But I'm willing to give it a try since you're so committed to the idea." She was bemused at how far this affair had come with someone she'd originally had no attraction to.

"Good. I'll tell Elissa in the next couple of weeks then give her time to find a place of her own and for us to settle everything. After that, you can move in. Is that okay?"

"I'm not in any rush. There's plenty of time." Michele recalled that on the first night she visited Nick at his house, the Goddess had said his house was to become her home. It seemed, despite Michele's protestations, that the Goddess' advice had been correct. Only time would tell if Nick was her true match.

MICHELE SPIED IT AS soon as Roger pulled up in front of her townhouse. Her front door was ajar. "Oh, my god. Look." She scrambled out of the back seat, pushing past Nick.

"Wait. Michele. Don't." He grabbed at her hand, but she was already bolting to her townhouse.

Roger and Nick chased after her, catching up just in time as she swung the door open. They stood at the threshold in shock.

"Oh no," she wailed.

"Darling, don't go in. Roger and I will look around first." Nick left her at the doorway and with Roger close behind, began to pick his way through her townhouse. Its once neat and disciplined appearance was now unrecognizable due to the upended furniture and shattered possessions strewn everywhere. Nothing had been spared. They made their way through the debris, checking the garage and laundry, then tiptoed upstairs to see if any intruders were still there. Finding the place empty, they returned to Michele who slumped against the doorway in disbelief.

Roger rushed outside to call the police.

"There's no one here." Nick put his arm around her, and she edged forwards.

Every inch of the floor was smothered in her ruined life — broken chairs, emptied drawers, discarded possessions, every item torn, ravaged and splintered. Looking around her at what had once been her comfortable little home, she felt numb.

"My car?" Her swampy eyes blinked at Nick.

"Graffiti, smashed windows, slashed tyres." He swallowed hard.

She sagged a little more.

"Take me upstairs," she whispered.

"I don't think you should go up, darling. It's just more of the same."

"No, Nick. I need to see." Pulling her shoulders back and with her chin lifted, she was determined to climb those stairs, with or without him.

Without a word, he obliged and took a firm grip on her hand.

Weaving their way past crushed picture frames, ornaments, cushions, occasional furniture and more ripped clothes choking the stairs, raw emotion scratched at her throat. They entered her bedroom and her hands clamped across her mouth, stifling the primal yelp that tried to escape. Her cherished Lautrec posters and lamps lay smashed in the war zone that used to be where she slept. Like remnants from a derelict clothing sale, her bed linen and clothes had been slashed, hiding more treasured personal items underneath.

"Darling, no more. Let's go downstairs and wait for the police." He tried to guide her away from the ruin.

She broke free of him. "No. This is my home." She forged through the wreckage to her bathroom, her once tranquil sanctuary. The image of her precious dancer's makeup smeared on the walls and all her accessories broken on the floor seared into her brain, driving the emotion higher into her throat.

"Who would do this?" She spun around with tears burning her face seeking an answer from Nick. But as he reached out to shield her, she caught sight of what he obviously didn't want her to see. A symbolic eye with a cross slashed through it, like some evil talisman, inscribed on the wall in her favourite red lipstick.

She ran from the room tripping and stumbling, trying to find a safe place. Hiding behind her bedroom door, she curled herself into a ball, rocking and sobbing with her eyes closed, trying to block it all out.

Nick crashed after her then knelt beside her. "Darling, please come away from here. We have to go downstairs and touch nothing. The police will be here soon."

"Who would do this to me?" She whimpered like a lost child.

"I don't know, darling. But I'm here. I'll look after you."

"I can't believe this has happened, just when everything seemed to be going so well. Why, Nick, why?"

"I don't know, darling. But we have to go downstairs. Come on. Let me help you up."

"Puss Puss? Where's Puss Puss? Oh God," she cried, trying not to imagine the horrors that had befallen her new pet, her mother's treasured companion.

"It's okay, darling. Puss Puss isn't here. She's with SallyAnn, remember?" Nick enfolded her into his arms, and she wanted him to absorb her fear, her pain. To bear it all for her.

Trembling, she struggled to her feet with Nick accepting all her weight. Dazed and undone, she allowed him to lead her downstairs and out to the limousine.

"Roger, stay with her, please. I'll be back."

NICK RAN BACK INTO the townhouse and began his search. Trying not to disturb too much evidence, he scoured downstairs until he found the box of Michele's parents' wartime love letters. Although some of the contents remained inside, others were scattered everywhere. Those around him that were still intact he plucked from the floor and returned to the box. Scanning for more memories, he bundled up any photo albums within arm's reach. The sound of sirens foretold his time was nearly up so he jammed whatever else he could into the box and dashed back to the limousine.

He thrust the box at Roger. "Put these in the boot where they can't be seen. Behind our luggage."

Without question, Roger obeyed.

THE NEXT FEW HOURS were a haze of flashing blue lights, endless questions and police stamping in and out of Michele's home. By the time Detective Graham Thompson arrived, she was too exhausted to register his presence as significant. However, Nick missed nothing.

Striding up to greet Cindy's fiancé, Nick outstretched his hand. "I assume since you're here, there's a connection between this catastrophe and your narcotics division?"

Graham side-stepped the question. "I'm not at liberty to say anything, Nick. However, I see you're pretty good at piecing together jigsaw puzzles."

"As I thought," Nick said with a nod. "It's the symbol they scrawled on the bathroom wall, isn't it? It's somehow connected with a drug gang or something?"

Graham pursed his lips. "If you'll excuse me, Nick. I have work to do." Before going into her townhouse, Graham leaned into the car and spoke briefly to Michele. Looking up with a final nod to Nick, he strode to the crime scene to do his job.

"I'm taking you home," Nick said to Michele. "Roger, we're leaving." Roger started the car while Nick slid in beside her. "Home to my place."

"Yes, sir." Roger pulled away from Michele's townhouse for the last time.

"But Elissa?" she squeaked, staring into Nick's determined eyes.

"My problem, not yours, darling." He squeezed her hand and steeled himself for the next catastrophe.

"I UNDERSTAND HOW AWFUL this is, but we have our own issues and one of them is her." Elissa's accusation hurtled down her arm in the direction of the guest bedroom.

Nick tried to quieten his wife, hoping Michele wouldn't hear their quarrel. "I suggested she come here tonight. It wasn't her idea. She said she could stay with one of her friends, but I insisted she'd be safer here."

"Really? So you bring her here and put me at risk." Elissa's fury grew.

He was done negotiating.

"Very well, Elissa." He stepped into her space. "We've had this discussion about Michele before. Neither of us has been happy for a long time, and the open marriage arrangement hasn't worked for either of us."

"Really? Well, just so you know, I haven't loved you long before she came into our lives." Venom dripped from her words.

"As I said, we haven't been happy, and this wasn't the way I wanted to broach the topic. I'm sorry, Elissa. But I want a divorce."

"What? So now you want a divorce? Well, that doesn't give you the right to dump me like a bag of shit you know."

"That isn't my intention. I'll make sure you're well looked after."

"You're damn right, you will!"

He ignored the threat. "Let's make this as amicable as possible. Due to the current circumstances with Michele having no place to live, she'll be staying here, with me."

"How dare you? This is my home."

"No, Elissa. This is *my* home. You still have your home in Sydney. I'll make available to you whatever you need to move back there if you wish."

"Are you serious?"

"In the meantime, we'll find a suitable apartment for you to live in until you decide what you want to do. I'll move into the other guest room until you find somewhere to live. I'm sorry. But I know this will be the best for both of us in the long run."

Using his best conciliatory manner, he approached his wife, but she glared at him, turned and retreated to the en suite, slamming the door behind her. He collected his clothes and heard her muffled crying behind the door. As much as he deplored what had just happened, he was resolute in his commitment to start a new life with Michele.

ALTHOUGH SHE COULD HEAR the battle blazing at the other end of the house, Michele couldn't quite make out what was being said. *It would've been so much easier if I'd gone to stay with Julie,* she thought. But Nick had insisted. Still, she was pleased to have a man around after what had happened. He'd tried his best to salvage her treasured memories, which made her love him even more.

Then another man appeared, his image flashing across her phone.

"Hey, baby, are you all right?" Mark's familiar voice swept around her, cradling her under his shoulder, protecting her.

"Mark, what are you doing calling me? I haven't heard from you for months."

"A police mate of mine on the Gold Coast called me and told me about this woman's place getting trashed and the fuckin' eye on the wall. I asked what the victim's name was and when he told me I couldn't believe it. Fuck. I'm so sorry."

"Sorry for what?"

"For everything. These are the bastards who've had a contract out on me and now it seems they've targeted you somehow. Maybe they did see us together at the Sugar Roll Club that night, or the strip club or Venezia Palazzo. I don't know. Fuck. Where are you now?"

She told him about her relationship with Nick and how he was taking care of her. She especially made a point of explaining Nick was going to divorce his wife for her.

"He sounds like a good man, baby. I'm happy for you." Yet his voice didn't resonate with its usual cheery tone.

"Listen." He turned serious. "I'm sure you'll be safe. These fuckers do this type of warning once and then disappear. Even if they're watching you, they'll soon see you're no threat to them. I've made sure the coppers will be doing twenty-four-hour surveillance on you for a while so there's no need to worry. You'll be fine."

"Fine? Really? Do you know what fine means?" Her reminiscence brought a lightness to their conversation.

"Sure do, baby. Frustrated, insecure, neurotic and emotional. Describes me perfectly. Anyway, I'm glad you've got someone looking after you and the boys in blue up there will take care of the rest. If you need anything, let me know."

"Thanks for the call, Mark."

"If you want, I'll give you a call in a few weeks to check on you?"

"No need. Save it, gorgeous. See you around." She released him from making, then breaking another promise.

"No doubt." His laugh danced on the end of the line as he ended the call.

Although his contact had quieted her concerns over the attack on her home, it had resurrected a ghost she thought she'd exorcised earlier that day.

~ ♥ ~

At Divinities early the next morning, the four girlfriends picked over their breakfast with much less enthusiasm than what the forensic officers had done the previous night at Michele's townhouse.

"You can cut the air with a knife," Michele said after telling her friends about the energy in the Stavros's house.

"Sweetie, come stay with Graham and me," Cindy said again. "We've got room."

"No, Cindy. You're with Graham now and the last thing he wants is a 'crime victim' living in your house. He's been wonderful just being on the case. You two have enough to worry about with your wedding coming up in a few months."

"Then come live with me until Elissa moves out," Julie said, sipping on her cappuccino. "I'm single and fancy-free at the moment. It'll be fun."

"I have Puss Puss, and you can't have animals in your apartment." Michele shrugged with a despondent sigh. "By the way, SallyAnn, I'll pick up Puss Puss this afternoon. Thanks for looking after her. Thank God she wasn't at home when those freaks destroyed everything. I don't know what I'd have done if they'd hurt her." Everyone shuddered. "At least at Nick's, she's with me, and we're both safe."

"I can't believe this happened. Just as everything was falling into place for you, 'Chele, and now this." SallyAnn leaned over and squeezed her friend's hand. "What are you going to do about all your stuff?"

"I can't do anything. Everything that can be has been bagged and tagged as evidence. Everything else is only any good for the tip. I still can't believe it either. Except for what Nick salvaged, everything's gone." Her voice trailed off while familiar tears brimmed in her eyes.

"At least this whole episode has brought things to a head with Nick. He's turned out to be a winner," Julie said. "I must say I'm pleasantly surprised. Seems you've cured him of his womanizing ways. He's turned into quite the hero."

"Yes, he doesn't appear to be the same philanderer I remember from all those years ago. I think he really loves you and his actions prove that," Cindy said.

"Agreed. A man should always love the woman a little more than the woman loves the man. That's the best recipe for a happy relationship." SallyAnn's relationship recipe often appeared in their chats and based on her success, it was an award-winner.

"Yes, Nick's a good man. Even though he's going through hell with Elissa, whenever he's with me he tries to shield me from his problems. He's even told me to buy whatever I need to replace what I lost. I don't know what I'd have done without his support and generosity."

"Honey, you make him sound like a charity organization. The man obviously adores you. But forgive me for asking, are his feelings reciprocated?" Julie asked.

"Sorry. I didn't mean it to sound like that. I do love him. It's just that things are so . . ." Again, her voice lost momentum, and she struggled back the emotion. "Why did this happen to me? Why didn't I know it was happening? Why didn't I hear the message? What's wrong with me?" She covered her face in shame.

Though her friends reached out to ease her pain, no matter how much they entreated she wasn't to blame, she couldn't rid herself of a guilt that made no sense.

CHAPTER TWENTY-SIX

SPRING 2000

OVER THE FOLLOWING MONTHS, Michele began her new life with Nick. Having found an apartment within the week, Elissa had left when Michele was absent one day. Since then Nick had tried his best to help her and Puss Puss settle into their new home. Building a domestic nest of her liking while piecing together her event management business, Michele did her best to retain her independence. Although Nick supported her financially whenever required, she suspected he was suffering severe financial strain due to the upcoming divorce.

One day she arrived home unexpectedly to find him with his head in his hands at the bar.

"Darling, what's wrong?" She hurried over to comfort him, and when he straightened Michele noted his reddened eyes, as if he'd been crying.

"Elissa is determined to cripple me financially. I'm willing to be fair and reasonable, but she isn't. It's not just us I have to consider. There's still my two children and their mother I'm supporting."

"I knew this would happen. You should've waited to ask her for a divorce. I would've been all right. What are you going to do?"

"I'll work it out, but it looks like I'll have to start again for a third time." He poured himself a generous slug of scotch which he swallowed without flinching.

"Is there anything I can do?" She rubbed his shoulder, wishing she could do something to ease his pain.

"Maybe you can ask that goddess of yours if she has any suggestions?" he said with a strained half-smile.

"Maybe you could ask her yourself. All you have to do is stop and listen."

"Stopping is not my thing."

"And listening is also a skill you seem to be lacking at times." With a sassy grin, she reminded him of the repeated theme of their quarrels.

He nodded in agreement. "Anyway, just be here. Be my queen. Together we'll build a good life. I promise." He clutched her hand and kissed it.

She smiled but didn't reply.

Since moving in, Michele had questioned herself whether being with Nick was the right decision. He'd swept her off her feet with a well-planned strategy yet oftentimes she felt as if she'd been duped. Not only did she have to pick up the pieces of her own life, now it seemed she had to pick up his as well. Perhaps she'd been right from the beginning, and he wasn't her type? Her carefree single days seemed long gone, and she once more performed the role of 'the other half' in a man's life.

AFTER SEX THAT NIGHT, which seemed more of a stress release for Nick than lovemaking, she lay frustrated and confused. Forcing herself to be still and listen, she eventually heard the mantra swirling in her mind. *"You are loved, Michele. There is nothing to fear. You can do no wrong. Heaven is all around you and you are free."*

What's going on and why am I here? she asked in the silence of her mind.

"This is your home, Michele. He is your match."

"But . . ." She could list a range of arguments against the Goddess's guidance, but each sounded selfish, insensitive and unloving.

Next to her lay a man who'd given up most of his life to be with her. In fact, they'd both lost close to everything in the past few months. But was it love or loss that pushed them together? All she wanted to do was run away. She heaved a heavy sigh. Deep within her, she felt this was the right place for her because the synchronicity that had brought them together was irrefutable. Yet every logical thought told her otherwise. She reached out to stroke Nick's slumbering back and resigned herself to stay onboard her Trust Airways flight with this man.

"Trust overcomes tension. There is nothing to fear."

With the familiar feeling of not knowing how the future would unfold, she trusted the command from flight control once more, murmuring as she drifted to sleep, "Over and out."

THE CHILDREN PLAYED ON the beach, yet this time she knew it was a dream. The confident little boy turned to the girl and said, "It'll be all right. I'm here. We can start again."

The little girl looked at him and in a tiny voice replied, "I know. We can start again."

EVENT MANAGING CINDY AND Graham's wedding proved a delightful distraction for Michele. It was like producing a stage show, and she and Cindy revelled in planning every detail. Dresses, suits, music, table settings, menus, entertainment, guests list, everything was meticulously itemized and double-checked. However, one detail required special attention.

"Hi, gorgeous, I was hoping you'd pick up." Michele used her brightest tone.

"Hey, baby. Good to hear your voice. Everything all right?"

"Yes, all good, and you?"

"Can't complain as no bugger'd listen." Mark chuckled.

"The reason I'm calling is about Cindy and Graham's wedding. Just as a little background for you, Cindy knows about us of course, however, Graham doesn't." She paused, giving him time to digest the facts.

"Yeah, I figured that when Graham and I spoke about your case a while back."

"I know you and Graham are good mates and of course you and Karen have been invited to the wedding. I'm just calling to say there'll be no issues with me if Karen and I meet."

"I wouldn't think otherwise," he said.

"Also, I just wanted you to know Nick knows all about our affair and there's no issue with him either."

"Sounds like a good bloke."

"Yes. He's a great guy, and we have no secrets, which I must say is refreshing." She waited an extra beat to see if Mark would bite. He didn't. "I just wanted to make sure you knew before the wedding. Our past is just that. Our past." She sighed, relieved she'd covered all the possible scenarios for Cindy's wedding and that now, nothing could go wrong.

"Great," he said.

She knew him well enough to know he wanted to say something else. "What is it?"

He hesitated. "There's something I need to tell you."

"What?"

"It's about New Year's Eve."

"I already know. You and Karen had a baby boy." Her voice remained cool and even.

"Yeah. I should've told you. I'm sorry. That's why I didn't call you after that. All too fucking complicated."

"No, you're too fucking complicated. You've lived a life of lies for so long you don't know what to do with the truth. But none of it matters, water under the bridge. I was just calling about the wedding and wanted to let you know that your secrets are safe with me, Cindy and Nick."

"Thanks, Michele," he said in a subdued tone.

"It's okay, Mark. Look, we were meant to meet, we had a fabulous time and now we can move on without anyone getting hurt. Right?"

"Right." His command of the situation had returned.

"I'll see you at the wedding. Bye, gorgeous," she said with affection.

"Bye, baby. See you soon."

~ ♥ ~

RATHER THAN A RAUCOUS hen's party, Cindy opted for a full day of spa treatments before the big day. Eight hours of massages, facials, manicures, and pedicures proved the perfect tension release and girlie retreat. By the end of the day, and with towels wrapped around their heads, Cindy, Michele, Julie, and SallyAnn luxuriated in the après-treatment lounge sipping green tea, feet encased in fluffy white slippers propped up on footstools.

Michele tucked her robe around her legs. "Wonderful day, Cindy. Good choice."

"Yes. It was fabulous," SallyAnn agreed.

Julie turned to face Cindy. "By the way, I'll be bringing a partner to your wedding."

Michele and SallyAnn stopped mid-sip, surprised.

"Really? Who is he?" Cindy asked.

"Well, you've all met him." Julie paused and shot a tentative look at Michele. "You actually know him."

"Really? Who?" Michele asked.

"It's Roger."

"What?" Michele gasped.

Cindy swung her legs onto the floor with such force, she spilled tea on her robe. "You mean that waiter from Venezia Palazzo last year? That Roger?"

"No. You're kidding, aren't you?" SallyAnn asked.

"Yes. That Roger. Roger Bishop. I'm sorry I haven't said anything until now. I still can't believe it myself." She studied her friends then hurried on with the story. "After that day at the hotel, Roger called me. Surprise, surprise. Aside from the terrific sex, we found ourselves wanting to be together more and more. It was most unexpected. Roger was also part of the reason I didn't want to marry Tom."

They nodded and waited for her to continue.

"Anyway, when Tom left at Christmas, Roger and I became exclusive, which in itself is strange for me. I know what you're thinking. What am I doing with a waiter? But he runs his own limousine business and he's been successful in other businesses so he's not an idiot. He doesn't need to work a lot as he's made some shrewd investments, but he likes the interaction with people, that's why he does the job he does when it suits him. I'm as gobsmacked as you are. Believe me. So now, Roger and I are in a relationship and we're ready to make it public." Julie's wide-eyed expression mimicked the faces of her friends. "Please don't be mad at me, Michele."

"I'm not mad at you. It's just a lot to take in all at once." Reaching out, she patted Julie's fluffy knee.

"Rest assured that even though Roger has been Nick's chauffeur all this time, he's never once said anything to me about what goes on between you and Nick. Not once."

"I'm sure he hasn't. Roger's always struck me as the soul of discretion." Michele mimed turning an imaginary key at her pursed lips.

"Well, sweetie. In my opinion, that's wonderful," Cindy said. "My three best friends will each have a wonderful man on their arm the day I marry Graham. I couldn't be happier."

Michele considered a moment then said, "It doesn't seem right somehow to be chauffeured around by the partner of one of my best friends. I'm sure Nick would agree. I hope Roger won't mind losing our account? We'd rather have him as a friend than a chauffeur."

"Roger already thought that'd happen. That's why we've waited as long as we did before telling anyone, to make sure we're both committed to this relationship. Just between us, Roger would much prefer to join Richie, Graham, and Nick as mates."

"Well, that's settled then. I'm sure the three amigos will be just as happy to have a fourth added to their ranks. Nick and I will find ourselves another chauffeur."

CHAPTER TWENTY-SEVEN

THE WEDDING

"**What a fabulous setting**," Julie said. "Everything is so beautiful. I really love all the wild roses strewn everywhere. The whole thing is simply stunning." She, Michele and SallyAnn sipped pink champagne under the rose arbour after the afternoon ceremony went without a hitch. The theme of blush pink and cream reflected Cindy's sweet nature, her love of all things vintage and the wedding of her dreams from *Steel Magnolias.* With her three best friends and Graham's daughter as bridesmaids in four shades of floating gossamer pink chiffon, the effect was truly romantic. Now as dusk approached, the reception lawn glowed with fairy lights adding a whimsical magic to the wedding.

"Yes, Cindy wanted magic, so I thought, what would Disney do? And this is what she got. She's happy so that's the main thing." Michele surveyed the wonderland setting she'd designed with quiet pride, wishing it was her special day.

Richie, Nick, and Roger chatted at the bar, unaffected by the feminine fairy-tale around them. Nick and Richie were most amused that Roger had now joined, what Richie affectionately termed, the male crusade against the 'Chorus Line of Always Bloody Right.'

"Yes, I'm learning that," Roger said with a hangdog expression.

"As bitter a pill to swallow as it is, I've always tried to live by the old adage, happy wife, happy life." Nick laced just enough irony in his voice for his mates to nod in satirical agreement.

"Aye, Nick, you may be right. But Jeez, they're a bloody hard lot to keep happy." At Richie's accurate observation, the three men laughed and ordered another round.

~ ♥ ~

"So, where is he?" SallyAnn scanned the mingling guests.

"Over there, by the tree." Michele flicked her eyes in his direction.

"Where?" Julie asked, not seeing anyone.

"There," Michele insisted but as she turned, Mark slid in beside her. Her skin tingled from the warmth radiating from his body and as she breathed in his scent, she was transported back to their week's long sex-fest.

"Hey, Michele, good to see you." His bright tone flooded over her like a cleansing waterfall. It'd been nearly a year since she'd last seen him, yet the impact he had on her body was just as intense. Despite his nonchalance and cheer, he typified the primal male of the species, verified by her twitching groin.

Exhaling, she smiled up at him. "Mark, good to see you again." Their eyes locked, charged with fierce passion and memories. She took another breath, hoping it didn't sound like a gasp, while he waited for her to take the lead.

"Mark, these are my two friends, SallyAnn and Julie." Both had been observing the sexual tension between the ex-lovers in silent amusement.

"Good to meet you, SallyAnn, Julie." He nodded with a dreamy smile while the women regarded him with more than casual interest. Returning his attention to Michele he said, "I hear you're responsible for all this," and waved his hand at the setting. "Great job, baby." His unrestrained term of endearment in front of her friends rattled Michele. On the one hand, she wanted to thrust her tongue into his hot, provocative mouth and on the other she wanted Nick to save her from her own fantasy.

Then he unleashed the full potency of his vivid blue eyes upon her. "Gotta go. See you later I expect. SallyAnn, Julie."

He nodded once more and flashed his killer grin. Before anyone could speak, he walked back to a group of other guests.

"Oh my, God, 'Chele. He is a compelling character." SallyAnn was as flushed from the encounter as Michele.

"Certainly is. And he's built. No wonder you had such a great time with him." Julie gave a naughty smirk. "Do you know if his wife's here?"

"She bailed at the last minute. Their son's sick or something. Mark's here on his own," she said, thankful not to have to meet Karen.

"And what about Nick? Does he know Mark's here?" SallyAnn glanced at their three men enjoying male bonding at the bar.

"Absolutely. I doubt they'll go out of their way to meet each other. I'm just leaving it all in the laps of the gods, so to speak."

"Good idea," Julie said. "They're big boys. They can sort it out."

"Has Roger said anything to you about recognizing Mark from Venezia Palazzo?"

"I don't think he's paid much notice yet. But I'll have a quiet chat with him if you want?"

"Probably a good idea. Mark will play his usual undercover role and not approach Roger, but best to be sure. Thanks, Julie." She gave her friend's hand a squeeze.

SallyAnn interrupted and nodded towards the bride. "Cindy's looking for us. Let's go, bridesmaids."

By the time the official part of the reception was over, the band began to rock, and the guests stormed the dance floor. Nick, Richie, and Roger did their best to keep up with their errant bridesmaids but as expected, the women out danced them. Surrendering, the three crusaders left their partners to burn up the floor while they retired to the bar again. Soon after, Michele excused herself to visit the bathroom, leaving SallyAnn and Julie doing the hand jive.

As she hurried around the corner into the passageway, she barrelled into Mark.

"Sorry. I wasn't watching," she said, catching her breath.

"That's okay. I was." He had that playful glint in his eyes. "It's really good to see you, baby."

"And you too, gorgeous." She looked up at him, remembering every inch of his body.

"I've been keeping up with your case through Graham. I hear there's been no further developments, which is good." Seeing his professionalism creep to the surface proved even more appealing to her. "As I said, I thought you'd be safe. We'll never catch who did it though."

"I know. Graham's already explained everything. I'm just upset about everything I lost more than anything. Anyway, how's everything with you?"

"Everything's pretty good. And from the way you look, everything seems to be very good with you." He also seemed to recall every inch of her body.

When he grabbed her hand to twirl her around for more than a cursory glance, Michele's inner sex goddess hit replay. Images, feelings, tastes, sounds, and smells flooded her memory like a pornographic movie reel, igniting her body with sexual tension. She tried to quell her mounting desire by diverting the conversation to the present man in her life.

"Would you like to meet Nick?" she asked, forgetting her previous vow to allow fate to orchestrate their meeting.

"Probably not the right time. Maybe next time I come up to the Gold Coast the three of us could catch up then?"

"Okay. Perhaps I'll see you before you leave tonight?" She wished she didn't sound so hopeful.

"Maybe." He leaned in to kiss her cheek but instead whispered in her ear, "You're still the horniest thing I've ever seen, baby." He buried his head into her neck with a tempting bite then returned to her cheek, planting a polite kiss there. Struggling to drag his gaze away from her, he smiled then made his usual self-assured exit.

Left with a fluttering heart and a flushed face, she tried to shake off his sexual confession. Like a silly schoolgirl, she fussed over her chiffon layers and tried to regain her poise on her way to the ladies' room.

Suddenly, SallyAnn appeared from behind an enormous floral arrangement. "What was that all about?"

"God, SallyAnn. What are you doing sneaking around like Detective Clouseau?"

"Well, what do you expect? You, Mark, a large vase of flowers for camouflage, I simply had to see what was going to happen. It's obvious you two still have something going on between you, that's for sure."

"That man does things to me I can't explain." Michele's words tumbled out of her, thrilled to be released.

"I can see that. You're nearly as pink as your dress. But I have to say there's something awfully familiar about him, but I can't put my finger on it."

"I can't seem to explain it. It's karmic I'm sure. There's some sort of past life thing going on here. I don't know. He drives me crazy." Michele tried to turn off the memory tape in her mind.

"But what about Nick?"

"Nick, I love. Mark, I lust. That's about the only way I can describe it."

SallyAnn's gaze drifted upward as she considered her friend's response. "Yes, I understand what you mean. I love Richie so much, but sometimes I'd just like to have a mad impetuous affair with someone. Just once, that's all."

"Really? Would you?"

"Probably not. But I do envy the sexual adventure you've been on. You've gone out and got some, a lot in fact. And look where it's brought you. To Nick, who's made your life so much better."

"He certainly has. But . . ."

"But what?"

"Sometimes I wish I could have them both. Nick as the good man and Mark as the bad boy. Now that would be a happy-ever-after-ending, wouldn't it?"

Michele hooked her arm through SallyAnn's, and they headed to the ladies' room fantasizing and chatting about having two men as lovers.

CHAPTER TWENTY-EIGHT

SUMMER 2000

"I REALLY CAN'T BELIEVE how this year turned out." Cindy pushed her instep forwards onto *pointe*. "I mean look at us."

Standing next to her at the ballet *barré* Graham had built in her costume room were her three best friends, all limbering up. With legs and bodies stretching in every direction, they resembled the classic ballerina images painted by Lautrec, without the period costumes. With no air-conditioning in the little room, the three dancers wore the bare minimum of dance gear, permitting the perspiration to bead and drip from their limbs into splotches on the floor. In contrast, Julie had opted for a swath of floating polyester over her tights, which her friends thought oddly out of place.

Propelling her leg into a side mount, Michele agreed. "I know. Amazing really. It was about this time last year that I met Mark, fucked myself stupid for a while then met Nick. I won big at the races, buried my mother and inherited her cat, had my home trashed, lost everything and ended up moving in with the man who wasn't my type. All of which brings me to today, living in a beautiful home, playing queen to a man who adores me. Even his kids are terrific. As John Lennon sang, 'life happens when you're busy making other plans.'"

Working on her stubborn Achilles, Julie spoke through clenched teeth. "Seems following the advice of your Trust Airways pilot paid off?"

"Yes. Seems Nick was your type after all?" SallyAnn exhaled hard and tugged her right leg back into an *arabesque*.

"It seems so," Michele said.

"It doesn't get much better than this for me." Cindy's face shone with married bliss as she slid like hot butter into the splits. "Graham and I are deliriously happy." She threw her hands above her head with a squeal of a can-can dancer.

"Good for you, girlfriend," Julie said, still coaxing her obstinate ankles. "Let's hope that when the honeymoon hormones wear off you still feel the same."

Cindy threw her other leg around into a split. "Julie, you're such a cynic at times. What about you and Roger? You seem deliriously happy."

Julie stopped stretching and with a soft smile said, "In fact, we are. Who would've thought I'd settle down happily with just one man in cohabitation bliss?"

The others agreed but before they resumed their self-inflicted torture regime, Julie turned serious. "Girls, I'm pregnant."

"What?"

"Sweetie, no, really?"

"You're kidding, right?"

"Yes. I'm pregnant." Her lips curled in a half-smile and her intelligent eyes twinkled.

"What are you going to do? Are you going to have the baby?" SallyAnn asked the critical questions while Michele and Cindy stood by in hushed incredulity.

"Roger and I've been over this a thousand times. Because I'm forty-four neither of us thought our chances of falling pregnant were very high, so at times we haven't been as vigilant with contraception as we should've been. So, this baby is totally unplanned."

"Well?" SallyAnn repeated her initial inquiry.

"I'm twelve weeks pregnant." She ruched up her polyester sheath to display her tiny mound of a belly.

SallyAnn screamed with delight. "Oh my God, you're having a baby!"

Michele and Cindy stared at Julie, who, with the widest of smiles creasing her face, nodded again. They all threw their sweaty arms around her, hugging and kissing, jumping up and down, asking all sorts of questions until with her usual expediency, she quieted the frenzy to explain.

"I did tell you that I've always wanted a baby so here's my opportunity. I'm scared as hell to go through with this but if I don't do it now, I'll regret it for the rest of my life."

"Well, as my mother would say, dance through your life without regret." Michele patted Julie's tummy.

"*Ces't magnifique*," Cindy said as she tiptoed around the expectant mother. "I can't believe we're having a baby. We're all going to be aunties and there'll be a little 'Stone' to look after us when we're old and grey, just like we talked about at Pearl's funeral."

"Actually, that's not quite right," Julie interrupted, bringing the curtain down on Cindy's performance. "The baby will be a little 'Bishop.' Roger and I are getting married."

The tiny dance space erupted in more squeals, laughter, and leaps.

"A wedding and a baby for the one of us who couldn't find the man with the right gene pool," Michele said, directing her 'tut-tut' finger at Julie. "From the very first moment I saw him at Venezia Palazzo I knew Roger was a silent achiever. Him and his silent trolley and his delicious Devonshire teas. Ha!" All the women laughed as they remembered that morning and how they had tried to embarrass poor Roger.

"Yes, and all I wanted to know was whether he liked cream as much as I did," Julie recalled, licking her lips in her trademark fashion, her green eyes flashing.

"Well, he certainly gave you lots of cream," SallyAnn said.

"And now you're having a baby." Cindy had resumed her sing-song performance complete with *pirouettes* and *pointe* patter to which they all applauded.

INSTEAD OF SITTING IN Julie's apartment on Christmas Eve drinking champagne and contemplating where their lives were heading, this year they celebrated the nuptials of Julie and

Roger Bishop in a low-key ceremony for about thirty family and friends at Nick and Michele's home. Pregnancy had begun to soften Julie's pragmatism, and she looked the blushing bride in a designer gown of ivory satin, strategically cinched to minimize her bump. Accompanied by Roger with his inimitable style and poise, they made a handsome, sophisticated couple as they pledged their 'I Dos.'

"Darling, you've done a wonderful job in pulling this together so quickly," Nick said, as they stood on the sandstone balcony of their house, his arm draped around Michele's waist. "You really are something, you know that?" He leaned in and kissed her neck, careful to avoid the single curl that cascaded from her up-style.

"Thank you. It is lovely, isn't it?" They surveyed their elegant gardens where the guests mingled congratulating the newlyweds. Brightly coloured Chinese lanterns dangled from the trees while the lawn glowed with more reds and oranges from candles burning in coloured bottles.

Deep feelings of contentment coursed through Michele as she crooked her arm through Nick's. "Thank you, for everything." She gazed into the depths of his dark eyes feeling loved the way Disney had promised.

"You're welcome."

She turned to face him. "When did you know you loved me?"

"From the moment I laid eyes on you. I knew I'd been searching for you all my life."

"Really?" She remembered how intent he'd been on their first meeting to sit with her alone, listening to her prattle on about her new lover, her previous marriage, and her future dreams.

"Yes. Right from then. In fact, it felt like I'd been searching for you for lifetimes. And the strange experience you had that night when you thought you were levitating was my omen telling me I was right. That's why, no matter how hard you fought against it, I had to make you love me. I wasn't going to lose you this time." His gentle fingers caressed her cheek in his customary gesture of affection.

"And the kings and queens speech? Why do you keep talking about that?"

"I grew up in a Greek home where men are treated as the head of the household. I know you hate that way of living, but in my traditional world men are supposed to look after their wives, to keep them safe, so we're supposed to act like kings and the wives are supposed to act like their queens."

"But that leaves no room for the couple to be equal, to be united, to have their own lives and identity. It implies men are higher up on the hierarchy than the women." She could feel the familiar irritation stirred by his chauvinistic view on relationships building up within her.

"No, it doesn't. It just means men and women are different. That they balance each other. Like the two of us, we are equal, we balance each other. I've never asked you to give up your independence to be with me. Have I? I've never stopped you from doing anything you wanted?"

Michele nodded her agreement. That was true. There was no doubt Nick loved her unconditionally.

"I understand your need for independence, or at least, what you perceive as independence. But isn't there a tiny part of you that likes being taken care of?" He held up his hand, closing his finger and thumb toward each other as an indicator.

"Yes, I guess so," she said, recalling the safety and security Nick's presence in her life had given her.

"Darling, think back to what I said when we met. Actions speak louder than words. Have my actions not shown you how I feel?"

"Yes."

"Do you trust me to continue loving you like this for the rest of our lives?"

"Yes . . ."

Edging toward her a little more, his charismatic personality smouldered. "Darling, there's something I want to ask you." His voice trailed off, but his eyes asked anyway.

She held her breath, hoping he'd go no further. She loved him, but was she in love with him enough? *God*, she thought, *I must be crazy to not want all this.* She contemplated the lavish life he'd provided for her, yet there remained an emptiness she couldn't understand.

She scanned his face and realized he was watching her body language with his usual expertise. His ability to know what she was thinking was uncanny. Perhaps they had been together in a past lifetime? Realizing she'd wandered to another time and place it took a few moments for her focus to return. Even so, the ensuing silence hung in the air like the lanterns on the trees, full of drama.

Nick redirected the conversation. "Tell me, did you ever hear back from that lawyer friend of yours who was going to investigate your missing sibling?"

"No, as a matter of fact, I didn't. There's been so much going on since I spoke to Ben, I've forgotten all about it. I'll give him a call after New Year's and see what's happened." She looked at her watch. "I need to get inside and check on the caterers."

"You go ahead, and I'll play host out here. By the way, did I tell you how beautiful you look this evening?" His eyes ran over her body encased in an expensive sheath of royal blue silk. The diamond pendant he'd bought her for Christmas accessorized the plunging neckline, drawing attention to her breasts which she knew he longed to touch.

"Yes, you did," she said with a demure smile, glancing down as she tantalized him with a slight shoulder shake. Then lifting her face, she looked into his eyes. "Thank you." She spoke the words with genuine sincerity. Not just for the compliment, but for knowing he'd read her signals and hadn't asked her to marry him.

"Not to worry, darling. There's plenty of time."

"I know I . . ." But as Michele tried to explain her residual feelings of fear and loss, he pulled her close and eliminated her anxiety with a tender kiss.

CHAPTER TWENTY-NINE

NEW YEAR'S DAY, 2001

AT LAST SHE SENSED the loving embrace and heard the gentle mantra repeating itself in her mind, "*You are loved, Michele. There is nothing to fear. You can do no wrong, Heaven is all around you and you are free.*"

Since moving in with Nick and becoming a part of his hectic life, she'd given little time to herself. Now, having completed the mammoth task of cleaning up after their New Year's Eve party and with Nick settled in for the day with his newspapers, she retreated within. Even though she was a little out of practice, she still found her peace within minutes, in much the same way her body revitalized its cellular memory to execute moves she'd not danced in years.

She focused her mind on a vast lake with shafts of light dancing across its still, dark surface. Once all other thoughts were expelled, she opened the conversation with her standard question, "Is there anything I need to know at the moment?" Then practising the lesson of patience, she waited until an answer came.

"*Close but not close enough,*" the Goddess said.

"I don't understand. Not close enough to what?"

"*You will know when you're there. Soon.*"

Confused by the ambiguity of the Goddess's counsel, she decided to ask a more specific question.

"But is being here, with Nick, the right place for me?" She still suffered from doubts about giving up her single life and freedom despite her deep-seated desire for a Disney happy-ever-after ending.

"Trust overcomes tension. Trust you are in the right place and the right time. Trust."

"Are you sure?"

"He is your match, Michele. You have been together before. He is your king."

"Not you too? This king and queen thing is wearing a little thin."

"A king's role is to please his queen. You will see."

Then her mind snapped to black, like a theatre at the end of the show when the stage manager switches off all the lights and the cast and crew go home. Inky blackness enfolded her, and she drifted into higher consciousness. On a molecular level, she remembered the little boy and girl playing on the beach together. Except this time, they weren't alone. In the background sat a king and a queen on thrones watching them.

The confident little boy turned to the girl. "It'll be all right. I'm here. We can start again."

Before the little girl replied, the king spoke in a deep, sonorous voice, "Children, you are safe. We are all here."

Michele searched for meaning, but the scene dissolved, and she returned to a quiet state of heightened consciousness. Gradually opening her eyes, she noticed the missed calls and messages from SallyAnn flashing across her phone.

"Thanks for calling back. Are you busy? Can I pop over to see you?" The distress in her friend's voice brought Michele back to third-dimensional reality with a jolt.

"Of course, honey. What's the matter?"

"I'll tell you about it when I get there."

"Is everyone all right, Richie, the kids?"

"Yes. Yes. They're fine. It's me I need to talk about. See you soon." SallyAnn was gone before Michele had time to say goodbye.

WITH THE DOOR TO Michele's home office closed, SallyAnn wasted no time. "I've done a terrible thing." She sprang up from the chair and paced up and down the room.

"What? What have you done?"

"Last night at your party. I don't know what came over me. I just lost all control. Oh God, what am I going to do?" She spun the rings on her fingers around so hard that red welts were forming.

Michele reached out and grabbed her hands, forcing her to sit down. "SallyAnn, stop. What are you talking about?"

"It was your ex-friend-with-benefits. Mr Grey Suit, who looks like Jude Law."

"Craig? What about him? What did he do?"

"It's not what he did. It's what we did." She dropped her face in her hands.

Michele stared at her girlfriend. "Go on."

"Well, you know how handsome I thought he was when we spied him at the races? And you know how much I've been looking for a change? And how much I admired the sexual adventure you'd been having? Well, you bundle all those elements together and throw in too much vodka, dancing and . . ." She winced at the memory.

"What did you do?"

"He cornered me at your party last night in the bathroom and we . . . Oh, God," she moaned, returning to attack her fingers.

"For God's sake SallyAnn. What happened?"

"Lots of grabbing, kissing, touching, he wanted me, and I wanted him," she said as if it was obvious. However, the only thing obvious to Michele was the crimson flush accelerating up SallyAnn's throat.

"But did you fuck him?"

"No."

"Did he finger you?"

"Absolutely not."

"Did you give him a hand job or a head job or vice-versa?"

"Of course not."

"So, why all the dramatics? You just got a little hot and sweaty for a couple of minutes with Craig. He's very charming and you've had the hots for him since you first saw him. I don't think it's such a big deal unless you intend taking it further?"

"No, I do not intend taking it further. It was a mistake. I lost my head. I just don't know what to do about it." Her current regret obviously replaced the remembered thrill.

Clasping her friend's hands in her own, Michele spoke with calm consideration. "Listen, what happened could be seen as a lack of judgment on your part. It happens. You just made your fantasy a reality for a few minutes. That's all. I think you're beating yourself up too much about it."

The colour drained from SallyAnn's face. "I feel so guilty I want to throw up."

"The best thing to do is tell Richie."

"Oh, God. I can't. He'll be devastated. He'll divorce me." SallyAnn's voice squeaked through the fear clenching her throat.

"No, he won't. Listen, you remember how awful it was for me when Adam used to go out, do the 'beats' to pick up men for sex and never tell me about it? I intuitively knew something was going on and it used to drive me crazy because he'd never admit it. I thought I was going mad, like I was some sort of insane, jealous bitch, which I knew I wasn't. His secrets made me doubt myself. Then he'd finally fess up, proving that what I thought all along had been true. You remember all that?"

SallyAnn nodded like a small child beginning to understand a parent's advice.

"Well, you can't do that to Richie. He's too intuitive. He'll know. He deserves better. He deserves to know the truth. You must tell him, SallyAnn. If you don't, this will only get worse."

"But what will he do? Oh God, I can't."

"He'll forgive you. It was just a bit of slap and tickle. Anyway, you've always said a man should love the woman a little more than the woman loves the man. Well here's your chance to put that relationship recipe of yours to the test."

"But I'm so scared." SallyAnn's body remained tense.

Michele looked into her friend's eyes, "Honey, marriage is not the place to have secrets. I was on the receiving end of living with a man who kept secrets. In the past twenty years, you've had this one tiny transgression. Don't keep this a secret. Believe me, Richie will be okay. You have to give him the chance to show you how much he loves you."

"But he'll never trust me again."

"Yes, he will. The trust you both have is far stronger than this one tiny episode. You'll see." She hugged her friend for long moments until SallyAnn's anguish began to subside. In a more cheerful tone, she added, "It's just like taking a flight on Trust Airways. You don't know exactly where you're going or how long the trip's going to be or where you'll end up, but you can always trust on it ending well. And it does."

SallyAnn gathered her reserves. "You're right. I can't keep secrets from Richie. I'm just going to tell him and trust everything will be all right. There's no other option." She stood up ready to return home.

"Good girl. I can come with you if you want?"

"No. I have to do this alone. God, how did I get myself into this stupid situation?"

"Remember that old saying, 'the grass is always greener on the other side'? I think most of us keep looking across the fence wondering if it's true. All you did was leap across the fence for a few minutes and then you realized the pasture you've been in for the past two decades is much greener."

"How did you get so wise, 'Chele?"

"Because you're in exactly the same spot as I'm in now." This was the real answer to her procrastination about committing to a future with Nick.

Michele escorted her friend to the door. "Anyway, what I've learnt is the grass isn't any greener. It's just different. Go home and tell your husband. Then together you can make your grass even greener."

Giving her friend the biggest hug, SallyAnn turned on her best 'eyes, tits and teeth' and strode off to her car, readying herself to see if the truth would indeed win out in the end.

~ ♥ ~

STROLLING THROUGH THE HOUSE, Michele went in search of Nick and found him reading in the garden. She encircled his thick, strong neck with her arms, kissing him on his newly shaven and fragrant face.

"Would you like to join your queen in the spa on this first day of the year?" she purred into his ear.

He folded his newspaper. "Sounds like a wonderful start to 2001. I'll just go and switch it on. Would you like a drink?"

"Yes, please. Some bubbles would be perfect."

Set in the indoor-outdoor pool and with an uninterrupted view to the lush gardens outside, the position of the spa in the middle of the vast entertainment room was a dramatic statement. Its powerful Feng Shui and circular shape proved irresistible to countless house guests who'd slither into its watery magic during their stay. For Michele, it had become her new personal sanctuary, replacing the tiny bath in her townhouse.

Within fifteen minutes, they nestled together, sipping French champagne, with steam wafting upward and wrapping like a warm veil around their shoulders. The whooshing sound from the swirling water tuned out the everyday noises, adding even more serenity to the setting. Relaxing back against the spa jets, Michele watched the day's brightness filter into their beautiful home. Her home.

"Cheers, darling." He tapped his glass to hers.

"Cheers." She did likewise. "This is so perfect, darling. Years ago, I wrote in my goal-setting journal the type of house I wanted to live in. And here it is."

His dark eyes intensified as a knowing smile curled his lips. "And all with a man who you thought was not your type?"

"Yes. I did, didn't I? But now I know you are my type. You're the perfect match for me."

"Really?"

"I thought being with you stopped me from being myself, stopped me from being independent and doing the things I wanted to do. But now I know that's only true if I make it so. With you I have security. With you, I have the space and freedom to explore more of myself without having to worry about the mundane things of life."

Placing his glass on the edge of the spa, he reached out to take her glass. "Darling, I cannot tell you how happy that makes me. I've waited all this time to feel your love for me. And now I have."

He reached over and clasped her face in his hands, tracing his thumb across her lips. Leaning closer, he kissed her. The match ignited and they combusted in a slow, intense burn.

His hand slid up to cradle her head while the other cupped her buttocks, pulling her to him. The intensity of the kiss travelled down the length of her body unlocking a deeper spiritual hunger. Driven by a passion she'd not allowed in her life since being given up for adoption, she let unconditional love course through her body. Like a deep restless river bursting through an impassable dam, her spirit reached into his, merging. As one, they swirled in the rushing waters, entangled legs hugging tight, making love. Real love. Ever deeper into each other they ventured, feeling an unwavering trust binding them, across lifetimes. The water thrashed across their bodies, and they exploded into bliss, sealing their destiny.

Spellbound, they lingered in the moment, holding tight. Quiet moments passed and when they drifted apart, the more subdued rhythm of the water washed over them, cleansing their heightened senses. For the first time, she believed they were sexually compatible.

"More champagne, darling?" he said, casually.

"Thank you. That was wonderful."

"As I said, we just needed a little practice and a whole lot of love." He kissed her cheek. "Darling, will you marry me?"

Although her old doubts and fears tried to resurface, she held firm and trusted.

"Of course I'll marry you. Every man needs a woman to be his queen. And just like the game of chess, the queen protects the king." With this simple analogy, she no longer concerned herself with relationship hierarchies, royal or otherwise.

WITH THE FESTIVE SEASON in full swing, Michele and Nick stayed home, soaking up the sun and each other. Julie and Roger gallivanted around South America on their honeymoon while Cindy and Graham played parents to his daughter for the school holidays. On Richie's suggestion, the O'Brien family flew out to Hawaii for some quality time. One week into their holiday Michele's phone buzzed with a text from SallyAnn:

"Having the best time. Best holiday ever. Best sex ever with my wonderful husband. You were right. The grass is greener at home! See you soon. Love SallyAnn xxx"

~ ♥ ~

SQUINTING FROM THE SUMMER glare, Michele answered her phone, "Hello. This is Michele."

"Hey, baby. Why so formal? It's me." Mark's bright voice matched the sunlight.

"Hey, gorgeous. Sorry. I'm sitting in the sun. Didn't see your name."

"I'm coming to the Goldie in a couple of weeks and thought maybe we could catch up?"

She looked over her sunglasses at Nick basking like a lizard on the other side of the pool. "Maybe. Wait a minute. I'll ask Nick." She flattened the phone to the sun lounge and said, "Mark's coming to the Gold Coast in a couple of weeks and wants to know if we can catch up. All of us, not just him and me." She added the last phrase although she wasn't entirely sure that was his meaning.

"Sure. Why not?" Nick said. "Tell him to come here."

She returned the phone to her lips. "Sure. What day were you thinking?"

"How about Thursday night, the twenty-fifth, the night before Australia Day?"

"Okay. Thursday the twenty-fifth, six P.M. at our place," she said, with Nick nodding in agreement.

"Don't worry about food. I'll grab something on the way. Text me the address, and I'll see you then."

"Okay. See you then." She looked at Nick waiting for him to speak, but he didn't. Closing his eyes, he returned to his sun worship with an enigmatic smile on his face, leaving her alone with thoughts of her ex-lover's impending visit.

CHAPTER THIRTY

THURSDAY, JANUARY 25, 2001

NO MATTER WHAT SHE did, she couldn't stop her hand from shaking as she applied her lip liner, so she leaned her elbow on the cabinet to steady herself.

"My, my. We haven't been this nervous in a while?" Her sex goddess stretched like an awakening tiger, sending shivers through Michele's body.

Although the familiar sexual excitement had resurfaced, so much had happened over the past year that it only added more confusion to how best to approach Mark's visit. A final assessment of the floor-length purple dress she'd chosen and the drama of its Grecian styling, made her feel more confident, quietening her nerves a little. If she could handle catastrophic nights re-blocking shows when over thirty per cent of her dancers were missing while cajoling lead artists onto the stage during domestic arguments, she could handle tonight. With a deep breath and a wiggle of her hips, she smoothed her dress, admiring how the filmy over-layers swished. At least she looked the part, the self-assured hostess, queen of all she surveyed.

"So?" she asked out loud, but there was no answer. The Goddess had given her advice that morning with more cryptic messages around the usual themes of trust overcoming tension, love being all around and there being nothing to fear. Yet Michele couldn't settle the churning in her stomach. Even opening night nerves had never felt quite this daunting. To have Mark meet Nick in their home seemed like tempting fate and though she was more than capable managing difficult clients and events, the thought of handling these two men if things went sour was not a task she anticipated with eagerness.

~ ❤ ~

"So, DARLING, LOOKING FORWARDS to your boyfriend's arrival?" Nick teased as she settled onto her bar stool.

Nick wasn't a stupid man. Michele suspected he knew that she still carried strong feelings for her undercover lover, and if things had been different, she and Mark would've started a serious relationship. Who knows? It could've even led to marriage. It occurred to her that Nick's agreeing to have Mark visit them tonight was more than a friendly gesture. It was a calculated move on his part. Maybe he wanted to meet this mysterious man whose appeal still had a hold over her. She watched Nick behind the bar, realizing he orchestrated the entire evening at home on his territory, knowing that if he wanted to make Michele happy, being jealous wasn't going to work.

Nick's devilish grin lit up his tanned face and with his cuffs rolled up and his white silk shirt offsetting his darkly burnished olive skin, Michele thought his resemblance to a Greek god was uncanny. Summer suited him well. "Cat's got your tongue I see. This boyfriend of yours certainly seems to have a hold—"

"Stop. He's not my boyfriend, he's my ex-lover." She did her best to keep the past and present separate.

"Maybe, but who knows what might happen tonight?" Nick winked, giving her a mischievous smile. Instead of continuing the banter as usual, Michele fell silent and pensive.

"What's wrong?" he asked.

"Nothing. I'm just on edge. I don't want this turning into some sort of Contest of the Alpha Males or worse."

"Darling, don't worry. Everything'll be fine." At the mention of the magic word, the doorbell rang with a bright, cheery tone much like the man who rang it. "Trust me," Nick called after her as she sashayed to the door.

With his blue jeans and white T-shirt clinging to his strapping body, she noted nothing had changed much. Mark still oozed animal magnetism stamped with his killer smile.

"Hello, baby. Good to see you." He bent down, giving her a friendly kiss on the cheek and his provocative scent curled around her face like wisping memories.

"Hey, gorgeous. Come in and meet Nick." Ushering him into the entertainment room, she felt her hips swaying just that little extra. No matter how she tried, every molecule in her body betrayed her.

"Old habits die hard," her sex goddess quipped. Michele tried not to walk like a seductress but failed.

Remaining behind the bar, Nick offered his hand over the countertop. "Pleased to finally meet you, Mark. What would you like to drink?" The depth of his voice exuded control while his smile was genuine and warm.

Taking his hand in his massive paw, Mark shook Nick's solidly. "Good to meet you too, Nick. I'll start with a cooling ale if that's okay?"

While the two men metaphorically danced around each other, Mark accepted secondary alpha-male status in Nick's territory. Michele watched the men focus on each other, searching for an ice-breaker, a common thread that might bind them. Since Sydney was Nick's hometown, they shared similar geographic knowledge and recollections of the city's progress which gave rise to easy conversation.

By the second round of drinks, she discovered Nick's past included well-known underworld figures, giving further insight into a darker side she'd glimpsed in him when they first met. As the men chuckled about Mark's copper days and the crooks he and Nick knew, it became evident to her both men were like old mates, having a drink at the pub. The men relaxed and her eyes danced between them, comparing them, enjoying their differences and how they complemented each other. Yet it was Mark's features that held her attention, the crystal blue eyes and wicked smile, his inherent power and the graceful rhythm by which he survived. She wondered if she could ever stop loving him.

Nick studied his guest closer. "Did you ever go to a swinger's club called Gypsies about fifteen years ago?"

Before answering Mark paused, studying his host just as intently. "Yes, I did. I was working undercover at the time."

"You weren't as big as you are now, a bit flabby if I recall. And you had a beard, long hair pulled back in a ponytail and you called yourself Neil. Is that right?"

"Yeah." Mark's face lit up. "Fuck. You weren't bald then. You had black hair and an evil- looking goatee beard. You were a bit thinner too if I remember correctly?" He glanced at Nick's little paunch.

Both men laughed out loud, leaving Michele unsettled. "What? What is it?"

They looked at each other, working out who was going to begin. Nick took the lead.

"Elissa and I sometimes went to swingers' clubs and once or twice, if she didn't feel like it, I used to go by myself if they had a night when single men could go without a partner." He handed the conversation over to his guest with a nod.

"I was working undercover doing a deal at Gypsies on a night this fella of yours was there."

"No way. Don't tell me you two met years ago?" Michele said.

Nick picked up the story again. "Not only did we meet. We partied hard that night. Remember?" The devil in his smile shook hands with Mark's.

Mark continued. "That night there was this girl at Gypsies, who was looking to have a threesome with a couple of blokes. So, Nick and I did the honours." Both men slapped a high-five across the bar.

'You're kidding me. I've fucked each of you and yet you two had already fucked some girl together. I can't believe it." She looked from one to the other in amazement.

"It's true. It was a long time ago, but I remember it being a great night." Nick cracked open a bottle of champagne and began pouring.

"Too bloody right. She was a hot little number. What was her name?" Mark cast his mind back through the haze of years of drug use.

"Nicole. Her name was Nicole." Nick's mind was razor-sharp.

"That's right. Little Nicky, have some more pricky." Mark's laugh was as big as him.

Michele smacked his shoulder in mock disgust.

Nick handed fresh glasses of champagne across the bar. "Whenever she started to slow down that's what you'd say to her."

"Fuckin' hilarious it was. She just put her brain in a box that night, and we told her what to do. I can't believe it's you." The giant dashed around the bar to give his old fuck-mate a bear hug.

"This calls for a real celebration," Mark said, walking back to his stool. With respect to his male host, he held up a bag of angel dust. "Would you like some coke, big fella?"

"Why not?" Nick gave a relaxed shrug.

After slipping a credit card out of his wallet, Mark cut up the cocaine on a black marble cheeseboard that Michele fetched while he and Nick rabbited on about old times. Propped on a stool, she delighted in watching her fiancé hold court while her ex-lover's sheer presence beside her brought back treasured memories. To have the two men she loved most in the world together laughing and joking like brothers awakened a secret stirring within her.

"Let's have a hit of this." Mark bent down and snorted two long lines of coke. He then plopped down on the barstool, passing the note to her. Blowing back one line of dust, she offered the note to Nick, who didn't hesitate.

"I never knew you did coke?" she asked, while tweaking her nose.

"I never have. But this seems like a bloody good time to start." The other two applauded as he leaned in and dragged too deep a sniff, making his eyes water. But he handled the hit with only the slightest shock, his Greek pride preserved.

Mark stared at Michele, transfixed, much the same as she remembered him looking at her when they first met. The chemistry between them was as powerful as ever. Breaking away from his gaze, she scampered off to turn up the music.

"Since you two are old mates from way back, I think it's time to party." She skipped around in the middle of the room.

"Abso-fuckin-lutely," Mark said, striding over to join her.

Nick sauntered around from behind the bar and with the rhythm of Janet Jackson's music filling their senses, they uplifted their glasses.

"To you, darling. I'm a very lucky man." Nick toasted to his soon-to-be wife.

"Yeah, baby. What can I say? He's a lucky man."

"To both of you. I think we're all lucky. And to Trust Airways who took good care of me all the way." Each took a hefty swig from their glass.

"Let's dance," Michele said.

While she and Mark began to carve up the floor with their dance moves, Nick returned to his power position behind the bar. The rhythm of the music amplified the crisp buzz of the cocaine creeping up their bodies, enhancing the already festive mood in the room. With arms outstretched, she began to swirl around her dance partner, expelling all previous anxieties of tonight's meeting.

"You're still the horniest thing I've ever seen," he boomed over the music, stomping around her. With Janet singing 'Together Again,' they danced as if nothing between them had changed.

"I'm so happy." She threw her arms through the air. Then a thought snapped to mind, and she dashed behind the bar and whispered to Nick.

After he nodded his approval, she sprinted from the room like a cheetah.

Still jigging to the music, Mark sauntered over to the bar, gesturing toward her departure. "What's up with her? Everything all right?"

"Yes, she's fine." Nick grinned like the cat that ate the proverbial canary as the cocaine made its inaugural occupation of his body.

"You know what, mate, she's not in the least bit frustrated, insecure, neurotic and emotional." Mark smirked, wondering if she'd told Nick everything.

"You're right. She's not fine. She's amazing. Thanks for not leaving your wife for her."

"You're most bloody welcome, Nick. You're a better man than me, and she deserves the best." The two men toasted Nick's good fortune and Mark's candid self-appraisal.

"Okay," she called about ten minutes later.

"Let's sit down. It's showtime." Nick led Mark to sit on the edge of the spa, then he changed the track on the CD and dimmed the lights. He readied himself next to his reprobate mate to the sound of tingling chimes descending the octave. Mark sprang to his feet, clapping with frenzied enthusiasm.

Nick laughed, pulling him down. "Sit down, relax."

As Janet Jackson moaned, Michele glided around the threshold like steam in a sauna. Her summer-tanned body clad in black everything — lacy G-string, frilly bra, stay-up stockings, opera-length evening gloves and killer stilettos — arched against the door jamb. By her side was a rope, limp yet eager to be turned on.

On the first lyric and with unfettered sexuality, she began to prowl toward her audience of two. Every muscle rippled, every move seemed executed spontaneously, as only years of dance training can produce. Her audience was besotted. With graceful poise and long elegant strides atop come-fuck-me shoes, she captivated them. The power was hers. When she sashayed past them, their eyes travelled every inch of her body, not daring to look away, obviously longing to be the rope that would soon taste her deliciousness.

While Janet begged to be tied up, Michele wrapped the prop around her wrists above her head, thrusting her crotch at them before sinking into a deep open-legged squat, only to clamp her legs shut with an audible slap of female flesh. She dragged herself upright and with her knotted hands acting as a chastity plate hiding her pubis, she paraded up to them, enslaving them with her eyes.

Singling Mark out first, she placed her foot on the edge of the spa so the heat from her snatch could warm his face. He remained still, entranced by the offering as she squirmed and rolled her hips to the grinding rhythm. Then with a gentle kiss to his drooling lips, she lifted her leg high above his head and moved to her other audience. Pivoting languidly in front of Nick, she stretched forwards to expose her arse divided by a delicate strip of black nylon. It hid deep between her cheeks and called out to be freed from its captivity. Paying no heed to its call for liberation, Nick leaned in and licked each buttock. Michele held her downward position for a moment longer as her sex quivered, hoping one of them would touch her dripping desire.

Then slinking away like a water python, she continued her raw display of carnality in the dance. She was wild and divine. Her sex oozed and her wet panties crawled up between her folds to be swallowed by her hungry cleft.

Returning to Mark, she pushed between his legs until her sweating body was pressed against his. Singing along with Janet to be tied up, she bent down, kissing his face, watching his jeans bulge with desire. He reached out and rubbed his hands over her arse, drawing her to him, breathing her in again. Then he slipped a finger between her legs from behind, making her gasp with delight. Taking command, she stepped away while he licked his digit, his face glowing with lascivious intent.

Since Nick hadn't yet sampled her desire, she threw her leg over his lap, straddling him. Grinding at his cock and with her hands raised high above her head lashed by the rope, she met his gaze, giving him consent. He slithered his hands, finger by finger, up her thighs while Mark looked on mesmerized by the thrill of the spectacle before him. Perspiration streamed down her body saturating her panties until they clung to her wet skin accentuating the shape of her mons. Her ravenous open folds, just visible beneath the shadowy gossamer film, glistened as Nick gently slipped his fingers in either side of her panties, ready to plunder. He pulled her apart for a few moments and the cool air assaulted her slit making her shudder. While the men, with salacious stares, watched the sweat trickle into her private parts, Michele unleashed her dominating sex goddess.

Clamping her mouth onto Nick's, she sucked and bit at him hungrily. In an instant, Mark was behind her on his knees, unfurling his tongue on her arse, pulling her G-string aside so he could lap at her unobstructed. With a gasp of pleasure, she unsealed her mouth and dropped forwards into Nick's lap. Though struggling to hold her weight in her bound arms, still she elevated her buttocks to her diner's hungry face. Mark tore her panties from her, driving his tongue deep into her cleft. Groaning, she buckled at the knees, her face spearing deeper into Nick's lap.

"Fuck me please," came her muffled cry.

Without hesitation, Mark bundled her up like he'd done many times before. "I got you, baby."

Nick motioned to Mark to deposit their prize on some cushions he'd hurriedly positioned on the carpet. With her smooth mons exposed atop the bolsters, her plump breasts bursting from her bra and her stockings, gloves and high heels still in place, they prepared to work on her.

Caressing her thighs with his hand, Mark leaned his shoulder into her crotch without allowing their flesh to touch.

Nick whispered into her ear, "My queen begs to be fucked by the two of us, yes?"

"Oh yes please," she said, with sexual agony coursing through her body.

"Then your wish is our command," Mark purred into her snatch without making contact. Though her musk called to him to eat at his leisure, he controlled his appetite, waiting for his host's approval.

Nick stood up and undressed, motioning Mark to do the same. Michele looked up at her two favourite men with their rampant cocks above her, and moisture dripped from every orifice of her body. If one of them didn't start soon, she'd come out of sheer anticipation.

She reached up to grab a cock in each hand, tugging at them to get to the floor. Kneeling beside her, they soaked up the silky coolness of her gloves and the tantalizing massage she bestowed upon their cocks.

Mark reached his hand toward her crotch, and Nick peeled back her bra releasing her breasts to pop forth like champagne corks. Then with mouths sucking on each breast, fingers circling and probing her sex and a cock in each of her hands, her body spiralled with primal urges.

Moaning and writhing one way, then the other, she sought out a cock for her oral enjoyment, while their mouths and fingers devoured and teased her breasts, slit, and arse.

"I need to suck cock," she groaned, to which Nick obliged, thrusting his rock-hard rod into her mouth. She sucked with ravenous delight, as her other lover thrust his fingers deep within, hammering her to her first orgasm which exploded with shattering force.

"Right, let's go." Mark sprang down between her legs, throwing them apart to devour her clit and quivering sex. While he growled at her, his tongue darting in and out, Nick sat astride her shoulders so she could take more of his manhood. Every time Mark brought her close to climax and she tried to cry out, Nick gave her more cock, stifling her pre-orgasmic screams.

Her body was such a seething mass of uncontrollable sensations she thought her head would explode. Then as Mark fingered her to another climax, Nick tore his cock from her mouth. She let out a blistering scream to accompany her orgasm and she ejaculated over Mark's face, which he relished by lapping at her pummelled flesh.

Like dancing a gruelling twenty-minute can-can, Michele's muscles screamed for relief, stretching her endurance to its limits. But no matter who partnered her or his expertise, there could be only one star in this performance. And it was going to be her.

"Oh God, this is fucking fabulous." She flipped over to sit on her haunches, looking at her lovers.

Nick eyed off her open, glistening slit. "That's what's fuckin' fabulous." Like a lizard, he slid in under her, clamping his mouth around her hanging clit to punish it once more. As she rode his face, Mark plunged his tongue into her accepting mouth, rubbed her nipples between his rough fingers then sucked at them in the same rhythm he could hear Nick sucking at her sex.

Michele moaned as Nick fingered her, bringing her almost to climax before fucking her with his tongue. "I'm so hungry for cock. Two cocks."

"That's easily fixed." Mark sat opposite Nick, and with their feet touching and their legs spread as wide as possible, their cocks stood at attention together in the middle.

"Suck on both of these, baby." With his and Nick's cock in his hand, he waved them around like night batons.

"Yum." She crawled forwards like a feline predator and maneuvered her mouth over their throbbing cocks. Their size proved challenging, but she stretched her lips over the top of them and began to work them with her tongue. The heat and smoothness of having two cocks jostling for position in her mouth made the ache return between her legs. Judging by the moans of her partners, they ached for more as well. When she bent over to take more cock in her mouth, the cool night air contracted her snatch, but insistent fingers still entered her from behind, working in tandem, opening her up. One set stroked forwards teasing her G-spot while the other set swivelled backwards triggering a new sensation. Together the two men fingered her without mercy, blowing her again, while she demolished their cocks.

She collapsed and rolled over onto Nick's lap.

"I'll be back." Mark sprang to his feet and headed to the bar.

"Are you all right, darling? Is this what you wanted?" Nick sounded concerned.

"This isn't what I planned, but I'm loving it. Having two men at once is amazing. I feel like Diana, the huntress, and you two are my prey." She reached up and kissed him for more. "But are you okay with this?"

"Of course, darling. Watching you get so turned on is very exciting. We're all enjoying ourselves." He bent in giving her a tender kiss.

"Ta, da!" Mark held the cheeseboard with three lines of coke. "Here, baby, you first."

She snorted back a line with a *Bewitched* wiggle of her nose.

"Now lie back."

She obeyed and though exhausted, her body still craved more. After Mark tucked pillows under her arse, raising her snatch above her hips, he looked at Nick. "You're gonna love this big fella." He scraped a line of coke onto her mound. "When you snort it back to her pussy, leave a little at the last and lick it into her clit." Nick followed the instructions making her moan with pleasure.

"Now my turn." Mark lined up his hit and by the time his tongue rubbed coke on her clit, their bodies had fired up with more insatiable desires.

With her hips held high, Mark rammed himself into her, fucking her limp while she sucked on Nick's angry cock hanging above her head. Then spinning around, she took control and wagged her snatch in Nick's face for him to have his share, which his cock didn't hesitate to accept. On hands and knees with Nick fucking her sex, she wrapped her mouth around Mark's strapping cock, and he fucked her face. Then arching back on his massive thighs, he held her head until he exploded, giving her all he had. Without breaking tempo, Nick plunged himself deeper until he too unloaded himself inside of her.

With cum in her mouth and her snatch, she clambered to her feet, every muscle aching but joyously alive.

The men lay spent on the floor, obviously appreciating her staying power while they tugged their cocks back to life. Ever on show, she cavorted over to change the track, and with Janet singing "My Needs," she danced around her two decadent lovers, lost in a world without inhibitions and taboos.

No longer needing encouragement from her sex goddess, she danced as if she'd just graduated to the realms of the Gods and Goddesses, reigning over her life in a fiercely independent, feminine way. If taking two men as lovers was so empowering, she vowed to partake of this divine pastime more often.

One after the other she stood astride her men's shoulders, riveting their gazes to travel up her legs to the glistening jewel tucked between them. Then with grinding hips, she lowered herself down into a deep squat, giving each of them a private, close-up of her open wet slit, reigniting their primitive instincts. On cue, they lifted themselves from their resting place clambering to bury themselves once more.

The night became a delirious sexual dance as they fed off one another's cravings, lustful bodies, and secret passions. They couldn't get enough of her nor she of them. Hours later, Michele found herself sandwiched between her debauched men. Having more body bulk, Mark lay beneath her, his rampant cock wedged tight and deep into her snatch. Behind them knelt Nick.

She felt the cold, slick lubricant smear across her arse. "I'll be very gentle, darling. Just relax."

Registering Michele's look of surprise Mark cuddled her onto his chest, lifting her arse to his fuck mate. "It's okay, baby, just go with it."

Penetrating her little by little, Nick edged his hungry cock into her anus. At first, the sensation was alien to her body, but she gave herself over to it and discovered an intensified sexual experience. Once inside, their cocks overfilled her, stretching her with their insistence. Her body loosened, and when the three of them found an even rhythm, she surrendered to this hedonistic orgy of three. With the tempo quickening, being fucked simultaneously in her screaming snatch and her no-longer virginal arse, Michele and her lovers exploded in a simultaneous orgasm, and she finally quenched their obsession. Like Diana, she was the vanquisher of men.

~ ♥ ~

AT FIRST LIGHT, THEY lay dozing and battered in the Stavros' king-size bed. Michele lay in the middle, entwined by the men who loved her most and who she trusted not only with her life but with her secrets. She mused on her current situation and smiled at the sleeping, contented faces of her twin Prince Charmings. Although not a traditional happy-ever-after, she appreciated the irony of the occasion.

Twisting her head to Nick, she realized he was the devoted king with whom she could spend her future. He was doing whatever it took to make his queen happy. He promised, he delivered, he matched.

Then turning her attention to Mark, she couldn't help but feel that familiar love for him. On a deep level, he connected her to a wildness of spirit they both possessed. He'd unleashed her, he'd set her free. She'd always love him for that. There was no denying their connection, yet, like wet paint on a canvas, it remained smeared and unclear.

For Michele, the three of them shared an untamed force; a love so extreme, so powerful, so trusting most people could never understand it. Even if they did, they'd disapprove. It was more than sex. It was a deep life-affirming pact of two men who loved one woman and she them, not equally but differently. Trust paved the pathway through taboos. She lay between her two magnificent men and realized she was in seventh heaven.

When sleep finally claimed her, with it came a gentle voice. "*You are loved, Michele. There is nothing to fear. You can do no wrong, Heaven is all around you and you are free.*"

CHAPTER THIRTY-ONE

FRIDAY, JANUARY 26, 2001

MORNING BLOOMED WITH THE innocence of a new world in the Stavros garden where Nick and Mark sat sipping coffees on the white, wrought-iron garden setting.

"Bloody great way to start Australia Day, mate," Mark said.

"Yes, it is." Nick leaned his elbows on the table to steady his coffee mug.

"You've got yourself a helluva garden here. It must take a team of gardeners to keep it looking this good."

Nick nodded. "It does. But my kids love it. They think that if they search long enough, they'll find nature spirits in the flowers."

Mark chuckled.

Neither had made any reference to the previous night's threesome since creeping out of the bedroom earlier to let Michele sleep. Because of an unspoken code, they avoided the topic and treated the day like any other. After showering and changing, they now enjoyed the mid-morning sunshine, chatting about inconsequential things like garden maintenance, kids and summer.

FEELING BRIGHTER THAN HER yellow sundress, Michele strolled over to join them. "Well, gentlemen, what can I say? Last night was wonderful. Thank you." She executed a petite curtsey accompanied by her best showgirl smile.

"You're most welcome, darling. I'm pleased you enjoyed it." Nick rose and walked over to kiss her on the cheek.

"Not sure what I can say?" Mark said with his usual mischief. "I just came over to meet Nick, and you took total advantage of me."

"Here we go again. Going undercover one more time," she said. "Now, do you want breakfast? I can do bacon and eggs if you like."

The two men accepted her offer of a hot breakfast when her phone rang. "Who could possibly be calling me on a public holiday? Talk amongst yourselves for a minute." She waved the phone then disappeared into the kitchen to take the call.

RETURNING A FEW MINUTES later with a mug of coffee, she slid into a chair opposite her lovers. Gone was the cheery expression she'd first greeted them with. Instead, her face was pale and drawn, and her heart raced.

"Darling, what's wrong?" Nick asked.

She stared at Nick. Trust. Truth. Nearly the same. One letter can make all the difference. Same as one phone call.

Recognizing she'd have to manage this event with her usual aplomb, she reverted to her trusty 'eyes, tits and teeth' technique and began. "That was Ben."

Before Nick could interrupt, she looked at Mark. "If you recall, I'm adopted, like you. Before my mother died last year, she spoke about a missing sibling. I thought it was just her dementia talking but since she was the last of my family, I needed to know whether what she said was true or not. I got a lawyer friend of mine, Ben, to dig around for me."

Catching the pause, Nick asked, "So, what did he say?"

"He discovered that my mum gave birth to a boy just before she met and married my father. She'd placed her son up for adoption and it seems she couldn't have any more children because of complications after his birth. That's the reason why they adopted me. It makes sense because Mum talked about my having a brother just before she died. Obviously not a blood brother, but in her mind, I'm her daughter and she'd given birth to a son before that. When Mum got more disoriented, she rambled on about who was going to look after my brother, and that I'd have to look after him now."

She sipped her coffee, doing her best impersonation of calm confidence.

"Well that's good news, isn't it, darling? There's someone out there who's related to your mum. In some ways, he's like missing family. I'm sure he'd be thrilled to know more about his biological mother." Nick sounded delighted her search had been fruitful.

"Yeah. Good for you, baby," Mark added.

"Did Ben tell you this guy's name and how you can find him?" Nick asked.

"Yes. He did. I know how to find him. That's the easy part." She looked from one man to the other, her eyes coming to rest on her guest. Then with a deep swallow, she said, "The hard part is his name is Mark Miller."

A silent scream exploded, drowning out everything.

Michele's mouth clenched shut as her hand sealed her lips, forbidding them to say more.

Nick sat motionless.

It was obvious Mark tried to absorb the body blow he hadn't seen coming, but the impact was too great. "No fuckin' way!" Like steam erupting from a geyser, his voice hurtled into the air, splashing its scum upon them.

"It seems so." Michele kept her voice even and low. "My adoptive mother, Pearl, was actually your birth mother." Michele's stomach spun like a low-level tornado while the day around her remained remarkably quiet and still.

"No fuckin' way." Mark shook his head in stubborn disbelief, his voice rasping in his throat. "This Ben guy has it all wrong. There's no fuckin' way your mother gave birth to me then adopted me out. Why would she do that?"

"That's what I asked Ben. From his investigations, it seems mum had been raped, and you were the product of that rape, so she gave you up. Then she met dad not long after that, and though he was willing to adopt you, the adoption records were closed back then, so they never knew what happened to you. The government has since opened old adoption records over the past couple of years, and Ben was able to track you down and piece this together." With a compassionate gaze and a tender smile, she tried to quieten Mark's anguish.

"No fuckin' way." This time, he said the words with a little less fright and fight.

"I know it's a lot to take in. But I trust Ben, and if he says it's true, I believe him."

Mark snarled.

"It's strange, but SallyAnn seemed to pick up on something. Wait here a minute." Michele rushed into the house and returned with some photos she scattered onto the table. "Look at these. These are pictures of my mum, your biological mother, Mark."

Mark leaned over the photos, studying them. Michele watched his face, hoping he'd see it. Suddenly, his eyes misted over.

"See, you have mum's piercing blue eyes." Michele pointed to the similarity. "And look at the shape of your faces. They're the same." Michele held the photo up for him and like a magic trick, the more he looked, the more obvious their physical likeness became. "I think this is what SallyAnn saw. First, when she saw the photos I'd taken of you when we were at Venezia Palazzo, and then at Cindy and Graham's wedding. She said there was something familiar about you. I think she was picking up the genetic resemblance between you and mum, your mother, but she couldn't explain what she was seeing."

Mark growled like a cornered beast. "Your adopted mother being my birth mother just doesn't work for me. This shit is too fuckin' weird." He sprang up and paced away.

Michele watched him prowl the gardens and longed to comfort him. But she knew he needed time. Then the recurring dream she'd had since she first met Mark, of the little boy and girl on the beach, flashed in front of her eyes.

"It was a dream of two children playing as if they were brother and sister. When you met him all these years later, I did say you were close but not close enough. Now you know why you feel what you feel. Why it was so hard for you to let

go of each other. You were meant to find each other." The voice of the Goddess swirled in Michele's mind.

The past eighteen months' worth of cryptic messages and roller coaster of emotions began to make sense. Her mother had given birth to Mark after a traumatic rape and had adopted him out. Pearl must have carried the guilt and shame with her for years. Then when her mum and dad tried to bring him back into their lives, they couldn't find him. So, they adopted Michele. Both she and Mark bore the same scars. Both had been broken and damaged. Their unresolved feelings of guilt, shame and emptiness had remained as guideposts to find each other and to bring them to this final destination.

When Mark marched back, it was obvious he'd had no such epiphany. The despair and entreaty in his eyes cried out to Michele. Her heart ached for him, but she remained silent.

"So you're telling me, although we're not in any way genetically related, your adoptive mother is my birth mother, and instead of me living with her all my life as her son, you've been living with her as her daughter?"

Michele nodded.

"But what do you want to do about this? I mean, do you want us to play happy families like a brother and sister, which is obviously what your mother, my birth mother, was trying to tell you? I'm not sure I can do that because I love you more than a brother should love a sister."

She cast a sideways glance at Nick who remained stony-faced. If she expected any indication from him as to how he felt about Mark's confession of love, she certainly wasn't going to get it now. She was on her own. With a deep breath, she began without knowing what she was about to say.

"Fly Trust Airways," the cheery little slogan resonated in her head.

"Listen, I'm as shocked as you," she directed her opening statement to Mark, like an attorney to the jurors. "This news does my head in. But aren't you in the least curious to know what your birth mother was like? How wonderful a person she was and what a loving mother she's been to me?"

Mark shrugged and sighed. "I guess so."

"I know we were meant to meet each other. What we did to and for each other in that first week we met will go down in the annals of my time, as pure awakening. Without what happened between us I'd never have met Nick, and he's the best thing that ever happened to me." She glanced at her soon-to-be husband with deep affection, which he reciprocated with an air kiss.

She returned to Mark. "As for you, without you, I'm not sure whether I would've ever truly trusted myself. Because of you, I let myself go, I learnt to be daring, sexual and alive. You gave me permission to do and feel things I never thought I could. You let me be me, to be free." The deep fondness for her lovable, incorrigible rogue flooded through her body.

"Thanks, you did the same for me too," Mark said. "You taught me to let the past go. To trust that life was going to work out better than it'd done before." His killer smile began to creep back across his face.

Michele smiled in return. "As an adopted child, I've always believed your parents are the people who love and raise you, not the vehicle who gave birth to you. But you have the opportunity here to know your birth mother through me. We could be each other's family for the rest of our lives. I'm sure this strange connection is why we were so drawn to each other and why despite everything, we couldn't let go of each other? It's like destiny pulled us together." She implored Mark to consider what she was saying.

He nodded and resumed his seat. "Maybe you're right." He waited a beat while his mind seemed to arrange his thoughts. "No matter how much I felt for you, I knew I had to stay with Karen. Just as well I trusted that gut instinct, hey?" A touch of brightness settled back into his expression.

Michele took his hand in hers. "Just as well indeed, seems we both fly Trust Airways. The thing is, we now have a chance at something more. We can have each other, we can love each other, just in a different way. You're one of the two men I love most in the world. I don't want to lose you. But I don't want sneak around and the three of us just have sex together.

I love you more than that, and I think you love and respect me more than that, too."

As she opened her heart to Mark, a deep peace welled up within her. The emptiness of all those years of not belonging disappeared. She'd found him, the big brother she'd always longed for. "I don't have to feel guilty about my feelings and neither do you. You don't have to go undercover to visit us. No more secrets from Karen. We can be a family if you want?"

Staring into his clear blue eyes, she reached out and touched his rugged yet boyish face. Breathing in his masculine scent, the familiar stirring in her groin no longer surfaced. She was free of the attraction and now she was free to love him as the family she'd longed for. Her voice was as soft as her touch on his face. "It doesn't matter what's happened up to this moment. I'm sure mum would've wanted us to be together. What do you say, gorgeous?"

Mark's eyes raced over her face, as if longing to be repaired, to be whole again.

"Well?" she asked again. Either he'd choose to become part of her life or he'd simply go undercover once more and she'd lose him forever.

"Well, my life's been pretty fucked up since my adoption. And I'd like to know about my birth mother, try to reconnect with where I came from, I guess. Okay, let's give it a try."

Scraping his chair back, he caught her up in a mammoth bear hug and spun her around all but squeezing the air out of her. Once more, Michele cried over Mark, but this time they were tears of joy, and she noticed he too shed some tears. At last, they were one. Not as lovers, but as family. When they sat down and clasped each other's hands, Michele suspected they resembled the children in her dream. Innocent, united and inseparable.

"Well, a more perfect day for all this couldn't have been chosen." Nick smiled at the two of them.

"What do you mean, darling?"

"It's Australia Day, the day to celebrate the founding of the colony of Australia, of its community. And here you two are, celebrating the founding of your new relationship as a family, of sorts."

"Yeah, you're right." Mark crushed her closer to him.

"Darling, thank you." She reached over to hold Nick's hand. "It's a wonderful Australia Day. Now I have a real family, you, my soon-to-be husband and your children and Mark as my adopted big brother. Life doesn't get much better than this."

"As I've always said, darling . . . happy wife, happy life." He brushed her cheek, celebrating in her joy.

"Mum was right . . . Now I can dance through the rest of my life without regret. I finally feel like I belong. Thanks to both of you." She kissed both men on the cheek and a deep serenity welled up within her. She was where she was meant to be, home.

"Time for breakfast. How do you like your eggs, Mark? We've got a lot to talk about. And then you'll need to bring Karen and your son up here to meet us."

While she prattled on, she looped arms with her fiancé and Mark, her feet dancing a little two-step.

Mark glanced sideways at Nick. "Looks like your kids were right."

"What do you mean?"

Mark cocked his head at Michele scampering between them and laughed. "You have got fairies in the garden, big fella."

"It would seem so, mate. It would seem so."

THE END

STAND-ALONE CONTEMPORARY ROMANCE FEATURING STRONG HEROINES AND PAGE-TURNING PLOTS

TEACH ME

When destiny beckons, what is a girl to do?

At twenty-four, Samantha O'Brien scores her dream job as a dancer at the famous Moulin Rouge, only to arrive in Paris to find her well-laid plans in disarray. Fortuitously, Sam is rescued by the eccentric, tarot-card reading proprietress of Hotel Hollandaise, who cautions that Paris is for lovers, but not always love.

As Sam launches into her new career, she suspects that the show's super sexy, Sicilian stage director, Tony Di Falco is more than just a creative genius and hard taskmaster, leaving her to wonder whether secrets are best shared.

Meeting Philippe Lacroix, a struggling, young artist in Montmartre saves Sam from imploding under the pressure. He introduces her to the city of love, captivating her with his angelic good looks and sensuous touch. Yet the mounting attraction intensifies between Sam and Tony, and their tense, sexually charged relationship threatens to overwhelm them. But the show must go on.

Filled with backstage bitchiness, tough rehearsals, a sprinkling of cocaine and the French addiction to cigarettes, Sam grapples with her new life. Then without warning, her destiny changes literally before her eyes, and she learns that even in the most romantic city of the world, you don't find love, love finds you.

Teach Me is the second stand-alone Contemporary Erotic Romance in Diane Demetre's genre-busting series, Steamy Secrets. If you love strong heroes, hot sex and feisty heroines, don't miss this page-turning love story with a twist.

EXCERPT

By the time Philippe opened the second bottle of wine, they'd devoured their baguette and the sun was setting, stroking the sky in Monet-inspired colours.

"It's getting cold out here. Let's go inside, Samantha." Grabbing the wine and glasses, Philippe walked indoors while Sam cuddled Jasper to her chest and followed.

"Come on, Jasper. Time for your dinner," Philippe said.

At the sound of the magic word, Jasper sprang from Sam's arms onto the floor where he was promptly fed a bowl of dry cat kibble. While Jasper chewed through his dinner, Philippe sat on the side of his bed. Aside from a rickety table and two chairs, obscured by pencils, crayons and sketchbooks, the double bed, bedside table and a wardrobe were the only other pieces of furniture in the room.

"Sit beside me, Samantha." Assigning their wine glasses to the bedside table, Philippe shimmied back onto the bed using the wall behind him as a backrest. When she settled in beside him, he said, "I would like to paint you. A real painting, for my exhibition. Would you sit for me?"

"I guess so." She was surprised that he wanted to include a painting of her in his exhibition.

"*Très bien.* Let's begin now." Philippe sprang off the bed and dashed to the table, where he rummaged around for the right implements. Finding a large sketchbook and several charcoals, he cleared a chair and dragged it in front of the bed. "You are my queen of the can-can. Like the famous dancer La Goulue. Here, I will arrange your pose."

Philippe fluffed the pillows for Sam to recline on, and she wiggled into place with a giggle. With great care, he clasped her arm and tucked it under her head as support. Trailing his hands over her body, he manoeuvred her this way and that, edging slowly to her hips. The strength and gentleness of his touch as he rolled her forwards to lay on her side ignited a subtle warmth in Sam's groin. His hand cupped her bottom, rolling her back a little to just the right angle, and she wished he'd dig deeper into her from behind. Taking her top leg, Philippe cupped her knee, bending it to drag across in the foreground. For the final effect, he reached to her other leg and pulled it straight beneath her, running his hands down her long limb to her ankle.

"There, that will be a good starting pose I think," he said. "Are you comfortable?"

"Yes, I think so." She was anything but comfortable. Moist and ready, her sex flamed. Her nipples yearned to be teased and her arse screamed for grabbing. The seam in her jeans bit hard into the folds of her cleft. She began to unravel.

"Are you all right, Samantha?"

"Yes. Yes. I'm fine." But her dilated pupils and shallow breathing betrayed her.

She was certain Philippe suspected what she was feeling because a lazy lascivious smile graced his angelic face. Michele sensed his wild, artistic spirit swirl around her like an unpredictable tornado. Yet he remained calm and lowered his sketchbook and charcoals to the floor. Resplendent in a flowing white shirt and low-slung cargos that matched the colour of his delinquent golden hair, he fixed her in his gaze and strolled over to the bed. Gazing down at her, he moistened his lips and exhaled with a slight purr. "Perhaps I can be of assistance?"

~ ♥ ~

TAKE ME

How far would you run to find love?

Aiden Bishop is a successful young lawyer hiding out in sunny Spain to escape unsavoury clients in Australia. At twenty-seven, Ace as he's known to his mates, happens upon a local flamenco club in Seville where he's befriended by Rafael Flores and beguiled by Carla Armando — a famous flamenco couple well-known for their fiery performances both on and off the stage.

With ancestral links to the famous gypsy flamenco dancer Carmen Amaya, Rafael and Carla have mysterious Romani culture coursing through their veins. Sensing Aiden's love of adventure, they invite him on a road trip from the Costa Del Sol to Granada in search of Carla's true Romani gifts. However, as the trip stretches deeper into less travelled emotional geography, long-kept secrets are exposed.

Brimming with gypsy traditions, the passion of the dance, mysterious rune readings and intrigue, Aiden realizes that he may be able to evade his clients, but he can't escape his destiny no matter how far he runs.

Take Me is the third stand-alone Contemporary Erotic Romance in Diane Demetre's genre-busting series, Steamy

Secrets. If you love strong heroes, hot sex and feisty heroines, don't miss this page-turning love story with a twist.

EXCERPT

"Well, tango is like having sex. Except instead of being horizontal, you're vertical. Here. I'll show you." Carla slithered her right leg in between Aiden's, the top of her thigh easing towards his crotch. "Now when we dance tango, we have to remain locked in this position, so we move as one."

"Carla, if I remain locked in this position, I won't be doing any dancing."

She giggled. "Why not?"

"First of all, I can't move, and second, I'd rather be doing the horizontal tango." A half-smile lurked on his face and his eyes twinkled with mischief.

"I see," Carla said in a soft, sultry voice. Tiny tingles raced from her toes, surging to her face in a hot flush. He'd not released his grip on her, nor the intense stare in which he'd trapped her. "Well, Aiden. That is tango. Tango is love. Tango is passion. You must love your partner. You must want to be passionate with your partner." The more she spoke, the slower her speech became. Gazing into his eyes, she recognized he had the requisite love and passion to dance tango. She moistened her lips, noticing how the slight movement with her tongue seemed to mesmerize him. "Let's proceed, shall we?" She tried to direct his attention back to tango.

Not breaking his stance or stare, Aiden said, "I'm ready."

"I'm going to step back on my right foot, and you step forwards on your left. Ready and step . . ." As Carla stepped back, Aiden obeyed with his left. Unsure of the power needed, he pushed too hard, and they stumbled. Quick as lightning, he crushed her in his arms lifting her up before they fell. He found his footing for them both though her feet dangled off the floor. His chest heaved, and she could feel his heart beating as fast as hers. With her arms wrapped around his neck, her face hovered at kissing distance and the yearning she'd disregarded since meeting him, resurfaced with a vengeance.

"Are you all right?" he asked, his masculine breath resting on her lips, making them ache.

"Yes. Thank you," she said, whispering her unspoken permission to be kissed.

"I told you I had two left feet." Aiden still held her firmly in his embrace, seemingly unaware of her weight and unwilling to let go.

Naked under her caftan, Carla felt her nipples harden against his bare chest. Glancing downwards, Aiden moaned. Suspending her in one arm, he slid his other hand to cup her buttocks, dragging her closer onto his body. His hot breath scorched her neck, and she pushed against his cheek like an affectionate cat. With his face tucked into her neck, his breathing deepened like he was trying to suck the life from her. Big heaving breaths tied them together as they caught each other's tempo. Expertly, his supporting hand under her buttocks flexed and contracted, squeezing her arse and made Carla squirm with desire. Unable to stand the insistence of his hand any longer, she crawled onto him, wrapping her legs around his trunk. The thin silk of her caftan did little to conceal the wetness between her legs when her cleft opened onto his bare stomach. "Oh God, Carla," he groaned.

Wrapped like two desperate souls, they clung tight to each other — she like a frightened child reluctant to let go and he the championing hero to her rescue. "Carla."

AUTHOR BIOGRAPHY

Diane began her career as a schoolteacher before moving into the entertainment industry as a choreographer, director, event manager, dancer and actress, working in television and live theatre, and managing multi-million-dollar productions.

Following her onstage career, she spent many years as a stress & life skills therapist, keynote speaker and presenter, appearing on national radio and television under the pseudonym of the Goddess of Love.

For her outstanding contribution to the arts, Diane was awarded the 2019 SBAA International Women's Day Leader Award for Leadership in the Entertainment, Creative Arts and Media Industry.

She is an award-winning author of contemporary, genre-busting romance, suspense and mystery novels. Her intuitive insights into human behaviour are woven into her casts of characters, heightening the intrigue in her storytelling. Set in exotic locations, her stories are packed with emotional punch and feature empowered heroines who live life to the fullest, much like the author herself.

Connect with Diane

https://dianedemetre.com/

AWARD WINNING AUTHOR

> 66 . . . Dare to dream bigger than ever before, dare to forge our own path no matter how hard the challenges. But most of all, dare to be you and let the chips fall where they may. We are all warrior women with gossamer wings . . . It's time to roar! 99
>
> — Diane Demetre

Winner of 2019 SBAA International Women's Day Leader Award for Leadership in Entertainment, Creative Arts and/or Media Industry.

Diane was nominated as a finalist in the ARRA Awards 2018 for Favourite Romantic Suspense, for her novel *Retribution.*

In 2017 Diane won the Romance Writers of Australia Emerald Pro Award for Best Unpublished Romance Manuscript.

ISLAND OF SECRETS

Two love stories separated in time. Two women following their dreams. In a paradise littered with painful secrets, will love turn the tide?

1973. Cecilia "CiCi" Freemont has a restless soul and the voice of an angel. Leaving her privileged upbringing behind, she chases her dreams to the sandy beaches of an unspoiled Hawaiian paradise, Harbor Island. But life takes an unexpected turn when she falls for the island's young heir-apparent and her newfound adventure becomes too much to bear . . .

2017. Investigative journalist Tina Templeton has dedicated herself to the pursuit of truth. But when she inherits Harbor Island, her career plans take a confusing twist. Managing the sprawling island estate is tough business even with the help of aging cabaret singer, CiCi Freemont. Especially when a massive ecological disaster threatens to destroy her beautiful beaches — and the responding coast guard captain steals her heart.

As the investigation into the disaster reveals a 40-year-old mystery that could change their lives forever, will Tina find love among the secrets, or will CiCi's painful past dash her dreams on the rocks?

Island of Secrets is an epic love story. If you like generations-spanning drama, characters with hidden pasts, heart-warming romance and intrigue, then you'll love Diane Demetre's powerful novel in paradise.

~ ♥ ~

RETRIBUTION

Winner of Romance Writers of Australia Emerald Pro Award 2017.

She's a ballerina with a dark secret.
He's a retired sniper with a tortured past.
Will they find love or fall prey to a stalker's deadly game?

Professional ballerina Jessie Hilton wraps her battle scars in satin pointe shoes, but there's a deeper hurt that haunts her sleep. When a handsome man steps in to save her from a mugging, something about her hero makes her heavy heart leap. Though her career can't afford distractions, he may be her sole source of safety when she gains the unwanted attention of a relentless stalker.

Ex-sniper Brad Jordan survived his tour of duty, but a tragic accident cost him the lives of those closest to him. With his faithful border collie Whiskey by his side, Brad gets a second chance when he protects the beautiful Jessie from danger. When the ballerina's stalker grows more brazen, Brad's tactical training may be their only weapon against tragedy.

Will Jessie and Brad survive a deadly game or will the assailant destroy their chance at love?

Retribution is a stand-alone romantic suspense novel. If you like tough-as-toe-shoes heroines, second-chance romance, and page-turning plots, then you'll love Diane Demetre's heart-stopping saga.

PRAISE FOR DIANE'S WORK

An exciting and erotic read A refreshing genre-busting story of a divorced, older (I hasten to add by society's standards not mine) heroine who is determined to embrace her singledom while simultaneously casting aside her self- and societally-imposed sexual repression through casual erotic encounters. Diane Demetre offers a story that challenges our pre-conceived notions of what "women of a certain age" should or should not be doing and she does this in an empowering manner. The heroine embraces and cherishes her female friendships and though this aided in the flow of the plot, it also highlights the importance for women of having encouraging and supportive female companionship. Most importantly, we see the heroine herself allow the experiences of her new-found freedom to shape her own future thus enabling her to escape the repressive nature of her pre-divorce life. All in all, an erotic and exciting read sure to captivate and thrill readers of any age.

— AusRom Today

I found this to be an amazing read and I adore the author's writing style. I was captivated by the setting, the characters, the Romani culture and the story line twists and turns. A fast flowing novel with just the right amount of eroticism thrown in. I fell in love with one of the lead characters (Aiden Bishop) very quickly and the relationship between Rafael & Carla had me wondering what would eventuate next. Well done Diane Demetre.

— 5 STARS, Robyn Powers

This is the third book I've read by Diane Demetre and I was absolutely delighted! What a great read. It has everything: a great story line mixed with sensual exploration; mystery; spirituality and wonderfully complex main characters. Couldn't put it down. Loved Aiden – just gorgeous and every woman's dream. Looking forward to the next book.

— 5 STARS, Deborah Bispham

Demetre paints vividly the atmosphere of Paris and the Moulin Rouge with such detail that it adds yet another layer of intimacy to the story. A wonderful read that we highly recommend.

— AusRom Today

I bought this book and wow what a read! To every young woman it's a must! Life lessons learnt in an amazing story told! Though I had other things to do, I had to finish this amazing story! Bring on book 3!

— 5 STARS

A well-written erotic romance with its share of twists and suspense. Love the characters and the way the author describes Paris and behind the scenes of the Moulin Rouge.

— 5 STARS, Peter Brady

Michele, a former pro dancer, has finally extricated herself from a very unsatisfying marriage, & is ready for a chance to kick up her heels, sexually & emotionally. Intent on a one night stand, she finds, instead, Mark, a most inventive & attentive lover, something she has never experienced before. As she falls in love with him, against her better judgement, she finds that he has way too many secrets that threaten to derail their fledgling relationship. By the time Nick inserts himself into her life, insisting he is just her type, despite her thoughts to the contrary, Mark has disappeared & bad people are after both him & Michele. Under Nick's protection, Michele finally figures out what she wants from life, in a very good

heroine's journey. There's an abundance of very hot sex, & the love of a good man.
— 4.5 STARS, Alberta, ManicReaders

Fast Pace!! Erotic!! Read it in 2 days!!!! What a book Woo Hoo!!!!! Congratulations Diane Demetre, I thoroughly enjoyed your book . . .
— 5 STARS, Amazon

DIANE DEMETRE